W9-ANT-845

CROSS
MY
HEART

BOOKS BY D.K. HOOD

Don't Tell a Soul
Bring Me Flowers
Follow Me Home
The Crying Season
Where Angels Fear
Whisper in the Night
Break the Silence
Her Broken Wings
Her Shallow Grave
Promises in the Dark
Be Mine Forever

D.K. HOOD

CROSS MY HEART

bookouture

Published by Bookouture in 2021

An imprint of Storyfire Ltd.
Carmelite House
50 Victoria Embankment
London EC4Y 0DZ

www.bookouture.com

Copyright © D.K. Hood, 2021

D.K. Hood has asserted her right to be identified
as the author of this work.

All rights reserved.
No part of this publication may be reproduced,
stored in any retrieval system, or transmitted, in any form or by
any means, electronic, mechanical, photocopying, recording or
otherwise, without the prior written permission of the publishers.

ISBN: 978-1-80019-258-4
eBook ISBN: 978-1-80019-257-7

This book is a work of fiction. Names, characters, businesses,
organizations, places and events other than those clearly in the
public domain, are either the product of the author's imagination
or are used fictitiously. Any resemblance to actual persons, living or
dead, events or locales is entirely coincidental.

*To my readers, who have become
an extended family and wonderful friends.*

"The weather is an unpredictable beast. One day the sun caresses your skin, and the next a storm tears your world apart. I figure in time we'll be naming storm cells after psychopaths."

—David Kane

PROLOGUE

Late Thursday Night

Wind battered the small tent and howled through the trees, peppering the sloping sides with pine needles. The tent bucked so hard it could've blown away in a split second—but it wasn't the weather that had dragged June Harris from sleep, it was the thud and desperate cry. Had she been dreaming? She opened her eyes wide and stared at the tent flap, its zipper glistening in the moonlight as the wind slapped it against the opening. The intermittent view of the campfire, its ashes twirling into the night, came and went with each gust. She reached out to wake her husband, only to find his sleeping bag empty. "Payton, are you out there?"

Nothing.

The hairs on the back of her neck prickled in alarm. Something was terribly wrong. If he'd needed to go outside, he'd have zipped up the tent. Heart thundering, she scrambled out of her sleeping bag, dragged on her boots and coat, and then crawled to the entrance. The wind whipped her hair across her eyes and buffeted her hood, but she hadn't mistaken the *crunch, crunch, crunch* of boots over dead leaves. She shrank back as a tall shape moved out of the darkness wearing a long, flapping dark slicker. A stream of moonlight glistened on something in his hand. In blind panic, she backed inside and searched around for the flashlight. Gasping with relief when her hand closed around the familiar shape, she flicked it on and, heart hammering against her ribs, moved the beam over the trees. The figure had vanished but as she scanned the perimeter of the campsite, she made out someone sitting against a tree wearing a familiar red jacket. "Payton, is that you?"

Nothing.

"Payton?"

Straightening, she ran across the clearing and gasped in disbelief as the flashlight moved over her husband's face, frozen in a glassy stare of horror, and then to the arrow piercing his forehead. Shocked, she stumbled to a halt, not believing her eyes. The wind lifted Payton's hair and flipped open his jacket. Pine needles showered her hood like raindrops and prickled her exposed flesh. A twig cracked behind her, and she spun around, moving her flashlight in all directions, but only dark shadows filled the clearing. Heart thundering, she took a few steps closer to Payton, hoping to see a sign of life, a flicker of an eyelid, something. The smell of gasoline bit into her nostrils and as she moved closer, she could see the fluid dripping from Payton's inert body. With trembling fingers, she touched his ice-cold cheek and peered into unseeing eyes. Her stomach cramped as realization slammed into her. Payton was dead, and his killer was coming back for her.

Indecision froze her to the spot and, terrified, she let out a sob. Alone and lost, she had no idea what to do. June stared into the darkness; the forest vast and foreboding offered no escape. She ran back to the tent to call for help. On hands and knees, she ran her palms over every inch of the floor searching the ground for her phone, flinging bedding in all directions, but it was nowhere to be found. Panic had her by the throat. She had to get away, and scanned the campsite, spilling the flashlight beam over the entire area before venturing across the clearing. The embers in the fire glowed as she passed and a curl of smoke rose up and blew toward her. She'd closed her eyes against the ashes brushing her face when the *crunch, crunch,*

crunch of leaves came again. Heart thundering, she spun around and gaped in horror at the dark figure emerging from the shadows. She took a step back as her flashlight picked out a man in black. His long coat flapped in the wind and a crossbow dangled from one gloved hand. Terrified, she stared at him, trying to make out his features, but something was covering his face.

"You looking for someone?" His deep voice seemed to penetrate the wind.

June raised her voice. "I need help. Someone's shot my husband."

"You planning on starting a forest fire?" He ignored her pleas and kicked dirt over the glowing embers.

June, waved a hand behind her. "No—my husband. Didn't you hear me? He's been shot."

"I heard you just fine." The stranger's eyes glistened in the moonlight like liquid pools with no expression, dark and deep as if the balaclava covered the face of a ghoul. "He's dead, so of no interest to me. What's your name?"

Taking a step backward, June glanced between the man and the body of her husband. "June Harris."

"You'll make a fine addition to my collection, June Harris." His voice seemed to echo across the space between them like a whisper from a grave.

The stranger chilled June to the bone. The way he tipped his head to look at her through the gaping eye sockets in the balaclava was like talking to a skull. "Collection?" She darted her gaze in all directions, looking for a way to escape. "What do you mean by that? What collection? You're not making any sense."

"You'll find out soon enough." His cold, bottomless stare never left her face.

The impending danger radiating from him grasped her by the throat and she gaped at him, unable to move. As if in slow motion, the stranger raised a crossbow and aimed it at her. She flinched, but her attention had fixed on the bolt pointing right at her. She held up her hands, defenseless. "Don't shoot me."

"Now that wouldn't be fun." A chuckle came from deep in his chest as he took a step closer. "Run."

CHAPTER ONE

Friday

Lungs bursting from lack of oxygen, June ran through the forest again, screaming until her voice became a raspy croak. He'd kept her tied up all day and held meaningless conversation with her as if they were friends. He'd waited until nightfall to play his sick games with her again. He was the hunter and she his prey. As his footsteps pounded behind her, she scrambled under a bush; the smell of damp soil and scat crawled up her nose. Heart pounding, she'd tried to control her gasping breath but the slow *crunch, crunch* of his deliberate footsteps stopped close by. He'd hunted her down with ease. She peered through the branches to see his outline, a dark shadow above her.

"That was too easy, June Harris." His amused chuckle sent shivers down her spine. "It's dark, surely you can offer me more sport than that? Get up and try again. Run up the trail, you'll be able to see your way in the moonlight. I'll count to twenty."

Exhausted and with her heart threatening to burst through her chest, she crawled out from under the bushes and ran, tripping and falling into the pine needles. When he laughed at her, his complete lack of empathy terrified her. She stood on trembling legs and faced him. "Please let me go. I won't tell anyone. You have my word. Just let me go. I can't run another step."

"Nope. You don't get to decide your fate." Shadows hid his eyes, but he motioned her on with the crossbow. "Last chance. Head toward the mountain. If you reach the fork in the trail, I'll let you go, now run." He laughed at her. "Scream all you like, there's no one here to help you and you'll attract the bears. Won't that be fun?"

Terrified, June ran, dragging her aching legs up the steep slope. Branches lashed her cheeks and dead bushes caught in her clothes. With each gasping breath, the cold air seemed to be tearing holes in her lungs. Ahead, the mountain loomed out of the moonlight, not far now. She could just make out the fork in the trail ahead where the trees separated. Something hit her hard and searing hot pain sliced through her calf muscle. Crying out in agony, she fell face down in the dirt and then he was on her. As she desperately tried to crawl away, he watched her as if enjoying her pain before grabbing her by the feet and dragging her away from the main trail and along an animal path. The rough ground tore into her back. Rocks and dead twigs piled up beneath her, cutting deep. "Please stop. You're hurting me."

He said nothing.

Dragging her into a stinking cave, he pushed her over onto her face with one large boot. Trembling with fear, she froze in the pitch-black darkness until he turned on a lantern. He remained silent and just sat at the entrance staring at her as if deciding her fate. In agony, she looked down at the bolt piercing her leg and dry retched as her abductor rested his back against the entrance, opened a backpack, and feasted on hot coffee and sandwiches as if they'd been on a picnic. Horrified, she lay in shock, too frightened to close her eyes, until the early morning rays of sunlight pierced the gloom.

The cave had metal boxes stacked in one corner, and a crude attempt had been made to sweep the animal scat and small bones into a corner. Cool mountain air rustled the bushes covering the entrance, raising chill bumps on her exposed flesh. June stretched a little, testing her muscles. An explosion of agony shot through her calf. She bit down hard on her cheek, refusing to give her captor the satisfaction of seeing her in pain, and peered at the man rolled up in a sleeping bag blocking the entrance. The cave reeked of his sweat as if he hadn't washed for a week. She had no chance of escape, now he'd shot her. The searing torment would make it impossible to walk, let alone run.

Panic gripped her and, dizzy from lack of food and water, she stared at her injury. Exhaustion soaked through her, but if she had any chance at all she'd have to remove the bolt wedged through her flesh like a giant silver splinter. With trembling fingers, she pulled gently on the feathered end of the bolt and then gritted her teeth and slid it back through the muscle. Her cry had caught the stranger's immediate attention, and he watched her with an amused expression as if she'd become an exhibit in a zoo. A rush of nausea and light headedness made her sway but she refused to allow him to win. Sucking in breaths between clenched teeth, she searched her jacket pockets and found her cotton scarf. After tying it around the wound, she leaned back against the wall. Sweat ran down her face and stung her eyes, but she forced herself to meet his hard, cold gaze. "What do you want with me? Why are you keeping me here?"

"Get some rest." He closed his eyes and rested his head against the wall of the cave. "It's just more fun trying to catch you when you're fresh. It gets boring real fast if you're too exhausted to run." He wet his lips. "You'll get a chance to escape again soon enough."

June nodded. She understood what he wanted. He craved the chase of the hunt. "Then shooting me and not giving me anything to eat or drink is cheating. How can I run? I can hardly stand up right now. Or is it you can't handle the challenge?"

"You have a smart mouth, you know that?" He reached for a backpack, removed a bottle of Gatorade, and tossed it to her. "There you go."

June grabbed at the bottle and sipped the drink, then stowed half of it in the pocket of her jacket. If she managed to escape him, she'd need it later. She planned the way through the forest in her mind. During her last escape she'd run blindly, but as he dragged her to the cave, she'd become wiser and scanned the area for an escape route. If she could reach the trail, she'd have a chance of someone hearing her call for help.

As much as she wanted to, she couldn't close her eyes and rest. The image of Payton with the arrow protruding from his head was burned into her retinas, and her leg throbbed along with the rapid beating of her heart. Trying to control her breathing, she eyed the man from beneath her lashes. He was toying with her and trying to prove he could catch her no matter how many times she escaped. He was as cunning as a fox. There was no reasoning with him. She might as well be talking to a robot with scripted replies. It was as if she'd become a player in a video game running on a loop inside a crazy man's head.

June stared at him, waiting for him to pounce. When he went through his backpack and tossed her an energy bar, she frowned, unable to understand his logic. Had she finally gotten through to him? "Thank you."

"Don't thank me." He pointed at her. "I don't hunt down wounded prey. It's no challenge to me. I'll make a deal with you. Play the game and if you make it to the river, I'll let you go. If not, you'll be spending a long time in this cave." His dark eyes, like bottomless pits, moved over her. "I'll even give you a minute start to make it interesting. Rest up, Little Piggy—the Big Bad Wolf is locked and loaded."

CHAPTER TWO

Black Rock Falls, Montana

The early hours of Monday morning

Sheriff Jenna Alton ignored the sinister howling of the wind, shoved her feet into her boots, and wrapping her coat around her, headed for the front door. She stared at Duke, the bloodhound owned by her deputy, an off-the-grid special forces sniper, Dave Kane, and sighed. "Two in the morning? Since when have you needed to go potty at this time of night?" She paused to disable the alarm. "Come on then."

Freezing air rushed to meet her. It was late October, and with Halloween just around the corner, the first snow wouldn't be too far away. Floodlights spilled across the driveway of her isolated ranch to the dark cottage where Kane lived. A strange loneliness crept over her whenever he went away. She'd gotten used to him being around. He'd been seriously injured recently and unable to cope alone, had spent time recovering in her spare room. Kane was an old-fashioned kind of guy and once he was back on his feet had returned to his cottage. Now the house was so dreadfully quiet she could hear herself breathing.

As they had no cases to solve, Kane had taken the opportunity of attending a criminal profiling seminar out of Helena, with Special Agent Jo Wells, a behavioral analyst, and her partner, Special Agent Ty Carter. The seminar had speakers from all over the world, and she'd encouraged Kane to go. His skill in the field was substantial, but he craved more information and she would manage for one weekend. In fact, she'd spent the entire day hanging new drapes over the picture window in the family room. Apparently, changing the drapes to a more modern look had proved to be a little more challenging than she'd expected. Previously she'd unhooked one pair and replaced them, but the new ones required a rod of huge proportions. Determined to complete this not so simple job herself, she'd found a way around the obstacles that had plagued her and, after many trips back and forth to town to collect the tools she needed, had the new rod attached to the wall and the drapes in position.

Leaning against the porch railing, she waited for Duke to run around. She inhaled the fresh night air. Cold and invigorating, it carried the scent of pine trees and a hint of snow from the mountains. Lightning zigzagged across the horizon, followed by a low roll of thunder, and Duke let out a yowl and scampered back inside the house. A brave dog most times, he had his Achilles heels: storms, the vet, and baths. She watched him head into her bedroom and crawl under the bed and then turned to stare at the sky. The weather had been strange of late: high winds and dry thunderstorms that yielded no rain. After a dry summer and with no rainfall so far in fall, the frequent lightning strikes had become a threat to Stanton Forest. A fire could burn out of control in no time and although the forest wardens had maintained the firebreaks, everyone was holding their breath and waiting for the first snow. Shivering as a blast of ice-cold wind flapped open her coat, Jenna turned inside, reset the alarm, and fell into bed. At least she'd have a few hours' sleep before rising at five-thirty to tend the horses before heading into work. Deputy Rowley and Deputy Rio were quite capable of running things in her absence, but she liked to keep busy and her new office still needed arranging.

Sleep came easy until her black cat, Pumpkin, let out a snarl and jolted her awake. She rolled over to stare at the cat. Outlined in the window, she was doing a great impersonation of a Halloween decoration. Back arched, fur fluffed out, and her ears flattened to her head. With every yowl, her tail swished back and forth. The next second, a low growl came from beneath her bed. "Oh, for goodness' sake, what's wrong with the pair of you now? It's just a storm. Lie down, Duke, and go to sleep."

She covered her head with the blankets and ignored her pets. This time of the year, when people's minds turned to Halloween and all the spooky legends around it, everyone including animals were on edge as if waiting for something to happen. Her cat had arrived last Halloween splashed in blood, and the entire week had been consumed with death and destruction. This year the weather had gone bananas and was lighting up the sky with dry storms. She dozed on the edge of sleep, that lovely place where the body relaxes into the warm hug of tranquility, when a noise came from the direction of the porch. Duke shot out from under the bed. Pumpkin spat and hissed, walking sideways along the windowsill, her head turned and eyes slits in the moonlight.

"It's just the wind." Jenna patted the side of the bed. "Come here, boy. It's probably just a branch hitting the steps is all."

Duke's growl was deep and menacing. Jenna pushed back the blankets and yawned. "Okay, you win. Come on then, I'll show you everything is okay. No one can get in here, Duke, we're safe."

Thump.

What was that? Suddenly wide awake, Jenna sat up and shook her head. "Now I'm getting spooked."

It's just the wind. When Duke growled again and scratched at her door, she reached for the bedside lamp. "Okay, I'm coming." She flicked on the switch. No pale glow flooded the room. She ground her teeth. Just her luck. The bulb needed replacing. Reluctantly climbing from her warm bed, she went to the door and hit the switch on the wall.

Nothing.

A flash of lightning followed by a roll of thunder shook the house, sending Duke running for cover. Jenna bit back a laugh. "It's okay, the lights will be back on soon and we'll check the house."

As the house had a backup generator, if the storm had knocked out the power it would come right back on. She went back to her bed and sat waiting, counting for the few minutes it took to kick in. Time seemed to drag by and she reached for her cellphone. It lit up, fully charged, and she watched the clock; five minutes went by and the house remained in darkness. The last time the generator failed, someone had entered her home and tried to kill her. The cat yowled again. Its orange eyes fixated on something outside and the hairs prickled the back of Jenna's neck, echoing Pumpkin's warning. She'd never seen a bear on her property but it wasn't beyond reason, or perhaps a bobcat had ventured inside her boundary. When Duke came out from under her bed, braving the storm to bare his teeth at her bedroom door, she had no doubt that someone was in her yard. Heart thundering, Jenna slid out of bed and took her Glock from the bedside drawer, checked the clip, and slid one into the chamber. She had the best security money could buy, but without power it was useless. But whoever was out there had underestimated her. She might be alone, but she'd fight back like a wildcat.

CHAPTER THREE

The moon peeked through the dark clouds rushing through a stormy night. Glad the shadows had hidden him from view, he smiled to himself as he observed her, backlit in the windows. Out here with no one around she thought she was safe from prying eyes, and yet, he stood mere yards away from the famous Sheriff Jenna Alton. Her tough-guy bodyguard was conveniently away for the weekend. Now here she was, all alone with only a dog to protect her. Oh yeah, she had weapons, but he was smart. In the dark, she'd go for a chest shot and he wore a military-style vest to keep him safe.

The wind buffeted him as he moved closer to the house and threaded his gift onto a bolt and slotted it into his crossbow. He was an excellent shot and automatically made an adjustment for the wind. He aimed and hit the front post on the sheriff's porch dead center. The sound of the metal piercing the wood seemed to vibrate the stillness for a split second before another crack of lightning lit up the sky. He heard a dog barking and could imagine the sheriff running around in the dark. Once he'd gained access to her ranch, he'd cut the phone lines and set up his wireless disrupter. Disabling the power had been a breeze, and it didn't take a genius to find the backup generator. Just about every ranch around these parts had one, and with one single flip of a switch the sheriff would remain in the dark.

He wanted to scare her, make her aware she had a worthy opponent. The idea of her watching over her shoulder all the time for an unknown assassin excited him, but then she'd never had to deal with what would happen next. He'd offer her glimpses of him. He wanted to frighten her and be menacing from the get-go. Others had tried to disguise their murderous ways but he reveled in death. She'd be aware of him, sense him close by, and almost be able to touch him, but he'd always be one step ahead of her, waiting for the time to strike.

He'd play with her for a while, make her believe she could win, and then he'd draw his trump card. He couldn't wait to be there at the end, watching her as she took her last breath and knowing that evil always triumphs. He'd left a message, a small clue on her porch, and a gift for her in the forest unless the wildlife had spread the remains but he didn't think so. He'd taken steps to keep the scavengers at bay. His attention remained fixed on the house, and excitement gripped him when the drapes moved a fraction. He chuckled and stepped out of the shadows in full view but just far enough away to make her question if it was really a man standing in her yard or an apparition. At this time of year, when people's minds filled with stories of ghosts and ghouls, she'd never really be certain. The drapes shivered again, opening just enough for him to make out a pale face at the window. He grinned. She couldn't hear him but he'd sure gained her attention. "Your move, Sheriff—or should I call you Jenna?"

CHAPTER FOUR

The house creaked and moaned through another blast of wind. Unsure if someone had broken through her security, Jenna ducked down and crawled across the floor to grab her phone. The cool night seeped through her PJs. If she planned to face an intruder, she'd need a few things for protection, and shucking her light-colored nightclothes was one of them. Dressing fast in jeans and a black sweater, she pulled on socks and boots. Another *thwack* hit the front porch and convinced her that someone was outside. If they used a suppressor on their weapon, it would sound similar, but why would some idiot be shooting up her house? She added a spare clip to the pocket of her jeans and edged toward the window. Apart from the intermittent rays of moonlight threading through the clouds rushing across the sky, darkness engulfed her yard. Only the groans of the old wooden house and Duke's low growl disturbed the peace, and yet something had made the noise.

Jenna touched Duke's head. "Hush now, lie down and stay. I need to listen."

A bear or a bobcat would have sent the horses crazy, and yet not a sound came from the direction of the barn. The pony in her barn belonging to Anna, the daughter of Dr. Shane Wolfe, the local ME, and a close friend, was well known for squealing, even if a rat entered its stall, so she discounted the chance that wildlife had run onto her property. That left only one conclusion. Someone was outside. Anyone entering a Montanan's property in the middle of the night was either a fool or had an agenda. Lightning flashed and thunder rolled across the sky, and Jenna's heart missed a beat. The millisecond of light had picked out a man. He resembled an old-style western gunslinger from the movies. His long black slicker flapped in the wind like bat's wings and his cowboy hat sat low over his eyes.

Unnerved, she swallowed hard, glad of the warm handle of the Glock against her palm. She hadn't seen a weapon, but then she'd had the blink of an eye to examine the stranger. Lightning flashed again and the man had vanished. Disconcerted, Jenna closed her eyes. The sudden flash of light had sent red spots dancing across her vision. Had she imagined the man? Was her mind playing tricks on her? She snatched up her phone, and pushing it inside her back pocket, headed across her bedroom and into the hallway. From here she had a direct line of vision to the front door, and the windows on either side gave a clear view of the driveway. Nobody lurked on her porch and the glint of the metal on her cruiser was the only thing visible in the dark.

Lightning bolted across the sky and the hairs on Jenna's body stood at attention as the figure of the gunslinger turned to face her before darkness descended again. This time she hadn't missed the crossbow aimed at her or the strange green glow of his eyes. Pushing down a surge of panic, she ducked under cover and headed down the hallway. *Thwack.*

With her back to the wall, she edged to her office. The room held screens for video surveillance. It also held her gun safe. This room always had the shutters closed. After the last psychopath had gotten through her security, Kane had replaced the door with one reinforced with steel on the off-chance Jenna couldn't make it to the safe room hidden beneath the barn. She chewed on her bottom lip and swirled the combination on the safe. Inside she had an arsenal of weapons but chose a hunting rifle, loaded it, and slung it over one shoulder.

It was one man, taking potshots at the house to scare her, but she had a team not twenty minutes away. She placed her Glock in the back waistband of her jeans, pulled out her phone to call Rowley, and then stared at the screen in disbelief at the NO SERVICE message. "What is going on here?"

Without power the landline would be out as well, but she lifted the cordless receiver and checked. A wave of uncertainty washed over her at the silence. If she wanted backup, she'd need her satellite phone. They had three satellite phones at work and she issued them when the need arose. Dave had one in his truck and she had one in her cruiser, but that was parked out front and there was no way she'd risk going outside. She stared at her tracker ring. Same with her ring. No wireless network meant it was useless. She pushed her phone back inside her pocket and moved back into the hallway. Lightning flashed and the window beside the front door exploded inward, sending shards of glass spinning across the wooden floor. A *zing* went past her ear and a crossbow bolt hit the wall inches from her head. Rolling into cover, she pulled the Glock from her back, rose to her knees, aimed, and emptied the clip out the shattered window. Another bolt zipped past and stuck in the door behind her. A shudder went through her, and memories she'd have preferred to remain buried erupted to the surface. Controlling a wave of panic, she shut them down and slipped the new clip into her weapon. She readied herself for a fight, but she wouldn't give him the advantage of remaining in the hallway with windows all around. If he wanted a fight, it would be on her terms.

Jenna peered back up the hallway and, keeping low, crawled to her bedroom door. Pumpkin had vanished, likely scampered to a safe place, but Duke was edging out the door on his belly. She grabbed his collar. "Come on, we'll be safer in the other room."

Once inside the office, she bolted the door and went to the gun safe. After swapping her rifle for one of the automatic weapons, she checked supplies. She had everything she needed to wait this guy out, including a bathroom. It would be light in a few hours and Kane would be on his way home, but if he was delayed, she already had a contingency plan set in place. If she didn't show at work or answer her phone, Rowley would be hightailing it out to the ranch to check on her before nine. The closet held the latest in liquid Kevlar vests and pants, sets made for her and Kane courtesy of the government and via Shane Wolfe. With Shane's finger on the pulse of new innovations for the elite military and Kane's value to POTUS, no one was taking any chances.

Reluctantly, she laid down her weapons and suited up. Liquid Kevlar solidified if hit with a bullet or knife. The unique material wasn't bulky like the old-style bulletproof vests and designed for combat so they didn't restrict movement. As lightning bombarded the sky and the house shook with rolls of thunder, Jenna paced, constantly checking her phone. Perhaps lightning had struck the tower close to her ranch. If so, a crew would be out soon to put things right. A whine from Duke caught her attention. He'd been braver than usual during the storm, but the last rolls of thunder had sent him under the table. She bent to look at his big brown eyes as a tremble went through him. She made her voice as coaxing as possible. "It will be okay, boy, you're safe in here and Dave will be back soon."

Bolts hit the shutters with a constant barrage of *thwacks*, and a cold breeze followed the tinkle of breaking glass. Jenna ducked down and placed her back against a metal filing cabinet and faced the door. How did he know exactly where she was hiding? Was this someone who'd been to the ranch? Only her closest friends would know Kane was away for the weekend, and she could count on one hand the names of the people who knew about the special room. The realization that someone outside her circle of safety knew about her personal life made her heart race. She stared into the darkness. This was one situation she must face alone.

Dragging in deep breaths, she tried to swallow the rising panic and rationalize the situation. Losing control now would be the death of her. She'd trained for situations like this and needed to find that calm, logical place inside her mind and just deal with it. *Think it through, Jenna.*

Taking a firm grip on her nerves, she pictured the man outside, standing staring at her. His intimidating attitude designed to make her believe she was no threat to him. It was a typical domination technique used by psychopathic killers, wife beaters, and bullies in an attempt to scare. There was more to this attack than a thrill kill. Someone out there wanted her dead, or a notch in their belt for killing her. She'd be damned if she'd allow them to take her down with a darn crossbow. Her mind went to James Stone, a killer she'd taken down some years ago. A man hellbent on killing Kane and then her for no other reason than jealousy. His weapon of choice had been a crossbow before he mutilated the bodies of his victims. He'd blamed her for the reason he killed, but he was locked up for life. The memory of him sent shivers down her spine—he would have stopped at nothing to see her dead. Shaking her head to dispel the terrifying images of his victims from clouding her judgment, she ground her teeth. The man outside could not be Stone and whoever he was, she refused to play his game and would stand her ground. No one could get through the reinforced mesh on the windows and if they did, she'd be waiting for them.

Determined and loaded for bear, Jenna gave Duke a pat on the head. "It's going to be fine, boy. No one is coming through that door alive." She swallowed her uncertainty, not able to voice her concern. She ground her teeth as glass exploded, pinging across the wooden floor.

He's coming.

CHAPTER FIVE

It had been an interesting weekend, but Dave Kane woke as usual at five and stared at the ceiling in his hotel room. At this time of the morning, he'd usually be out tending the horses. He sure missed Jenna and being on the ranch, but he'd gained a lot of information over the weekend. The seminar had been engrossing and he wished he'd had Deputy Rio's incredible recall to remember all the techniques used by the specialists in their field of psychopathy. He'd ordered the DVD and would be using it to refresh his memory. His mind went to Jenna. If he had his way, he'd have been on the first flight home after the seminar, but Jo wanted to dine with old friends and, although reluctantly, he'd joined her with Carter. He had little choice in the matter. They'd given him a ride in the FBI chopper and would be dropping him at the medical examiner's office before heading home to Snakeskin Gully. With a helipad on top of the building, it made life so much easier. He'd left his truck, affectionately known as the Beast because of its high-performance engine and bulletproof capabilities, in the ME's parking lot.

He rolled out of bed and, after stretching his tight muscles, he completed deep breathing exercises to expand his damaged lung. The pain still caught him unawares, and the specialist had forbidden him to resume his vigorous daily training schedule. He padded to the shower, taking ten minutes to shave, shower, and dress. His military training was part of who he was, and being ready in any situation was part of his life. He usually kept himself mentally and physically in shape for any contingencies. The injury had slowed him down some but he'd recover. One thing for sure, it hadn't stopped him shooting the wings off a fly.

He'd surmised that Jenna had some military qualifications from the get-go. The way she'd trained Deputy Rowley came as close to a drill sergeant as she could get. The young man worked out three nights a week at the local dojo and never missed his time on the gun range. He'd married Sandy, a local girl, last Christmas, and they had twins due late December. It would seem his circle of close friends was getting larger by the year.

He'd missed Jenna's company over the weekend. They'd been working side by side for a few years now and had become more than friends, but Jenna was an independent woman, not to mention his boss, and they'd needed to remain professional on the job at all times. They'd agreed to keep their involvement secret from the rest of the team to maintain normality.

When a knock came on his door, he frowned. He'd ordered room service but wasn't expecting it until five-thirty. It seemed being with an FBI delegation had its rewards. The kitchen had been open to them at all hours over the weekend. He opened the door, surprised to see Ty Carter pushing a breakfast cart, and grinned. "Morning. Are they having staff shortages?"

"Very funny." Carter wheeled in the cart. "I know you eat early and I called down and told them to add my order to your cart. I offered the girl a twenty and she handed it right over. It's just as well I wasn't planning on slipping something into your food." He pushed the cart to a table before the window. "I eat alone every day and having someone to talk to is an indulgence I don't plan on missing out on." He turned and looked at the Doberman who'd shadowed him inside the room. "Lie down, Zorro. We won't be long."

Kane took in the FBI special agent and ex-Navy Seal. They worked well together. Carter had his ghosts to deal with and had spent two years off the grid living in a cabin in the woods fighting his PTSD demons. Dressed in a clean shirt, blue jeans, and cowboy boots, his shaggy sun-bleached blond hair still hung to his collar even after their trip to the barber. One thing for sure. Carter didn't resemble any FBI agent he'd worked with, but his persona suited him just fine now he was investigating crimes in the wild west.

Kane followed him to the table and lifted his meal from the cart. "What time are we leaving? I'd have like to have gotten back to the ranch last night to help Jenna with the chores this morning. The storms have been bad over Black Rock Falls. I hope the roof is still on my cottage."

"She'd have called." Carter poured coffee from a two-cup pot and took a sip. "Wouldn't she?"

Kane swallowed a mouthful of eggs and shook his head. "Nope. She wouldn't disturb me unless there was a homicide and then I guess she'd have enough backup with Rowley and Rio. She's an independent woman, she knows who to call for help if disaster strikes."

"We'll be leaving at six-thirty. Jo is keen to be home before her daughter leaves for school." Carter smiled. "When you're done here, we can head down to the lobby to wait for her. If we're not delayed, you should be home before Jenna leaves for the office."

As Kane finished his meal, his phone pealed out Rowley's ringtone. He frowned and took the call. "Yeah, Jake, what's up?"

"Have you spoken to Jenna this morning?" Rowley sounded anxious.

Kane glanced across the table at Carter. "No, I haven't spoken to her since yesterday. She told me she'd be busy hanging new drapes in the family room over the weekend. Maybe she turned off her phone and forgot to turn it back on. You were on the 911 callout, right?"

"Uh-huh." Rowley cleared his throat. *"Well, I called just before. I figured she might need some help with the horses but she didn't pick up.*

The message said her phone was unavailable. I had the same response with the landline and she didn't pick up her sat phone. We had a dry storm here last night, but it didn't affect the power here but it could have out at the ranch. She's on a different grid to us."

"The backup generator would have kicked in, so something's not right." Kane stared at his watch. "It will be light soon. Grab Rio and head out to the ranch. We'll be leaving here as soon as possible."

"I'll call Rio now." Rowley disconnected.

"Trouble?" Carter loaded up the cart and stood.

A knot tightened in Kane's gut. After trying Jenna's number and getting the same message, he pushed his unfinished meal away. "I'm not sure. Jenna's not picking up her phone. Rowley's been trying to reach her for some time." He stood, reached for his jacket, and shrugged it on. "We need to go. Can you hurry Jo along?"

"Sure. But I have a SatSleeve for my phone." Carter glanced at Zorro. "Stay." He headed for the door.

As Carter's room was right next door, he returned in a few minutes with the phone pressed to his cheek.

"She has the satellite phone in her cruiser, right?" Carter's eyebrows met in a frown. He waited for what seemed like ages and then left a message. "Jenna, it's Ty. Call me on the satellite phone. It's urgent."

Uncertainty crawled over Kane like a rash from poison ivy. "She'd have parked right outside the front porch. Something's wrong."

"Meet us in the lobby." Carter motioned Zorro to follow him and headed for the door.

Kane nodded. "I'll be right behind you."

Worry for Jenna clamped Kane's gut. They'd made a lot of arrests in Black Rock Falls and put many murderers in jail. In the investigations many people had their noses out of joint when they came under scrutiny, especially if they'd faced lesser charges from crimes they'd uncovered during the investigation. Some people and their families held grudges for years and might figure Jenna was an easy target. She was far from it, but out at the ranch all alone, she'd be able to handle one or two assailants—but for how long? He knew Jenna, and she'd never kill anyone unless they threatened her life. Kane took his weapon from the bedside table and slid it into his shoulder holster. After doing a quick sweep of the room to make sure he had everything, he picked up his bag and headed out the door for the elevator. He checked out and turned as Carter and Jo came into the lobby.

"Has something happened to Jenna?" Jo had toast wrapped in a paper napkin and carried a bottle of water under one arm. She balanced her suitcase on wheels against one leg, and her eyebrows raised in question.

Kane waited for Carter to check out and they all headed for the door. "I'm not sure. We can't reach her."

"We'll go straight to the ranch." Carter headed for their rental car. "With the power out, she might be stuck inside. The gates would be locked, right?" He got behind the wheel and started the engine.

Kane dumped the bags inside the trunk. "Yeah, but I checked the generator before I left. It was working fine." Worry for Jenna seeped through him in an ice-cold chill. "If they'd gotten inside when she was asleep, they could've had the jump on her. With the storm last night, Duke would have been hiding and maybe not given her a warning."

"This is like déjà vu." Jo slipped into the back seat. "It was a nightmare when that psychopath broke into the house. But this time she's all alone."

"Jenna's tougher than you think." Carter started the engine. "And if someone broke in, they wouldn't be expecting a fight."

CHAPTER SIX

Exhausted and frozen to the bone, Jenna had remained with her back pressed up against the filing cabinet, weapon aimed at the door. The rifle had gotten heavier by the minute and she wondered if her ice-cold fingers could pull the trigger. Only adrenalin kept her alert, and bursts of it had flooded her bloodstream the moment the front door of her home crashed open. She tried to control the fear welling up inside her as boots thundered over the wooden floor and a person searched the rooms, invading her privacy. Anger rose as the intruder went through her home like a wrecking ball. Things hit the floor and she made out the tinkle of glass breaking.

The door handle rattled and a shoulder first and then a boot slammed into it, shaking the lock. A normal door would have flown open with a kick aimed beside the lock, but the steel door and frame held. Taking a steadying breath, Jenna aimed the AR-15. If anyone came through that door, their intent was clear. A muffled sound of cursing had Duke's hackles rising all down his back. His skin had drawn back from his teeth, exposing his canines, and he barked a warning.

Recalling Kane's orders to his dog, Jenna kept her voice low and calm. "Take cover, Duke." She sighed with relief as he crawled under the desk but kept up a steady low growl. "Good boy."

The assault on the door continued but no weapon was fired. Whoever was out there was only carrying a crossbow. The footsteps came again and scratching came at the door. Jenna held her breath as blows shattered the wall beside the door. God help her, the intruder had found the tools in her utility room and was attacking the wall with a hammer. She rested the rifle on her knees and stretched her fingers. Her weapon would shred the wall but leave her exposed. She had to find cover and scanned the room. As the noise became louder and wood cracked as loud as gunshots, she stood on legs numb from sitting, placed the rifle on the filing cabinet, and moved everything from the desk. She tipped it over and then dragged it into place. The cracking of wood shook the walls as she heaved the metal filing cabinets around the table. With Duke safely inside, she grabbed her weapons, clips, and a bottle of water and hunkered down.

Muscles aching from overexertion, Jenna took slow, even breaths. She doubted he would get through the steel mesh lining the walls that Kane and Rowley had discreetly covered with drywall. The knowledge the room was protected didn't slow her racing heart, or ease the dread enveloping her. The barrage of blows stopped and footsteps clattered through the house. She listened intently, and then sighed with relief at what had disturbed the intruder. Sirens cut through the early-morning silence like the answer to a prayer. She glanced at her phone. It was almost six-thirty. Who was coming to her rescue? She didn't care, but she hoped they'd be prepared for a lunatic with a crossbow. She pushed to her feet and shook out her stiff limbs. Her head ached and her hands trembled, but she'd made it through alive. She patted Duke, glad he'd been with her. Scanning the room, she shook her head, recalling the argument she'd had with Kane about constructing the secure room. Kane, Rowley, and Wolfe had spent weeks working on it to keep it a secret, but they'd forgotten to add one thing: a trapdoor. If the intruder had set fire to the house, she'd have been trapped inside. She grimaced at the thought of being burned to death. "An escape route is the next thing on my list."

The sirens had gotten louder, two vehicles by the sound of it. The wail stopped and she could imagine her deputies checking the perimeter, looking for a threat. Footsteps clattered down the hallway and she heard Rowley's voice.

"Jenna." He rapped on the door. "It's okay, we've cleared the house, you can open the door."

After laying the AR-15 on the filing cabinet, she picked up her Glock. Experience told her to act with caution. She unlocked the door and stood back, aiming her weapon. The door opened slowly, and Jake Rowley and Zac Rio peered at her.

"Are you okay?" Rio examined her face. "The house has been trashed."

She slid her weapon into the back waistband of her jeans, pulled off her Kevlar vest, and heaved a sigh. "Yeah, I'm good. How bad is it?"

Peering into the hallway, she drew a breath at the damage. The front door was hanging off its hinges and broken glass sparkled in the early morning sun. She peered into the family room to find chairs had been tipped over, and books that had been ripped from the shelves had spilled into the hallway.

"I figure they were looking for something." Rio grimaced. "It might be better if you leave Duke in the office—there's glass everywhere."

Jenna shook her head. "He's been shut in here most of the night, he needs to run around." She turned back inside the room.

"I'll take him outside." Rowley moved past her and heaved the dog into his arms. "He weighs a ton. Kane's on the way." He looked over his shoulder. "What the hell happened here?"

"I'll explain when you get back." Jenna looked at Rio. "We'll do a walk-through. This is a crime scene. Use gloves."

As Rowley came back into the house, she heard her phone buzz a message. She pulled it out and replied. "Thank God, my phone is working. It's been out all night. It's a message from Kane saying he's on his way. I've seven missed calls. The storm must have knocked out a wireless tower and the power."

"No, it didn't." Rowley looked concerned. "No one else lost power. Is the landline working?"

Jenna headed for the kitchen and lifted the receiver. "Nope, it's out." She stared at the kitchen, and it appeared to be intact apart from muddy boot prints all over the floor. "Rio, get shots of the prints and document the scene. Rowley, come with me. I need to see if the horses are okay and check the generator." She headed outside, picking her way through the glass, and whistled to Duke.

As they headed to the barn, Jenna's phone chimed Wolfe's ringtone. "Hi, Shane."

"I'm just checking to see if you're okay." Wolfe cleared his throat. *"We have a problem. Someone smashed the side window of my van last night and took the remote control for your gate."*

A cold chill crawled up Jenna's spine. "Yeah, they did more than that, they came here, disabled the power, the generator, and my phones, broke in, and tried to kill me using a crossbow. I locked myself in the safe room and waited him out, but he's trashed my house." She stared at the open door to the barn. "I'm at the barn and it's wide open. Rowley is with me and we're going inside to check the horses."

"I'm on my way." Wolfe disconnected.

Pulling her weapon, Jenna turkey-peeked around the barn door, glad to see the horses' heads peering over their stalls. When Duke ran inside and Pumpkin jumped down from a bale of hay and rubbed around her legs, she heaved a sigh of relief. "It's okay, these two are a great warning system. There's no one inside."

"I'll clear the area, just in case." Rowley slid through the door, keeping his back to the wall, and edged into the barn, moving from place to place. "All clear." He holstered his weapon.

Jenna cast a quick eye over the horses. "I'll check the generator and then turn out the horses into the corral, there's plenty of fresh grass in there to eat. I'll tend to them once we've secured the house."

"Copy that." Rowley walked to the generator and shook his head. "It's been turned off is all." He flicked the switch and it rumbled into life. "It's working fine. Where is the power pole? You have a switch inside the power box, here, right?"

Jenna nodded. "Yeah, it's the one out front of the house, on the left of the driveway. Do you figure he waited until I was asleep, used the remote to get inside without triggering the alarm, and then disabled the power?"

"Yeah, that seems feasible." Rowley headed to the horses, and speaking quietly, had their halters on in a few minutes. He handed the lead rein on Anna's pony to Jenna. "I'll take the horses."

As they headed for the corral, the sound of a chopper broke the still morning. "That will be Carter." She quickened her step to get the horses into the enclosure before the chopper arrived. "The horses are getting used to the sound of the chopper now. They'll be fine." She shut the corral gate. "Let's check the power."

The power to the house had been cut by tripping the switch. Jenna shook her head slowly and turned to Rowley. "This guy knows too much about me. He had information about the power, where to find the backup generator, and that I was alone all weekend. He's someone close. Who the hell is he?" She waved at the house. "I'm going to look over the exterior and see if he left us any clues."

Jenna headed back to the house, moving slowly searching for footprints and looking for anything to point to the identity of the intruder. As she moved closer to the porch, her attention fixed on the number of bolts peppering her house. They seemed almost methodical in pattern, apart from one, fixed in the post on the porch. She stared at it long and hard. It appeared to be different from the others. Something was pinned to the wood. Had he attached a note? As she stepped closer, a shiver of horror stopped her in her tracks. The intruder had pinned a bloody ear to her house, complete with gold earring. She took a step back as her gaze fixed on the message below it, written in mud on the porch: *You're next, Jenna.*

"Oh, that can't be good." Rowley removed his hat and bent to examine the muddy scrawl.

Numb with disbelief, Jenna looked at him. "That's a direct threat from James Stone. Those were his last words to me."

CHAPTER SEVEN

Relief was quickly replaced by concern when Kane stared at the message from Jenna. He pressed his mic to speak to Jo and Carter over the noise of the chopper. "Jenna's okay but someone tried to kill her at the ranch. It was well planned. Someone broke into Wolfe's van and took the remote control for the security system."

"It sounds like they know her pretty well." Jo shook her head. "Have you employed any strangers to work on the ranch lately or had anyone drop by?"

Kane thought for a beat. "Only the guy who broke in gunning for you, and he's locked away with a never to be released order. It can't possibly be him." He looked at Carter. "How long?"

"We'll be there in five." Carter glanced at him. "Jenna knows how to handle herself. You worry too much about her."

"This is Black Rock Falls, remember?" Kane narrowed his gaze at his friend. "Just when you think everything is back to normal, something weird happens and the nightmare starts all over again."

"So, it seems." Carter grimaced. "Cute little town you have here."

The chopper headed over Main and far below Kane could see the Halloween decorations beginning to appear on front lawns. The early morning mist swirled from the river and spilled over the lowlands. Ahead, the usually blue endless sky looked troubled and a collection of gray clouds hovered over the horizon. The chopper dropped lower as Jenna's ranch came into view. Kane scanned the area and made out the horses in the corral and three sheriff's vehicles in the driveway. He noticed Wolfe's van heading through town, but no other vehicle traveled the road to the ranch or lurked along the side of the highway. When they landed, his attention went straight to Jenna. Her pale face peeked out from under her hoodie and she stood arms folded across her chest, waiting for him with Duke leaning protectively against her legs. Rowley was dusting what was left of the front door for prints. He gaped in disbelief at the damage. "Holy cow, it looks like someone took an ax to the place."

"How did they get inside without power?" Jo unbuckled her harness.

Kane shrugged. "Once someone breaches the perimeter, glass breaks and doors can be kicked in. That's why we converted the office into a secure area." He pulled off his headset and headed for the ranch house, ducking to miss the still rotating blades.

Surprised when his dog didn't dash to greet him, he headed straight for Jenna. He could see the damage to the renovated interior they'd worked on all summer. "Had a bad night, huh?" He put one arm around her and peered into her eyes. "Did you see who did this?"

"Nope, not exactly." Jenna leaned into him, obviously exhausted. "I did get a glimpse of him in a flash of lightning. Maybe five-ten to six feet, long coat, cowboy hat, and glowing green eyes." She gave him a determined look. "I know it's close to Halloween, but he did have glowing green eyes."

Kane gave her a squeeze. "I'd say he used night vision goggles. So, he came prepared. Anything else you remember?"

"He left a message." Jenna pulled a disgusted face, walked to the end of the porch, and indicated to a piece of flesh hanging from a crossbow bolt embedded in a post. "I only just found this. It's an ear, and that's the same threat James Stone made to me when they hauled him off to jail." She pointed to the muddy writing.

"Yeah, I remember." Kane examined the message and then moved to the bloody ear and sniffed. "It's fresh." He removed his Stetson and scratched his head. "Has anyone gone missing over the weekend?"

"Nope." Jenna indicated toward Rowley. "Everyone had power and phones except me, and no one has called in a missing person's report." She looked at Kane with a concerned expression. "James Stone used a crossbow in his murders, and the message is something only he would know. It's not something we made public, but how can he be involved? He's locked up, right?"

Kane nodded and pushed up the rim of his hat. "We would have been notified the moment he escaped; the prison warden knows he's gunning for you." He looked at Duke. "He looks a little shell-shocked. Is he hurt?"

"No, he's fine, but he hasn't stopped shaking. It was pretty harrowing for him. First a violent storm and then some guy trashed my house and tried to break into the office. I'm not surprised he's distressed. I'm trembling all over. He let me know someone was outside and it gave me time to get to safety. Thank God you reinforced that room. I just holed up and waited him out. If he'd made it through the door, I wasn't too worried. He had a crossbow and I had the AR-15."

Kane smiled at her. "No contest." He moved to her side. "What do you want me to do?"

"Take over the investigation." Jenna looked up at him. "I can't be involved with the break-in. When we find this guy, I don't want him getting off because of a conflict of interest. Rowley will walk you through and Rio is inside capturing the scene." She indicated to her duffel. "I've packed a few essentials, and I really need to sit down for a spell."

"Why don't you head over to my cottage and get some rest? You can grab the rest of your things later. Carter and Jo are staying for a while, and I saw Wolfe heading this way. I'll wait for him and once we've finish processing the scene, I'll write up a report. The damage will be covered by insurance and I'll get someone out here to secure the house today."

"How are we going to stop this happening again?" Jenna shuddered. "This crazy has access to my ranch. He'll come back the second he knows I'm alone."

"That's not going to happen, Jenna." Kane shook his head. "We'll need a different access system. Wolfe will know what to do. We'll just cancel all the remotes and replace them. I'll go with Carter and get what we need from town and drive the Beast home." He waved a hand toward the house. "Don't worry about the damage. Everything can be fixed."

"There is one thing." Jenna pulled her jacket tight around her. "I think we need a trapdoor in the office. If the intruder had set fire to the house, I would've been trapped."

Kane rubbed her back. "I'll see to it before you move back into the house. Now go and get some rest."

"Okay, thanks. I'm dead on my feet. Where's Jo?" Jenna looked around him. "Ah, there she is. I have a theory I want to run past her. We can discuss it later. I really need a shower and ten gallons of coffee." She headed down the front steps. "Come on, Duke."

When Duke just sat there staring at him, Kane squatted to rub the dog's ears and received a lick on the chin. "Good boy. You looked after Jenna all night. Go home—you'll feel better with a full belly and a sleep in your basket." He gave the dog a shove in Jenna's direction and watched him follow her to the cottage.

"You talk to that dog like he understands you." Rowley chuckled.

Kane frowned. "Duke understands me just fine." He went to Jenna's cruiser and pulled out a forensics kit, taking out gloves, evidence markers, and bags.

"What have we got?" Ty Carter came to his side and moved a toothpick across his lips. "Man, someone sure wanted to get to Jenna." He gave him a sideways glance. "Have any of her past convictions been released from jail lately?"

Kane shook his head and handed him gloves. "Nope, most of the dangerous ones are in for life." He indicated to the crossbow bolt. "We've had our share of unusual cases, but this is the first to leave an ear as a calling card." He indicated to the porch. "It's hard to make out now, but that's a threat written in mud. Here, look at the images." He held out his phone. "That just happens to be the last thing James Stone said to Jenna."

"Hmm, and yet he's locked up in jail with no communication with the outside world. That would take some doing. More likely whoever did this is trying to deflect the blame away from him and onto Stone." Carter indicated to his Doberman, Zorro, to stay with a flick of his hand and climbed the steps and examined the ear. "I'd say it's from a female. You don't see many guys around these parts wearing daisy earrings." He turned in a slow circle. "Dammit, we need a scope to follow the trajectory. Looking at the pattern, I figure most of these shots were made from the same location."

Kane scanned the area using his years of sniper experience and indicated with his chin toward the tree line. "I'd say he positioned himself there and walked toward the house. There are what—six bolts in a quiver?"

"Darned if I know." Carter patted his Glock. "I've never had the need to use one."

"Yeah." Rowley walked toward them. "Six bolts but he had more with him, I've counted eight. They're all the same, aluminum and a brand for a popular crossbow. I dusted a few for prints and there's zip. He was careful. No foreign prints in the house either."

"But he left footprints." Zac Rio stepped around the broken front door. "Size twelve work boots. I looked up the brand and they're made in the millions."

Kane nodded. "So, he wasn't too worried about leaving evidence, because everything he used was generic." He glanced toward the driveway as Wolfe's van pulled up outside the house and then turned back. "I hope Wolfe finds trace evidence inside." He walked down the steps. "I'll bring him up to speed." He looked at Rowley and Rio. "The intruder came through the gate using the remote, so he must have parked his ride somewhere close by. Walk down the driveway and see if you notice any tire tracks. If you find anything, we'll need images and plaster casts. Wolfe will have the kits in his van."

"When we're done, do you want me to tend the horses?" Rowley tipped back his Stetson. "It's no trouble."

Kane smiled at him. "I'd appreciate it." He headed to meet Wolfe and gave his daughter Emily a smile and Wolfe's assistant and badge-carrying deputy Colt Webber a slap on the back. "Thanks for coming out so fast."

"What the hell happened here?" Wolfe tipped back his Stetson, and his blond eyebrows rose in astonishment. "I'm real sorry this jerk found the remote in my truck. I had drugs inside but he didn't touch my medical kit. He went straight for the glovebox, broke it open, and took the remote." He gave Kane a steady look. "How did he know I carried a remote to Jenna's ranch?"

Kane shrugged. "We've all been thinking the same thing. It's someone close to us, but who?"

"We've all been working close for years now." Wolfe scratched his chin. "Rio is the only newcomer and I think he's solid."

Kane stared down the driveway at the two deputies and shook his head. "It's not Rio. I figure someone is stalking us and we just haven't noticed." He sighed. "Jenna is with Jo at my cottage. She's pretty shook up but okay. Rio has captured the scene, so I'll leave you to it and go see if the intruder left anything behind from his starting point."

"A crossbow is like a signature." Carter ambled along beside him. "Think about it. Any fool would know Jenna would be packing for bear inside the house. She could have walked out and dropped him with one shot."

Kane shook his head slowly. "You don't know Jenna too well, do you? The last thing she wants to do is kill someone. She'd rather take them alive and then find out what caused the attack. I figure she used common sense and retreated to a safe position. She had no backup and no communication. There's nothing in the house that can't be replaced. She doesn't have an attachment to things, I'm guessing you're much the same."

"True." Carter bent to examine a footprint. "Although, you are attached to the Beast." He grinned around his toothpick. "Don't deny it. That truck is your baby."

Kane shrugged. "It's insured and I'd just build a better one, but I'll admit I do have some attachment to it. Although, I figure if I lost my sniper rifle it would be like losing an arm." He pushed a marker in beside the footprint and used his phone to take a photograph.

"Over there." Carter pointed to a spot between the trees. "The grass is trampled." He edged around the small patch, peering at the ground. "There's nothing here. So, say he walked in from the gate, he wouldn't come straight here to his shooting position." He removed his Stetson, smoothed his untidy hair, and replaced his hat. "Hmm, how come Duke didn't alert her?"

"He did wake her but he hates storms. He tends to hide under the bed." Kane pointed to the barn. "From what Jenna said, the prowler was wearing night vision goggles. He'd have no problem moving around and would have disabled the generator first, then flipped the switch on the power box." He turned to look at the house. "He wanted to wake her and once he'd placed the ear where she'd find it, he aimed a few bolts through the windows." He rubbed his chin. "He didn't attempt to hide himself. I think he was trying to scare her."

"There's no accounting for stupidity." Carter marked the area with crime scene tape and then looked at him, hands on hips. "If he knows her enough to get in here, he should've known she had weapons. Who walks into a gunfight with a crossbow?"

Kane led the way back to the house. "That's exactly what's worrying me."

CHAPTER EIGHT

Bear Peak, Stanton Forest

He nudged the woman awake. She hadn't moved since he'd left her and she'd fallen asleep, exhausted or from blood loss, he didn't really care. He enjoyed the terror in her eyes and the funny little grunts she made behind the gag. He'd never gotten that response with animals. The defiance, the cursing, was sublimely human and something that kindled a deep-down excitement in him. After reading about people who enjoyed killing, he'd realized he was just a different kind of normal. Men hunted, women hunted, and some committed unspeakable crimes on each other. He smiled to himself. Some went to jail and others killed under orders and walked free. Some had the right to kill and some didn't. How could any normal person fathom the reasons behind the law? He had the right to hunt and carry a weapon, and there was nothing on his license that mentioned he couldn't hunt people. Every game animal had a season and pages of rules and regulations. So, any logical reasoning would suggest it was open season on anything else.

He held up the lantern and used the tip of his boot to get her attention. She looked comical with one ear missing. The bleeding had been impressive but then her little heart had been pumping like crazy when he'd sliced it from her and held it up like a prize. Now the wound had crusted over and just seeped a little, adding to the black stain on her jacket and shirt. Watching her run from him had ignited a primal urge to hunt. He'd stalked her, brought her down with one bolt to the calf but left her strong enough to walk at his command. He glanced around the cave and smiled. It was set up just right. Over the weekend he'd allowed her to escape twice, hunted her down, and dragged her back. He'd left her tied and gagged all night, but playtime was over. He yawned. It had been a long, eventful night but all good things must end, and he had other things to occupy his time. He nudged her again and she turned brown, angry eyes on him. She hadn't become submissive. Many did, but this one was wild, and he liked that about her. Fighting back made her interesting to him.

"Get up." He pulled her to her feet and touched her tear-stained cheek. "It's time for you to go now."

She tipped back her head and made those grunting sounds again. Like a Neanderthal man trying to create a language. He shook his head and pulled out his knife, laughing at the way she shrank back and screamed against her gag. "I just want a lock of your hair, to remember our time together." He grabbed a handful and sliced it through with the blade. It was long and luxurious and he tied it in a knot, sniffed the fragrant strands, and then pushed it inside his pocket. "Don't move or you'll lose the other ear and maybe your nose." He dived into his backpack for a roll of black gaffer tape.

Methodically, he wound the tape around her chest and down to her bound hands. He moved to her legs, wrapping them from ankle to knee. Soon she resembled a shiny black mummy. All she needed was an ancient Egyptian mask and a sarcophagus. He pushed her and she fell heavily onto the ground with a satisfying thud. He had everything ready; he'd planned this day for months. In the roof of the cave, he'd installed a pully system similar to those hunters used to dress their game in the forest. He wrapped the chain around her ankles and hoisted her to the roof of the cave. He watched her wriggle and squirm. Her shocked eyes made his heart race, and he liked that she understood what would happen next. Soon she became still and he crouched to look into her funny upside-down face. "It's been fun, June, but I have to go."

He ran the blade down her cheek and the panic in her eyes sent a rush of euphoria through him. It was always the same, and he embraced the power surge from knowing he controlled the glow of life and the spark inside every living thing was his for the taking. The cut was tiny but effective, and it didn't take long until the light left her eyes. She'd grown weak and was no longer a challenge, and the urge to play with her had vanished. He grabbed his backpack, extinguished the lantern, and headed out into the sunshine. As he strolled along the trail, he could hear voices in the distance. The sound triggered a need to forget his day job and hunt again. Nothing came close to the anticipation of the kill. His excitement in the hours before entering the forest reminded him of the times his father had taken him to buy ice cream. The eagerness of selecting the flavor, the taste as the ice confection slid over his tongue was a treat most kids took for granted, but for him that small window of time with his dad had been special. And like his time with—*What was her name?* It had been exciting but, like the alluring wrapper of an anticipated treat, she no longer served a purpose. Who thought twice about the food wrappers they'd tossed into the trash? He chuckled and shook his head. "Now that would be some kind of crazy."

CHAPTER NINE

Exhausted, Jenna dropped into the chair at Kane's kitchen table and caught the coffee Jo slid across to her. She added the fixings with extra cream to cool the brew. She sipped and allowed the night's experience to settle in her mind. A shiver went down her spine and she lifted her gaze to Jo. "Thanks."

"I know you've explained the details of what happened last night but there's more to this than you're saying." Jo turned a concerned expression on her. "I know something is on your mind or you have a hunch who's behind this attack. I'm a great sounding board. Talk to me, Jenna, and then try and eat something. You look like hell."

Jenna's gut feeling insisted that the man trying to kill her was familiar, but no one she considered made sense. She wanted to explain but she wondered if her reasoning was sound after such a disturbing night. An eerie sensation refused to leave her and she fought the constant urge to keep looking over one shoulder. "Being alone with someone hunting me down was an experience I've tried not to repeat, but last night was too darn familiar, like déjà vu."

"How so?" Jo leaned forward on the table.

Jenna peered at Jo over the rim of her cup. The smell of coffee was somehow comforting to her shattered nerves. "A couple of years ago I dated a lawyer by the name of James Stone. He didn't take rejection too well and became a nuisance. In the end Dave warned him off, suggesting we were in a relationship, and Stone backed off."

"What's that got to do with last night?" Jo stood and dropped bread into the toaster and then retrieved butter and jelly from the refrigerator. "He can't still be stalking you, can he?"

Jenna shook her head. "Nope, he's in jail for life without parole. He was living a double life. Top-shot lawyer by day and on the weekends, he ran a human hunting racket via the dark web." She shuddered. "Not only did he hunt down couples for his clients to murder, he killed the clients as well and kept their bodies in a cave out of Bear Peak."

"And you caught him?" Jo buttered toast and slid it across to Jenna. "Eat."

Jenna added strawberry jelly and nodded. "Yeah, but Stone came close to killing Dave. We were hunting him down in the mountains and Stone shot Dave in the head and he fell down a ravine, busting his knee. Worse still, he had amnesia and didn't remember coming to Black Rock Falls. When I went to help him, he didn't recognize me. Trust me, when Dave aims a gun at you, he means business." She stared at the toast and shook her head. "It was a nightmare." She bit into the toast and chewed slowly, recalling the terrible weekend. "In the end it came down to Stone or me. I took him down but wanted him alive. He blamed me for his killing spree and it's not something I can forget in a hurry." She lifted her gaze to Jo. "When I saw Dave's headshot and him falling over the ravine, I kind of lost it. I thought he was dead."

"But you were calm and detached when you faced Stone?" Jo sat down and looked at her closely. "That's what our brains do under stress. They can react either way. It's the fight-or-flee response. People like us train to cope in these types of situations and pull up what's necessary to survive. Your professionalism on the job kicked in and you fought back." She took a drink of her coffee. "It's a chilling story, but what significance does this case have to last night's incident?"

The images of Stone's victims impaled with crossbow bolts ran through Jenna's mind in a flash of horror. "Two reasons. One: Stone used the crossbow like a signature, but he wasn't exclusive; he did carry a rifle and knife. The second: although we've brought many killers to justice, Stone made it personal. He wanted me dead and blamed me for turning him into a killer. You should have seen him at his trial, he could have given Ted Bundy tips on charisma. My gut tells me he's involved. The crossbow attack is him saying, 'Don't forget I'm coming for you, Jenna. We have unfinished business.'"

"Then we'll need to find out if he's escaped ASAP." Jo reached for her phone. "Although if he's still in custody, you might have to consider a copycat killer."

Unsettled by the thought of a copycat killer with her in his sights, Jenna pushed both hands through her hair. "That's all I need." She looked at Jo. "Make the call. If it is Stone, at least we'll know who we're up against."

As Jo made the call, Kane and Carter came through the front door. She turned to look at them and held a finger to her lips to stop their chatter, but Jo stood and walked into the hallway. "Jo's calling the county jail to make sure James Stone is under lock and key."

"So, you figure he's behind this attack?" Carter dropped into a chair beside her and pushed back the rim of his Stetson. "Kane mentioned the crossbow but honestly, Jenna. Stone isn't the first killer to use a crossbow. It's probably a coincidence. For instance, did Stone leave ears as his calling card? Or take them for trophies?"

Jenna shook her head. "No, but the crossbow and the intent reminded me of Stone. I'm wondering if he has a follower out there."

"It's possible." Kane filled two cups with coffee and handed one to Carter and then refilled Jenna's cup. "Although, because of the macabre nature of the case, details of the murders were withheld from the media. Only we know he blamed you, so this has to be someone else." He sat down and added liberal amounts of sugar and cream to his cup. "One thing for sure, a woman is missing an ear. That message was loud and clear, but is he advertising the fact he's murdered someone or is he holding them for ransom?"

Jenna moved her attention over Kane and Carter as they removed their Stetsons and almost self-consciously ran their hands through their hair. They had their sleeves rolled up, but apart from that, she would have walked right past them in the street. She leaned back in her chair and stared at them. The usual jeans and casual shirts had been replaced by suit pants and dress shirts. It was obvious both had visited the barber, although Carter's sun-bleached blond locks looked as if he'd visited a stylist. His hair still hung over his collar but was fashionably untidy. Kane, on the other hand, looked slick, his dark hair trimmed to perfection. She must have been in shock not to notice the change in them before and wondered just how much she had missed during the home invasion. She cleared her throat. "I guess we'll have to see if anything comes in today. Perhaps Wolfe can use the Snapshot DNA Profiler or whatever it's called, again and we'll be able to get some idea of what the person looks like who's lost the ear."

"I'm sure he will." Kane smiled at her. "He'll be by later to give you an update. He is arranging for some of his friends to come by and secure the property."

Jenna understood by Wolfe's "friends" he meant a government team would be by, no doubt by chopper, to secure the ranch. Having POTUS watching over their security meant things happened fast when necessary. She nodded. "Thanks." She was going to ask about the conference when Jo's voice came from behind her.

"Stone is under lock and key." Jo walked into the kitchen. "He has visits from his lawyer, that's all. His mail is opened and read before he gets it, he's not permitted to send anything from the jail. There's no way he can communicate instructions or discuss his case with anyone who may be a fan." She sighed. "I spoke to the warden and because of Stone's notoriety, they keep a very close watch on him. Apparently, he is a model prisoner and spends most of his time in the library reading law books and making notes. Maybe he's writing a novel?"

"So, it will be a wait and see situation." Carter finished his coffee and stood. "We'll head off home now. Jo wants to see her daughter. Our resources are at your disposal if necessary and as it's quiet in Snakeskin Gully right now, if you need us, just pick up the phone."

"Thanks." Jenna smiled at him. "I appreciate you coming by."

"Any time." Carter pushed on his Stetson and looked at Kane. "I'll drop you at the ME's office so you can pick up your ride."

"Okay." Kane turned to Jenna. "Unless you need me here? I could get a ride back to town with Rowley?"

Jenna shook her head. "Go, I'll be fine. I'll leave Rowley and Rio in charge of the office today and we'll see if we can chase down anyone with a missing ear. I want you here to watch over the repair crew when they arrive."

"Roger that." Kane bent to examine her face and frowned. "You should go and rest. There's nothing you can do at the moment. Wolfe will be at least an hour, and Rowley and Rio are out looking for clues. No one will disturb you."

"Sure." Jenna stood and gave Jo a hug. She'd enjoyed her last visit with her daughter, Jaime. "It was good to see you again. Say hi to Jaime for me."

"I will." Jo smiled at her. "I've a feeling we'll be back soon. This case is intriguing."

A cold shiver trickled down Jenna's back, as if someone had filled the back of her shirt with snow. She swallowed the rising apprehension. "I'm not sure if that's the word I would use if this is a copycat killer of the Stone murders. I'll send you the case files."

"I'll read them on the chopper and get right back to you." Jo squeezed her arm. "You do want my evaluation on Stone, so you can make a comparison?"

Jenna nodded. "Yeah, I'd appreciate your input." She grimaced. "If this is the same type of psychopath, we're in for a bloodbath."

CHAPTER TEN

The new Wild Outdoors store in Black Rock Falls impressed him with its range of goods, and he liked the fact it opened at six every morning to cater to the hunters' and no doubt the hikers' needs, selling everything most people would require. It was always busy, as people in Black Rock Falls liked to make an early start to the day. He inhaled the mixture of smells from leather to gun grease and scanned the floor from one end to the other. The massive store held everything from camping gear to bullets, and it was a great place to observe potential bait. Of late, the town had become a magnet for tourists, and even this late in the season when the first frosts were already glistening on the high country each morning, some folks still wanted to hike into the mountains. Returning to Stanton Forest after a time away had been like awakening the beast. Many things had changed in his home town, but the forest remained constant. So had the mountain ranges, lakes, and waterfalls, but the town had grown from a quiet place in the middle of nowhere to a bustling, busy vacation destination. The hordes of bright and happy faces surprised him considering the town's reputation for being murder central. It seemed to him, being a possible target only added to the excitement of their visit.

He examined a top of the range backpack from a display he would never have considered long ago, but now he had money to burn. The equipment he chose said something about him, as did his appearance. People tended to trust the clean-cut type and avoided those who looked as if they planned to mug them at the first chance. He'd been following a couple from Aunt Betty's Café, the local eatery, after overhearing their conversation about hiking into the forest. Tour guides were booked to capacity as people rushed to the area. The hiking season was coming to an end. The first snow would arrive soon and many hikers were discussing how long they had before the weather turned bad, what trails to take, and the designated hunting areas to avoid. Most of them he'd dismissed as unsuitable, but the young couple would be perfect. They'd been complaining about the availability of a suitable guide, the lack of maps, and were currently arguing about purchasing a GPS to take into the forest. The cost would mean they'd have to cut their vacation short.

He smiled to himself and zipped up his jacket, making sure the BLACK ROCK FALLS PRIVATE TOUR GUIDE patch was visible. How simple that had been to replicate. These days anything could be copied. The technology was amazing. From growing ears to replicating a human heart on a printer, a simple patch was a walk in the park. He moved closer to the couple and examined an expensive satellite phone sleeve. He bit down hard on his lip when the young dark-haired woman nudged her companion so hard, he yelped in pain. He turned and smiled at them but said nothing.

"Excuse me." The man looked at him with a pained expression. "I noticed you're a tour guide."

"I am. It's a beautiful day and I can't wait to get my hiking boots on." He sighed dramatically. "Unfortunately, the party who booked me for the next couple of days decided to hole up in Blackwater with relatives until after Halloween." He shrugged. "At least it gave me time to collect supplies."

"Are you available for hire—for Tuesday?" The man's face lit up with eager enthusiasm and he stuck out his hand. "Emmett and Patti Howard out of Sleepy Creek."

He couldn't respond with his real name and glanced around the store for inspiration. His attention settled on the crossbow bolts he'd stacked on the counter beside a box of Jerry's Beef Jerky and the fine new hunting knife he'd chosen. "Ah, nice to meet you." He shook the man's hand. "Jerry Bolt."

"Well, are you free or not?" Patti Howard pushed a strand of raven hair behind one ear. "We need a guide to show us the trails into the mountain and a safe place to camp overnight. We have a good sense of direction and once you show us how to get there, we'll be able to find our way back. We don't want to stay up there for days, there's so much to see in this area."

Jerry shook his head. "That's not a good idea unless you're familiar with Stanton Forest, but if you want some alone time, I could leave you there and I'll make camp some ways away and come back and get you later or the next day? Or I could take you to see some of the attractions before you hike back to town?" He shrugged. "I'm easy either way. I'm planning on heading into the mountains anyway, there's a few less busy trails I want to explore." He looked at Patti Howard. From the argument he'd heard, she handled the purse strings. "If you want to tag along, I'll show you a safe place to camp. If you decide you want a tour of the sights the next day, I'll only charge you the going rate for one day."

"That sounds great!" Emmett beamed. "What time do we leave?"

Amused, Jerry looked from one to the other. They looked so eager and trusting. It was a shame he had to seed the forest for his kills, but with so many people packing for bear, he needed to be careful. "Sure. Get your supplies together. Can you find your way to the parking lot at Bear Peak? You take Stanton until you see a road sign pointing to Bear Peak Lookout. Head to the parking lot and I'll meet you there at eleven-thirty."

"That seems awful late to start hiking." Emmett frowned. "We'll waste the entire day."

Feigning disinterest, Jerry looked away. He didn't plan on spending too much time with his prey. He had things to do, places to be, and waited a beat before returning his gaze to the couple and then shrugged. "That's the earliest I can get there. It's not a long hike to the campsite, and you'll have time to set up your tent and eat before it gets dark. Once you're settled, I'll leave and come back the next day to make sure you get back to your vehicle. Or we can spend some time exploring the forest. It's up to you. Either way, I'll have you back here before it gets dark."

"Okay." Emmett nodded slowly. "Are there bears up there? I have a rifle in my truck."

Jerry raised both eyebrows. "Of course, there are bears but they'll leave us be and I'll bring bear spray. You can't just go around shooting bears in Stanton Forest when you feel like it, the MFWP, that's the Montana Fish, Wildlife and Parks officers, will haul in your ass. You'd need a license and as grizzlies are protected, they'd need to be attacking you before you could fire on them and I won't allow that to happen." He looked from one to the other. "There are rules you need to follow when hiking and camping so you don't attract bears. I'll show you how to protect your campsite."

"Thank you. I'm glad we ran into you, Jerry." Emmett took out his wallet. "Do you want me to fix you up now?"

"Nah." Jerry laughed. "After is fine. I'll see you later." He turned away to select a backpack and then headed through the crowded store to the counter to pay for his purchases.

Outside, he made his way to the alleyway where he'd parked his truck and checked his supplies. He'd head out now, to see what chaos had been created at the sheriff's ranch, and then head into the forest to choose a suitable killing ground. He liked to make sure he had everything ready for a hunt. The anticipation of the kill made his hands tremble with excitement as he turned the key in the ignition. He turned in the direction of the sheriff's ranch, taking the backroad that led to the old pastoral trails. The sheriff couldn't have the security up and running yet. He smiled to himself. He'd hole up there to watch the excitement and then head into the mountains. He had plans to make.

People rarely used the parking lot at Bear Peak anymore as too many bodies had been found in the area, but it was perfect for his needs. He wondered if Emmett would bring his rifle and try to defend himself. The idea added another level of thrill to his task, and the risk of his prey killing him was a chance he'd be prepared to take. Nothing in life was certain, that was for sure. As he drove deeper into the pine trees, the view seemed to brighten, colors became vivid. Like a butterfly exploding from a cocoon, he'd started to enjoy life again, and if it was for only one more glorious day, so be it.

CHAPTER ELEVEN

Once the chopper lifted off, Jenna stared at the suit jacket over the back of the chair and Kane's bag by the front door. A restlessness crept over her. Sleeping was out of the question. How could she rest when someone had invaded her sanctuary? She didn't feel safe anymore in her own home. She walked to the door and flung it open and took in the view. The big blue sky had pushed away the storm clouds and she could see the snowcapped peaks high above Stanton Forest. She turned again to take in the rolling lowlands wearing their fall coat of many colors. Beauty had surrounded her like a warm hug and someone had spoiled it. She turned and looked at Duke, curled up in his basket beside the fireplace. He gave a shiver as if he joined her in her concern. Kane's loyal companion would have given his life to protect her, same as his master, and the thought humbled her. She went to the thermostat and turned up the heat and then went to Duke and pulled his blanket over him. One sleepy eye opened and Duke licked her hand. She stroked his silken head. "Go back to sleep, everything is going to be fine."

Jenna made her way over to her house and surveyed the damage with a clearer head than before. The sturdy front door had been ripped off the hinges, and that took some strength, but inside had been trashed. Her new lamps and coffee table were in pieces, windows smashed, and the only picture of her, taken at a cookout with her friends, had been crushed under the heel of a boot. The new rug in front of the fire was covered in glass. She'd been proud of the renovations, and everything she'd worked on with Kane and her friends had been destroyed, apart from the darn drapes in the family room. She swallowed hard. All those memory triggers gone forever. Shaking her head to crush the remorse, she remembered the reason she didn't collect personal items. Nothing from her past life existed and always being ready to run meant she couldn't leave any clues behind.

"Jenna." Shane Wolfe walked up beside her. "I'm just about done here." He glanced around. "He didn't touch your bedroom, and the kitchen looks fine. The drawers were open and a couple of your knives are missing from the block. I've collected samples from all over, but I doubt he left anything we can use apart from the ear. No fingerprints on the bolts, no hair, fibers, or any trace evidence. The bolts are sold everywhere, same with his boots."

"He must be strong to have ripped the door off the hinges, Shane." She stared into his concerned face. "This security is supposed to be the best available and yet he got in with ease and could have murdered me in my bed. I didn't hear a thing. If Duke and Pumpkin hadn't alerted me, I'd probably be dead."

"It was my fault." Wolfe looked at her with his steady gray gaze. "I shouldn't have left the remote to the ranch in my glovebox. I had no idea anyone even knew I had one. He wouldn't have got in without it, but I'm arranging another fail-safe. We're putting a second backup generator in the cellar. Kane said there is an empty part of the cellar you converted, which will work just fine. We're also removing the power box from the pole outside. Most people have a switch inside now with a surge protector built in for storms. It can go in the mud room."

Jenna nodded. "I don't blame you, Shane, but whoever did this still has the control for the gate."

"Everything is being upgraded and will work through your phone now." Wolfe smiled. "Don't worry, Bobby Kalo the FBI whizz kid will make sure everything is hacker proof."

Jenna shuddered. "Unless someone cuts off my thumb."

"Then we'll incorporate a retinal scanner." Wolfe shrugged.

"So, they'll cut out an eye?" Jenna rubbed both her arms, suddenly cold. "That makes me feel a whole lot better."

"We'll keep you safe, I promise." Wolfe gave her a long look. "Do you want to come stay with me and the girls until this is sorted?"

Jenna shook her head. "Much as I'd love to, I've work to do and Kane's spare room will be just fine. I don't think anyone will get past him or Duke."

"Me either." Wolfe gave her a long look. Dave will guard you with his life, and I mean every word."

Jenna rolled her eyes. "Yes, I know, and I'd just gotten him out of being overprotective." She sighed. "It's not that I don't appreciate him, I do, but when he's worried about my safety, I lose my friend and he becomes a different person."

"You're lucky we've seen the real person. I only ever communicated with a professional, machine-like, emotionless soldier for a very long time." Wolfe lowered his voice. "When he decided to retire, his clearance was so high, as was his integrity, POTUS didn't want to lose him. He went through so many psych tests to see if he was sane, I'm surprised he came out the other side. It took him a long time to come down and even relax. I was retained as his handler even when he worked at the White House. He never lost his cool even when Annie died. He remained remote. I've only seen him crack twice, and the first time was when he thought you'd died, the second when we discovered who'd killed Annie, and yet you held him together. I wouldn't have been able to control him if that lunatic had killed you; he'd have been off the grid and out for blood and yet you kept him on track and calm." He squeezed her arm. "It's taking time but you're thawing the ice-man, however, he'll always be there lurking in the background. Years of living without emotion and killing on command takes a toll on a person."

Jenna pushed both hands through her hair. "I understand him better than you realize. That's why I try to keep things normal around him. I joke about his combat face and make sure he knows I like him, ice-man or Dave." She looked at him. "You have to admit, he's more relaxed now than ever before."

"He is." Wolfe turned as voices came down the hallway. "That's good. Emily and Webber have finished collecting samples." He turned back. "A crew will be here soon to secure the ranch. First, they'll arrive by chopper. They'll do a walk-through and see what needs to be done, and then expect trucks and a mess of people running around. I've stuck an 'off limits' notice on your bedroom door and locked it." He handed her a key. "Nothing was touched in there, but I secured it for your own peace of mind. You don't need to worry about people going through your belongings. If you have anything you need to keep private, you have time to remove it. I can help."

Jenna shook her head. "They won't be getting into my room, and the safe is in there. It will be fine." She rubbed her temples. "Will I have to supervise?"

"Nope." Wolfe led her toward the front door. "Leave them to do their job. They'll have the perimeter secured today and they'll be camping on the ranch, but it should be finished in a few days."

Astonished, Jenna stared at him. "How am I going to feed all of them?"

"They'll have a mess tent set up. Don't worry." Wolfe chuckled. "Stay in Kane's cottage until they leave. I'll have your new phones waiting for you by the morning."

"New phones?" Jenna frowned. "But I can access all my office files from my phone. It's indispensable."

"Trust me." Wolfe smiled. "Everything will be fine." He turned to his daughter. "Jenna is dead on her feet. Walk her back to Kane's cottage and make sure she rests."

Jenna shook her head. "Later. I need to speak to Rowley and Rio about running the office for a couple of days."

"They're not going anywhere for a few hours." Wolfe guided her to the door. "They're out making casts of tire tracks and footprints at the moment."

"Okay." Jenna turned to Emily. "You don't need to escort me, I'll go and rest, I promise."

"Sure, you will." Emily took her arm and led her toward the cottage. "Did you see Ty today all dressed up? He scrubs up well, don't you think?"

Jenna gaped at her. "You don't have a crush on him, do you?"

"Well... he is nice, and I am twenty-one next month." Emily looked suddenly serious. "I've worked hard and avoided relationships, but when I pass my finals, I'll be spending the entire year in residency working with Dad. It takes years more study before I can apply for board certification, but I think I'll have time to live a little."

"But Ty Carter?" Jenna chewed on her bottom lip. "He's sexist and a player. You're just attracted to his bad boy image. It will wear off in time." She wanted to change the subject fast. "So, did you find any evidence to point to who is trying to kill me?"

"Not a shred." Emily shrugged. "Don't worry, Dad will find something. He always does." She followed Jenna into Kane's cottage and sniffed. "I'm going to help myself to a cup of Dave's famous coffee. She pointed to the hallway. "Go and rest. Turn off your phone. I'll stay right here until Dave gets back."

"Okay, okay." Suddenly exhausted, Jenna yawned and gave her a wave and then headed for Kane's spare room. She kicked off her boots, flopped on the bed, and snuggled under the blankets. The troubles of the night drifted into insignificance as sleep claimed her.

CHAPTER TWELVE

Kane dropped by the office to explain the break in at Jenna's ranch to the receptionist, Magnolia Brewster, known as Maggie to everyone around. Nothing had come in about missing persons, and he gave Maggie the task of contacting the hospital and local doctors to find out if anyone had sought medical attention for a missing ear. Hoping Jenna would be resting, he took the opportunity to shower and change into his uniform. Well, if you could call black jeans, and T-shirt plus his sheriff's department jacket, a uniform. He kept several sets of clothes and boots in the locker room, often not having time to drive back to the ranch to change. He collected his belt and holster from the gun locker and strapped it on as he walked into Jenna's new office. He wore his weapon low on his thigh, to allow him freedom of movement and the fast draw of a gunslinger. Over the weekend of the conference, he'd opted for a shoulder holster. He never went anywhere unarmed, and hadn't for many years.

The fragrance of the honeysuckle shampoo Jenna used still lingered in the room. He'd caught the same scent in the hallway outside his room the previous night and had walked from one end of the hotel to the other looking for her. He'd wanted to call her but it was late and for a man who could fall asleep standing up if necessary, he'd lain awake a long time. If he'd been a superstitious man, he'd have believed she'd been trying to send him a message. He laughed. A few years in Black Rock Falls and the spookiness of Halloween was creeping into his life. Pushing away fanciful notions, he sat at Jenna's desk and opened her computer to search for reported missing persons across the local counties. He scanned the page as the reports came in and sent them to the printer. As an afterthought, he scanned the list of the convicted killers they'd sent to county. All were locked up and accounted for. He rubbed his chin as concern for Jenna's safety crawled over him like a swarm of ants. Whoever broke into Jenna's ranch knew too much about her. He must be someone very close to know such intimate details of her private life. She hadn't advertised the fact she'd be alone over the weekend. Nobody knew unless…

He pulled out his phone and called Bobby Kalo at the FBI field office at Snakeskin Gully. The young man had been recruited after an arrest as a black hat hacker. The kid was a genius with anything to do with IT. Kalo didn't have a dishonest bone in his body but playing with fire and hacking top-secret government databases for fun had almost landed him in federal prison for life. "Hey, Bobby, Dave Kane here."

"I'll have the new phones to you first thing in the morning, Wolfe can update the security protocol once the new system at the ranch is installed." Kalo tapped away at his computer and Kane could hear music in the background.

He's playing games. "I didn't call about the phones but I'll pass on the message." Kane cleared his throat. "So, you know about the attack on Jenna?"

"Yeah, anything else I can do?" Kalo sounded genuinely concerned.

Kane leaned back in the office chair. "Yeah, check out the conference we attended over the weekend. I noticed reporters there. Jo was of interest to them and did a number of interviews. I'm wondering if anything showed in the media about me being there?"

"Looking for five minutes of fame, huh?" Kalo barked a laugh. *"I'll look. Anything else?"*

Shaking his head, Kane rolled his eyes to the ceiling. "Nope. Trust me, that's the last thing I want, but if I was mentioned then someone would know Jenna was alone over the weekend. Anyone who knows Jenna wouldn't risk attacking the ranch with both of us there. In fact, I'm surprised anyone tried taking on Jenna with a crossbow. She is quite capable of defending her home, but having me out of the way as well made his odds better."

"Okay, let me see." Kalo hummed a tune as he searched. *"Ah-huh, yeah, you're here in a photograph with Jo. Nice suit. Italian? You're doing okay for a deputy."*

Kane rubbed between his eyebrows and sighed. "Did they name me?"

"Sure did…. Special Agent Jo Wells and her companion Deputy Sheriff David Kane from Black Rock Falls." Kalo tapped on his keyboard. *"The story went out on the wire. It would have made the local newspapers just about everywhere. The convention was a big deal for this state."*

"Okay, thanks." Kane thought for a beat. "We're hunting down a woman with a missing ear. Well, we're assuming it's a woman. Can you keep a watch on any missing persons or people seeking medical attention at hospitals with an ear injury?"

"You mean hack into hospital files over what time frame?" Kalo didn't seem at all fazed by the request.

Kane wrinkled his nose recalling the fresh meat smell of the ear. "From Thursday. We found the ear this morning but the perp could have kept it refrigerated for all I know. Wolfe will be able to tell us more later."

"Okay." Kalo sounded serious and the background music had stopped. *"Leave it with me. If I come across anything, I'll contact you."*

"Thanks." Kane disconnected and stood. He collected the printouts and slid them into a folder and then headed for the door.

He paused at the counter and waited for Maggie to finish speaking to one of the townsfolk. He gave the man a nod and turned to her. "Rowley and Rio will be back soon. Jenna will be working from home today at least. I'm heading back to the ranch now."

Before Kane reached the front door Atohi Blackhawk arrived looking agitated. He nodded to Maggie and grabbed Kane's arm. "We have to talk."

Kane stared at the hand on his arm and then back to Blackhawk's expression of deep concern. He was a close friend and although not officially on the team, the Native American tracker had given his time freely to assist them and was a good friend. "Sure, come into Jenna's office."

"No, outside." Blackhawk practically dragged him to the door.

"Now just wait up a second." Kane dug in his heels. "What's so darn important? You're acting crazy."

"You'll see soon enough." Blackhawk dropped his hand. "In my truck. I went to see Shane but the ME's office is closed. I called Jenna and got the answering machine, so I came here." He walked up to his pickup and pulled back the canvas cover. "Take a look. I figure it's human. One of the dogs brought it into the res. I bagged it and put it on ice." He pulled a cooler toward him and lifted the lid.

Kane leaned into the tray of the pickup and examined the fleshy bone with numerous teeth marks. The end had been crushed, but what resembled a part of a tattoo remained on the flesh. "Yeah, it sure looks like part of the lower leg." He turned to Blackhawk. "Bear attack?"

"There's not been a grizzly attack in years in these parts. This looks more like a black bear came across a body and chewed it up some." Blackhawk looked at him. "Has anyone gone missing?"

Kane shook his head. "Not that we know of yet, no, but perhaps this person hasn't been missed yet." He leaned in closer to the body part and sniffed. "Can you smell gas?"

"Yeah." Blackhawk dragged the cover back over the tray. "It was all over the limb. The dog's mouth was blistered from it and we had to wash it out. I haven't tracked this back to the source. I figured you'd want to be involved. The bears are feasting before hibernation, but they won't eat anything tainted with oil or gasoline." He frowned. "This is man's doing. Bears don't carry gas around with them. Whoever killed this person didn't want the wildlife spreading it around. I've seen this before. Do you recall the last time something like this happened?"

Vivid memories of finding bodies soaked in gas pinned to trees with a crossbow bolt rammed into Kane's mind like a cannonball. The nightmare that followed a gunshot to the head had been harrowing. The man responsible was locked up, but the attack on Jenna, the ear attached to the house with a crossbow bolt, and now a dismembered body part soaked in gas. The scenario was getting way too familiar. Concern gripped him. He composed his features and turned to Blackhawk. "Wolfe is out at Jenna's ranch. Someone trashed the house last night when I was away. She was alone too."

"Is Jenna okay?" Blackhawk's face filled with concern. "Why didn't she call someone?"

"She's fine." Kane straightened. "She couldn't call anyone. Her phone was out, and so was the power. I didn't find out until this morning when Rowley dropped by to check on her." He indicated with his chin toward Main. "Why don't you head out to the ranch and hand the remains over to Wolfe. He'll decide what to do once he confirms it's human. If he does, I figure I'll start at the res and follow Duke on horseback."

"It's human. No animal I know has a tattoo on their leg. You take the remains to Wolfe, and I'll arrange for horses from the res to save time." Blackhawk stared into space for a beat. "Four and a packhorse should be enough for your team. I'll come along too. I wouldn't want you getting lost up there. The forest is very dense, and there are many glacial ravines around Bear Peak."

Kane slapped him on the back. "Great, thanks. I'll grab the supplies."

"This is bad business." Blackhawk's face held an expression of sorrow. "Too many use our forest for murder and the spirits will not rest easy until you find this menace." He handed the remains to Kane, climbed into his truck, and, shaking his head, drove away.

Unsettled, Kane stared after him. He had great respect for the beliefs of Blackhawk's people, and as he turned and stared at the pines marching up the side of the mountain to disappear into the morning mist, a great sadness fell over him. He considered the forest, mountains, and falls an incredible gift that too many people abused. Just absorbing the beauty of them had kept him going, especially in the beginning. After losing his wife, he'd left behind his time in the White House protecting POTUS and his years as a sniper to arrive in Black Rock Falls to start a life created in fiction, with a new face and name. He carried a ton of hurt and anger, but this town had soothed his soul. The forest and mountains seemed to know he needed solitude, and then he'd met Jenna. A sheriff new to the job, a little unorganized at first and fiercely independent. He'd picked her as a special agent from the get-go and believed her to be a plant. Jenna, on the other hand, was convinced he'd been sent by the cartel to take her out. It had been an interesting few months but he wouldn't change anything about his job as deputy sheriff or working with the people who'd become his surrogate family.

He made his way back inside the office and gave Maggie an update. She bustled around making coffee and filling Thermos flasks. It was cold in the mountains and anything could happen. Kane made a quick call to Aunt Betty's Café for supplies and then pulled out the saddlebags. He packed everything they'd need and hauled them out to his truck. Ten minutes later, he'd made his way through the bouncing plastic pumpkins strung up along Main and sidestepped the grinning skeletons and ghosts adorning the storefronts to get back to his truck. The townsfolk were going all out this year and were out in droves repairing and decorating the town after the storm.

He drove slowly through town and turned onto the highway heading for the ranch. Lights flashing, he accelerated, enjoying the roar of the engine and the wind blowing in his face. The smells and sights of late fall surrounded him on his journey in peaceful normality, but as he turned into the ranch the hairs on the back of his neck bristled with a primal instinct that warned him someone was watching. He slowed and reversed back to the gate and then moved forward slowly, scanning the trees. Many criminals returned to a crime scene, but this one would have to be pretty dumb to hang around with the entire team on the premises... but then there was no reason to a psychopath's mindset and if someone was killing people in the forest and nailing ears to Jenna's house, anything was possible.

CHAPTER THIRTEEN

He'd decided he liked the name: Jerry Bolt, and he could almost see himself signing his name in blood on the face of Patti Howard. He lifted his fingers to his lips and licked across them, almost tasting the metallic tang of blood. The anticipation was rebellious now, screaming at him to forget the sheriff and concentrate on Patti. He chuckled. Patti's name would become redundant the moment he issued the order to run. He had such plans for her, but soon she would just be another part of his collection. What would he keep of hers? He liked a small remembrance, a token of their time together. He couldn't explain why the names faded as the light went from their eyes, but the moment he touched their belongings it brought back the intense rush of the moment they'd died. It was not like any other memory. He could see himself as if he watched from outside his body. It was like an exciting movie. It made his heart race, and knowing it was him taking their lives made it surreal, like an incredible dream. The scent and feel gave him a rush of sensation so intense it took his breath away, but then the craving started again. It became so powerful he couldn't function. The planning helped some, it occupied his mind, but doing was so much better than thinking, and right now he needed to move to the next hunt.

He took one more look at the ranch and then dropped the binoculars. He'd seen enough of the sheriff's team to recognize them all on sight. The last one to arrive in the black truck had almost blown his cover. That one was astute, and he'd need to be more careful dealing with him. He shimmied backward down the hill overlooking the ranch, and once out of view headed back to his truck. The old road was still carved out of the land as he remembered. The barbed wire that once divided the prime cattle grazing had been left to rust. One thing for sure, the sheriff wouldn't fall for the same trick twice. He'd learned everything about her and she was as smart as a whip. The night's effort would keep her busy for a day or so and give him time to enjoy himself in the forest. He ambled to his pickup and pulled off the cover and stowed it in the back, and then climbed behind the wheel. He'd hidden his white truck under a camouflage tarpaulin just in case the chopper he'd seen leaving decided to return. He'd used the cover many a time to avoid detection, and it was worth its weight in gold.

CHAPTER FOURTEEN

For some reason, whenever Jenna fell asleep totally exhausted, she dreamed of the beach. A sunny day, not hot but just nice, and walking on wet sand on the edge of a blue ocean that went on forever. Of late, she hadn't been alone. Dave had been there, walking just behind her. She couldn't see him but kind of sensed he was there. He gave her a wonderful feeling of security, and when she lifted her face to the sun a peace came over her, leaving all her worries behind.

"Jenna."

It was Kane's voice dragging her away from her idyllic Shangri-La. She squeezed her eyes tight shut, not ready to leave yet. "Do we have to leave so soon?"

"Well, you can stay, but I figure you'll want to be involved in the search." Kane's fingers closed around her arm and gave her a little shake. "Atohi's dog found human remains in the forest. We're heading out to the res to track down the rest of the body. Are you coming?"

Reality came crashing down like an avalanche, and Jenna opened her eyes and looked at him. Dressed to travel, with his Kevlar vest under a thick winter jacket and a woolen cap pulled down over his ears. "What time is it?"

"Almost ten." Kane glanced at his watch. "We're meeting Blackhawk at eleven. We need to move along."

She swallowed hard. "What did the dog find?"

"A part of the lower leg, just above the ankle and some ways up. It was chewed up some. The bears or the dogs had gotten to it before Blackhawk noticed it."

"Oh, so we're assuming this is the owner of the ear?" Jenna yawned and pushed her hair from her face.

"Maybe." Kane narrowed his gaze. "It was pretty hairy and had a part of a tattoo. It could be male. Wolfe has already confirmed the ear is from a female, so we may be looking for two different people." He held out a cup of coffee. "Get this into you. If you're hungry there are sandwiches and coffee in the truck and I've packed the saddlebags with supplies."

"Thanks." The implications of two people dying over Halloween week again this year seemed too bizarre. "I hope Halloween isn't going to be spoiled every year by murders."

"It might trigger some people." Kane shrugged. "Anything is possible."

Jenna sat up, swung her legs off the bed, and searched for her boots. "Is Wolfe coming with us?"

"Yeah, he's leaving Webber to run the office and Em is coming with us. They've headed back to town to get their gear. Atohi said it was below freezing at the base of the mountain, so rug up and after what happened last night, a vest would be sensible."

Pulling on her hiking boots, Jenna nodded. "Sure. I assume we're taking the horses?"

"Nope." Kane leaned against the doorframe. "I've settled them in the barn, Atohi is supplying horses and a packhorse just in case we need to bring down a body."

"Okay." Jenna sipped her coffee and sighed as the rich aroma filled her nostrils. "We'll need vests for Blackhawk and Em. I don't want to put them in danger."

"Wolfe and Em are already suited up and I've a spare for Atohi. He was a little upset we didn't inform him you'd be all alone over the weekend. He said you should have called him." Kane's lips quivered into a smile. "It seems I'm not the only overprotective male in town."

"He knows I can look out for myself just fine." Jenna searched her bag for another sweater and then grabbed her jacket. "My vest is in the Beast."

"It's in the kitchen now, I'll get it. Finish your coffee." Kane headed down the hallway. "I'm ready to leave and we're meeting Wolfe on Stanton."

Jenna swallowed her coffee and then scanned the room for what else she would need. She'd grabbed a few days' clothing from the house, but some essentials were still locked inside her room. She smiled. Kane had rescued her duty belt from the house, her gloves and woolen cap. She dived into the bathroom, washed her face, and tied back her hair. The couple of hours' sleep had worked wonders, and when she returned to the bedroom Kane handed her the vest. She dropped it over her head and pulled on her jacket, hat, and gloves. "What's happening about securing my house?"

"I emptied your safe, and gun locker. All your valuables and documents are now in my safe. You can go get anything else you need later." Kane narrowed his gaze. "No one is getting in here. My backup generator is working just fine." He met her gaze. "The team are here and have their orders. POTUS wasn't too happy with the breach in security. The ranch will be secure by the time we get home. The cosmetic side may take longer, but you'll have more control over that side of things. All the broken furniture has already been removed and you can order the replacements. The insurance will cover any cost involved. The interior damage will be repaired by the team over the next day or so."

"Good to know." The feeling of someone violating her home hadn't left Jenna but she smothered it. She dragged up her last ounce of professionalism and nodded. "Okay, let's do this."

They met Wolfe and Emily as planned, and they set out in a convoy. As the Beast powered its way up the mountain ranges, Jenna dragged her gaze away from the panoramic views of Black Rock Falls and turned to Kane. "Everything you've told me and my first impressions still point to James Stone, and yet we know he's locked away. Is there a chance he could be manipulating people, followers or whatever, from jail?"

"That would be my first conclusion, but I don't see how he can." Kane's attention was fixed on the road. "Jo followed up on her phone call this morning. She wanted to put your mind at rest. Stone is monitored, the only news he gets from the outside is a newspaper. All his correspondence is copied, and as we speak Bobby Kalo is going over it, making sure a code hasn't slipped past the officials. We'll hear more later. There's a ton of mail, he has admirers, followers, but nothing is happening between them and Stone. He's not permitted to reply to anyone. There is no direct communication to and from the outside. It can't be him. Jo feels the same. He can't possibly be controlling anyone from inside the jail."

Pushing back her memory to the discussion she had with Wolfe about the dark web, she recalled a comparison he'd made at the time to explain how it worked. "Wolfe once told me the dark web was similar to a cartel. There are groups of likeminded people who would prefer to remain anonymous but at times they gather… like pedophiles, sooner or later they trust each other enough to trade. Maybe Stone's clients in the human hunting racket were widespread and some are still out there waiting for him to reactivate his web presence. They are supersmart and rich. If the newspaper is the only thing Stone gets from the outside, we should be looking closer. I'm convinced he's involved. I figure, if this is a couple someone has murdered, with the gas on the body and the crossbow bolts, it's getting too close for comfort." She turned in her seat and stared at him. The image of Kane falling over the ravine in a cloud of blood made her stomach cramp. "He tried to kill you, Dave. It wasn't just me, he wanted us both dead."

CHAPTER FIFTEEN

If the trip to the forest on horseback hadn't been to search for the remains of some poor soul, the day would have been idyllic. The wind that had tormented Jenna the night before had calmed to a gentle breeze, and although more storms had been predicted the day was crisp but not toe numbingly so. She rode beside Kane as they followed the dogs along narrow trails that zigzagged across the dense forest at the base of the mountain. Duke ran ahead, nose to the floor with no hint of exhaustion from the long evening awake, beside him another bloodhound belonging to Blackhawk by the name of Seeker. The dogs shared the same mother, although some years separated them. They hit a wider trail and the claw marks on the trees warned of bears close by. She turned in her saddle to Blackhawk. "Bears have been here."

"The marks are old and there's no scat." He waved her onward. "They're far away and hunt at night and dawn. I don't think they'd come close to a group of us. They're smarter than you think."

The trail ahead widened and she noticed Kane scanning the area, his head moving from side to side and all around. She rode closer. "What's up?"

"Nothing yet, but my gut tells me we're not alone." Kane's gaze shifted to her. "I had the same feeling at the ranch. It's a second sense that something isn't right." He sighed. "I can't see anyone but I've been watching for signs of trail cams. If you remember Stone used them to capture and stream his murders. I've seen nothing and at the speed Duke is moving, the crime scene isn't too far away."

Wolfe moved up behind them and pointed at Duke. The dog was sitting in the middle of the trail and Seeker barked twice and then dropped down. "What does that mean?"

"They've found something. And the air here is tainted with the smell of death." Blackhawk moved past them. "This could be the place." He waited for a few seconds, observing the surrounding forest, and then turned to Jenna. "Someone trampled the bushes over there, there are broken branches leading off toward the ravine." He sniffed the air. "Someone had a campfire close by. I can see ashes on the wind."

"The horses are getting nervous." The stallion Kane rode tossed his head and snorted. "Are you okay, Em?"

"Have no fear, the mare is placid." Blackhawk glanced at him and his lips quirked into a smile. "Not so your ride. He carries the name Black Devil, but I'm sure you can handle him. Be aware he might try to take a piece out of one of the others. He bites."

"So do I." Kane moved away from Emily and rode beside Jenna.

Jenna turned to look at him. It was hard to believe he'd been so close to death a month or so ago. He covered his discomfort well or had a pain tolerance above most people's, but she'd gotten to know him well and his usually fluid movements had suffered. The two stab wounds had gone deeper than she'd realized, and one had nicked an artery. He'd been forced to rest up and she'd seen how much it bothered him, but this week he'd turned the corner and was almost back to his old self. As he rode close to her, the stallion's teeth snapped. The bay mare she was riding was sure-footed but shied away, almost unseating her. She grimaced, seeing Kane's horse roll his eyes. "Just keep his teeth away from me."

"Don't worry, we're getting along just fine and I won't give him the chance to bite anyone." Kane reined in his mount and then wrinkled his nose as a gust of wind blew up the trail. "I smell rotting flesh and gasoline. The body is close by. That's a smell I won't forget in a hurry."

The scent of the pine forest had turned into a smell Jenna would never forget. Death had a stench like no other. It crawled up her nose and stuck to hair and clothes. Like the acrid lingering smell of smoke, a person carried it with them and most times everything she'd worn to a crime scene had to be thrown in the trash. She turned at a tap on her arm. Kane was leaning toward her, his horse sidestepping and eyes rolling as Kane thrust a facemask in her direction. "Thanks." Pulling it over her nose, she scanned the forest. "The trail opens out some ahead, we'll take a look." She turned in her saddle to speak to Emily. "We don't know what may be ahead, so stay alert."

"I'll be in between Kane and Dad. They'll cover me front and back." Emily smiled at her. "Don't worry, I'll be fine."

The trail turned to the right and opened up into a small clearing. A tent sat open to the elements, the flap waving and ashes from a dead campfire dancing in the breeze. Jenna's gaze moved past the tent and she made out a figure at the bottom of a tree. "Wait, Atohi, we'll go in on foot."

They dismounted, Jenna waited for Kane to come to her side and looked at the others. "We'll go in first. Watch our backs."

Jenna's heart pounded and bile rushed up her throat as she moved into the clearing. She peered into the tent. "Clear."

"The fire's cold." Kane moved beside her, scanning the clearing from top to bottom. "I can't see any trip wires but be alert."

Jenna nodded. "Copy that."

Step by step, she moved across the campsite, her attention fixed on the body of a man sitting upright. He stared straight ahead pinned by a crossbow bolt through his forehead to the tree. The head and torso were intact but wildlife had gnawed on his limbs. The lower part of one leg was missing. As she moved closer the underlying smell of gasoline wafted from him. His clothes and hair had been soaked but it didn't hide the stench of rotting flesh. Flashbacks of Stone's kills washed over her in a horrific rerun. It was as if someone had re-created the scene from one of his many murders. She stared around. The only thing missing was the mutilated woman. Stone picked couples for his clients to hunt. He disabled the male and made him watch as he or his client tortured the woman. The bolt in the head was the coup de grâce. He'd filmed everything and streamed it over the dark web, taking instructions on how to proceed from the highest bidder. Stone's clients never made it home and became part of a macabre collection of corpses held in a cave at Bear Peak. She turned to Kane. "There are two sleeping bags and backpacks in the tent, also a pink sweater. There's a woman missing."

"Maybe they had a fight and she killed him." Kane was checking the ground around the campsite. "This might be unrelated to what happened at the ranch."

"It's making my skin crawl." Jenna beckoned Wolfe. "Clear." She looked at Kane. "I can almost feel James Stone watching us and yet I know darn well he's locked up in jail. Who did this, Kane?"

"I wish I knew." Kane pulled on surgical gloves. "I'll search the backpacks for ID."

Trying to focus on the procedure and not the reality before her, Jenna dragged her gaze away from the staring eyes of the victim. "I'll examine the tent. Go with Atohi and recon the forest, the woman might be close by."

"Okay, but I'll grab the sweater. The dogs will be able to track her from the scent." Kane touched her arm. "Stone is in jail. Don't allow the memory of his obsession with you to overshadow what we have here now. It's creepy that this murder is so close to his case, but there has to be an explanation."

Jenna stared back at the body. "It's too darn close, and I'm not imagining the man who wrecked my home. I know you figure I'm not thinking logically but my gut is telling me Stone is involved. We have to find out how he is communicating with the outside before one of his disciples kills again."

"I know you went through hell last night and whoever doing this is a threat, Jenna, but I can read you like a book and the thought of Stone manipulating a copycat killer and sending someone after you is clouding your judgment." Kane's expression filled with concern. "You always think outside of the box. You're logical. This"—he waved a hand toward the corpse—"doesn't compute in your mind. It can't be happening because we know Stone has no communication with the outside world and then we come across a crime scene like this one and it's unsettling."

Unconvinced, Jenna nodded to appease him but she had no doubt, some way, somehow, James Stone was in the thick of it. "Okay, okay. Think outside the box, gotcha."

"If we find anything, I'll use the com." Kane headed for the tent, bent to snag the clothing, and then dropped it into an evidence bag. He gave her a wave as he headed to where Blackhawk was waiting with the horses.

As Jenna turned away from the corpse, Wolfe and Emily moved in to secure the site. Having a medical examiner on her team was a bonus. Wolfe's team documented the scene and she could concentrate on the investigation. She headed to the tent as Blackhawk and Kane followed the dogs through the surrounding forest. Inside the tent, she found two backpacks and bedding. She took photographs with her phone. The tent hadn't been disturbed. After pulling on surgical gloves, she leaned inside and grabbed the backpacks. She went through them methodically and found a woman's wallet, her driver's license but no phone, just like in the Stone case. A wave of panic shot through her and she straightened to stare all around her. This was like a recurring nightmare and she wanted to wake up. Pushing down the rising panic, she scanned the forest, seeing a threat in every shadow. In her mind's eye James Stone stepped out of the darkness, intent on murdering her with slow deliberation. It wouldn't be fast. Stone like to enjoy his kills and he'd make sure it would be an especially slow and painful death.

Forcing her mind back to reality, she shook her head, but panic surfaced in a hurry as the shadows turned into a dark figure heading straight for her. She gasped with relief when Kane walked into the clearing and stopped to speak to Wolfe. As he came to her side, she looked into his troubled expression. "Did you find the woman? I found her purse. June Harris out of Buffalo Ridge."

"Nope, the surrounding forest is disturbed, so she could have run away. The dogs lost her scent down by the creek. It's wide and fast flowing, she might have waded across it or fallen in and been washed away. Or someone carried her. It's hard to tell. There's nothing but rock alongside it." He indicated toward Wolfe. "The man has a wallet in his back pocket, no phone. That's what's left of Payton Harris."

A shiver went down Jenna's spine. "No phones, the man disabled. This is too close to Stone's murders. We have to keep looking. June Harris must be here somewhere or what's left of her." She shook her head slowly and then waved a hand toward the corpse. "I'm not paranoid. This has Stone's signature all over it."

CHAPTER SIXTEEN

Bear Peak

Returning to a crime scene was listed as one of the dumbest things a killer could do, but his fascination with death compelled him to admire his work in the cave before resealing the high-voltage barrier. The black cocoon hanging from inside of the cave, with its purplish, swollen, blood-filled face and bulging eyes, captivated him. The images he'd shared with likeminded friends didn't come close to the real deal. He'd watched videos but in truth the tantalizing smells of a hunt came in stages. Fear had a scent, and mixed with the sweat of a young woman, made him hungry to kill her. The first drop of blood, warm and intoxicating, was an experience he'd never gotten from a video, and now the luring odor of death called to him. He took one last look and stepped outside. The smell would cling to him, and although many hunters walking from the forest had the stench of an animal kill on their person, he chose to use a pine-scented body spray all over his clothes. It was an idea he'd come across on the internet to cover the odor of death. He chuckled—that or a mentholated spray seemed to work just fine. He climbed to the top of the boulder that concealed his cave, the snowberry bushes acted as a fine cover and he took care not to damage them.

A horse snickering caught his attention. Sound carried in the forest, especially alongside the mountain. The echoes of people's voices as they traveled sounded like ghostly whispers coming from all directions. He took out his binoculars and stared in disbelief at the group gathered in the clearing. The sheriff was hard to miss with her rank emblazoned across her jacket front and back. He grunted in disgust; the warning he'd given her hadn't slowed her down and now she had found his kill. He watched for some moments until the deputy and another man had moved into the forest behind two bloodhounds. He snorted. They'd find nothing. He'd hunted down his prey and herded her to the river. It was knee deep at this time of the year, fast flowing and wide, but it hadn't taken too much convincing to make the woman cross to the other side. In fact, she'd run some ways down the river before staggering up the rocks and heading straight for his cave. He'd enjoyed his time with her and removed the silken hair from his pocket and stroked it. "I'd like to stay here all day but I have to go."

He checked the soil around the cave for footprints but found nothing. The thick coating of pine needles had covered any trace of him. He glanced at his watch and, with reluctance, pushed the hair back into his pocket. After taking one lingering look at the cave, he headed along the animal trail bordering the foot of the mountain. In ten minutes' he'd be climbing the track to the Bear Peak parking lot. He stared into the tall pines. It was so good to be back hunting in the forest again.

CHAPTER SEVENTEEN

Kane pulled Wolfe to one side as Emily collected samples from around the body. The animals had made a mess of the victim and Em took it all in her stride. Nothing seemed to faze her. Although he'd tried unsuccessfully to calm Jenna's worries, the same thoughts filtered through his mind. He met Wolfe's gray eyes over his facemask and caught his lifted eyebrow. "You think Stone is involved too, don't you?"

"You know darn well I don't make conclusions on the fly. You shouldn't either, because we have no proof he's involved." Wolfe waved a hand toward the corpse. "There are similarities with the Stone murders but also significant differences." He inclined his head. "I'm guessing you'll need absolute proof to calm Jenna's nerves after what's happened, but even if I make that decision, she'll make up her own mind and you know as well as I do she is difficult to convince otherwise."

"On some things, maybe, but she's no fool." Kane sucked in a breath, suddenly glad of the mentholated balm under his nose. "This has Stone written all over it and I'm sure you have the same suspicions. How he orchestrated the kill and attack on Jenna is the mystery. Jo contacted the jail and has absolute proof that Stone has no contact with the outside world. How could he possibly be convincing likeminded killers to copycat his kills?"

"Here lies the problem with that conclusion." Wolfe opened his hands and spread them wide. "There are a ton of differences if you look closely but as we only have one victim, I can't make a valid comparison. One on one, Stone's murders were a little different to each other, and why? Because he had different accomplices at each scene."

Kane rubbed his chin and stared at the victim, now lying on an unzipped body bag. "The obvious comparisons I see are the crossbow bolt and the gasoline. They are a signature of Stone's MO and those particular details were never released to the media. So, what makes you believe this might be a coincidence? What am I missing?"

"Many things." Wolfe bent and rolled the body onto its side. "The only obvious injury the killer inflicted on this man is the head wound. Everything else you see, at first inspection, I believe are from animal origin. In all Stone's cases he used a hunting knife or other methods to sever the spinal cord. His intent not to kill but to paralyze the victim. He was then propped up against a tree, secured with a rope around the chest, and forced to watch Stone torture the female victim. The bolt in the head was the death blow. He used the gasoline to prevent wildlife consuming the body but it didn't stop something tearing off part of one leg."

Kane nodded. "Would that be the body part Atohi recovered?"

"Yeah." Wolfe's mouth turned down. "It looks as if the remaining half of a tattoo on his leg is a match to the body part I have on ice."

"He wanted us to find the victim and what was left of the female after he and his client had had their fun torturing her." Jenna had walked up behind them. "He didn't use gas on the female because he wanted her devoured by animals. She was an embodiment of the hate he had for me." She turned her attention to Kane. "Jo just emailed her workup on Stone. She figures by making the male victim watch, Stone was displaying his power over the female. She believes in his mind, each male was you, Dave, and he was showing you he could do whatever he wanted and you'd be powerless to stop him. He almost succeeded, didn't he?"

Kane took her by the shoulders and stared into her troubled eyes. "But he didn't. You took him down and now he's in jail." He shook his head. "If by some remote chance Stone is messing with your mind, you're allowing him to win. I'm not going to let anyone hurt you, Jenna."

"He knows you've been injured." A shiver went through Jenna. "That was in the newspaper, so he knows you're not at full strength." She chewed on her bottom lip. "But how did he know you'd be away at the weekend? Only our team knew."

Dropping his hands, Kane stared into the distance. The idea of Stone noticing him in the newspaper was so remote he hadn't told her. He looked at her and shrugged. "There was a picture of me with Jo at the conference in the newspaper on Friday." He sighed. "You have to remember Jo is a big name in her field. I honestly didn't know they'd taken a photograph of me until Bobby Kalo checked the newspapers."

"You knew?" Jenna's eyes narrowed. "You broke security protocol and didn't think it was relevant to inform me? I'd have taken precautions if I'd known."

Kane rolled his eyes. "Really, Jenna? Don't you figure I'd have called you the moment I found out if I'd known? Kalo only just told me. I spoke to him just before we left the ranch. I'd never risk putting you in danger, Jenna." He cupped her cheek. "When I left home, everything was sweet. We had no cases, there was no perceivable threat. You had the team behind you and the security on the ranch should have been enough. I'm not clairvoyant. I had no idea any of this would happen."

"Why didn't you tell me in the truck on the way here?" Jenna stared up at him, the anger in her eyes palpable. "It's relevant information and I needed to know."

Kane blew out a long sigh. "It's only relevant now we've seen the body and have a possible link to Stone. The intruder's only connection to Stone was the fact he used a crossbow. You said he dressed like an old-time gunslinger, long coat, hat, and Stone wore a mask and camouflage gear." He could feel Jenna tense under his palm. "Say I'd known about the newspaper article and called you before all this happened? You would have told me to stop being overprotective and that you could take care of yourself." He dropped his hand with some reluctance. "I can't win either way, can I?"

"I guess." Jenna rubbed her temples. "Okay, let's get at it. There's a woman out there with an ear missing." She pulled out her phone. "Now we have her ID, I'll call Rowley. He can hunt her down at the ER and local doctors. I'll ask Rio to put out a media release and a BOLO on her. We might have some information by the time we get back to the office."

Relieved that Jenna had dropped back into her professional mode, Kane nodded. "They must have arrived here in a vehicle. I'll call Kalo. Once we have the plate number, make, and model we can add that to the BOLO."

"Yeah, we'll need help to chase her down. She could be lying injured and need help. I want every man and his dog out looking for her within the hour." Jenna walked toward the horses. "I'll grab my satellite phone. The reception isn't so good this close to the mountain."

Kane took the satellite sleeve from his pocket and slid it onto his phone. He made the calls, and after his phone had chimed the receipt of a text with the information, he chatted to Kalo about his latest online game scores.

"When y'all have finished playing with your phones. I've a corpse to get on ice." Wolfe walked up behind Kane. "My team has bagged and tagged all the evidence. If you could assist in packing everything onto the horse, I'd appreciate it. I've a long day ahead of me and I want to get off the mountain."

Kane turned to look at him. "Sure, I'll get out a BOLO for June Harris and the vehicle and get right at it." He made the call.

After they'd packed the horses, they headed down the mountain, but even with the body sealed in a body bag the scent of death lingered. It would cling to his clothes and he couldn't wait to get in the shower. Kane moved his mount closer to Jenna. "Are you still riled with me?"

"No, not after you explained." She turned in her saddle to look at him. Her raven hair had dropped over one eye and she dragged it back behind one ear. "I don't care what proof everyone thinks they have about Stone's lack of communication. I know it's him. Something, an early warning system inside me, whatever, is screaming his name at me. He's involved, I'm sure of it."

Kane shrugged. "I often go with my gut feeling." He scanned the area, peering into the deep shadows, ever moving like a living entity as the wind rustled through the trees. "Believe it or not, I figure we're being watched. It can't be Stone unless he died and his ghost is haunting the forest, and although that might be an option for you, even after listening to Atohi's stories, I don't believe in ghosts. Trust me: if people could come back, they'd sure as hell be haunting me."

"Then it's someone we know." Jenna moved her mare away as Kane's stallion's teeth snapped an inch from her toes. "What do we really know about Rio? Let's face facts here, Dave. If we are living a lie, he could be too. They put killers in witness protection too if they roll over on their crime boss."

Kane shook his head. "No way. Wolfe checked him out with his people. Rio is clean." He rubbed the back of his neck. "I hope the woman shows and she's not out there somewhere being tortured. This murder was well planned. Who brings gas with them hunting? I figure what happened to Payton Harris isn't this killer's first dance and it won't be his last."

CHAPTER EIGHTEEN

The temperature had dropped considerably by the time Jenna returned to the Beast. Exhausted from lack of sleep and an adrenalin high that had lasted six hours or so, the cold wind was the only thing keeping her awake. She rubbed her arms with frozen fingers. Latex gloves did nothing to prevent the bitter cold of the northern regions of Stanton Forest. Getting the body and the mound of evidence Wolfe had collected into his van had been a long task. She had been grateful when Blackhawk had gathered up the reins of the horses and led them back to the res. Suffering a headache straight from hell and a backache that went from her backside down both legs, she tried unsuccessfully to climb into the Beast and just leaned against the door gathering her strength.

"Are you ill?" Kane closed the distance between them in two strides. "Headache?"

Jenna peered at him from under her lashes. Darn, even blinking hurt. "Yeah, and my back has seized up. The headache is a mystery, but the back must have been from sitting on a cold floor all night."

"Just stay there for a second, don't move." Kane hurried away and moments later came back with Wolfe.

"I'm fine, Shane." Jenna blinked at Wolfe. "I'm tired is all."

"Where does it hurt?" Wolfe prodded at her back. "Hmm, muscle spasms. I can give you something for that." He bent to go through his field medical kit.

The fact that as a medical doctor Wolfe preferred to examine the dead didn't bother Jenna. He'd flown a medevac chopper during his tour of duty, treated many wounded troops, and saved Kane's life on more than one occasion. She trusted him implicitly. "Thanks. I need to have my wits about me, no morphine."

"Sure, show me your hip." Wolfe prepared a needle, swabbed her skin, and jabbed it in. "There you go. You'll be fine after a good night's sleep." He looked at her. "Go home. You need to rest. You can work from the cottage if needs be. I'll be performing the autopsy on the victim in the morning at eleven."

"Thanks." She turned to Kane. "Can you help me climb in? My back is frozen." Then she remembered. "Oh, no, I'll ask Wolfe. I forgot about your injury."

The next moment Jenna landed softly in the passenger seat, the harness was strapped around her, and Kane had tucked a blanket around her.

"I'm fine." Kane narrowed his gaze. "It's been a month and I can start back on my regular exercises next week. I can do warm-ups now. The scan came back fine. There's no permanent damage, the doctor was just being cautious."

"That's good to know." Jenna smiled at him and leaned back in the seat with a sigh. The heat was running and the drug was working already. "Now if I had coffee, it would be perfect."

"Your wish is my command." Kane smiled at her. "I have coffee and sandwiches for the ride home." He closed her door gently. "I'll get Duke settled and we'll be on our way."

Stifling a yawn, Jenna nodded. "You're a lifesaver. I'd have dropped by the office but I don't think I'd make it up the steps right now."

"I hope you'll rest when you get home." Kane looked at her. "We need you at full strength, and you're tuckered out. You've given

Rowley and Rio their orders. The autopsy isn't until tomorrow, we have a BOLO out on the missing woman. I can handle anything that comes up." He sighed. "If I promise to wake you if we have a breakthrough, will you please go and get some sleep?"

Forcing to keep her eyes open, she took the cup he offered her. "Okay."

CHAPTER NINETEEN

Tuesday

It was dark when Jenna woke, and she peered at the bedside clock. The digital readout told her it was a little after five. She didn't recall getting home, let alone climbing into bed. Stretching tentatively, she sighed with relief. The pain in her back had gone. She'd slept through. Staggering to the bathroom, she showered and returned to the bedroom to hunt down her bag of clean clothes. With a smile, she stared at the chair by the door at the clothes she'd worn to the mountain with the smell of death clinging to them washed and in a neat pile. This was typical Kane. The military in him couldn't stand seeing an unmade bed, or a stack of dirty washing. His cottage was as neat as a pin and, like him, immaculate.

She dressed quickly and headed to the kitchen. The smell of coffee drifted down the hallway and a laptop sat open on the table, with pictures of Duke on a screensaver that ran in a loop. She peered into the family room, but Kane and Duke were missing. Duke slept in a basket by the fireplace and it was unusual for him not to greet her. She walked down the hallway. Kane's bedroom door was wide open, his bed made. Had he gone to tend the horses already? She poured a cup of coffee and added the fixings. Taking the cup to the window, she stared outside. Men moved around, going in and out of what looked like a mess tent erected in her paddock. The house had a new front door. It looked different from before. The windows on either side of the door had gone, replaced by ornate wood that suited the old ranch-style home very well. The windows now had security blinds. They looked strange, but after what she'd been through the idea of having a way to secure the windows was a relief.

After finishing her coffee, she pulled on a coat and woolen hat and headed for the barn. As she moved into the warm interior, she could hear Kane humming a tune. The smell of horses and the sharp odor of urine seemed welcoming after such a terrible weekend. "Morning. You're up early." At the sound of her voice Duke bounded out of an empty stall and nuzzled her hand. "What do you want me to do?" She rubbed the dog's silken head.

"I'm done here as soon as I've emptied the wheelbarrow." Kane closed the gate to a stall. "I'm leaving the horses inside the barn today as another storm is forecast." He took both handles of a full wheelbarrow and headed out the back door of the barn.

Jenna followed behind him. "Anything happen overnight in the case I should know about?"

"Nope. No sighting of the missing woman, nothing to report." Kane emptied the barrow and turned back to her. "Jo called last night to ask after you, and the new phones arrived this morning via a security team. I took the liberty of ordering a new rug for the family room. It's the same as the one you had and it will be here sometime today. Everything will be back to normal soon, although the paint smell may linger for a few days. The men Wolfe had sent here have been working around the clock."

Jenna smiled at him and pulled a strand of hay from his hair. He looked healthy and moved easily. Obviously, the long ride yesterday hadn't caused him any problems. "Good to know." She rubbed the noses of the horses. "You go and get cleaned up and I'll start on breakfast."

"There's a pile of hotcakes in the refrigerator, they just need reheating in the microwave." Kane smiled. "And bacon. I have a hankering for bacon, as many strips as you can fit in a pan, and crispy."

Jenna grinned at him. "I'll warm the maple syrup as well. I'm starving."

As they headed back to the barn, Jenna turned to him. "I'll call Jo later, after the autopsy, and get her opinion on my theory about James Stone."

"I've been giving what you said a lot of thought." Kane pressed in the code on the keypad to his cottage. "I figure unless we find June Harris dead and she fits Stone's MO we might be wasting valuable time. I say we treat this like any other case and hunt down suspects. Right now, we're surmising June Harris is missing. We don't know if the ear attached to your porch belongs to her. The two cases may be unrelated. June Harris could have killed her husband and dropped off the grid."

Jenna headed for the kitchen and washed her hands over the sink. "And if he strikes again?"

"If it's the same MO as Stone, then two murders the same takes the idea of a coincidence off the board." Kane headed for the bathroom. "Let's hope that never happens."

After stopping by the office to get a report from her deputies, Jenna discovered they'd been very active since the discovery of Payton Harris' body. Rowley had notified the forest wardens and made sure everyone who went through their station was aware they had a potential missing person and showed them June Harris' picture. Atohi Blackhawk had called and offered to take a group on horseback with their dogs to search the area across the river from the campsite where Harris was murdered. With the news media broadcasting June Harris' image on the hour, if she was anywhere in the area Jenna hoped someone would see her or the couple's vehicle and call the hotline. After sending Rowley and Rio out to check the remote places people might park their vehicles out of Bear Peak, she went with Kane to the ME's office for the autopsy.

The sterile environment and antiseptic smell did little to hide the stench of death hovering in the air. After settling Duke inside Wolfe's office, they suited up in the alcove outside the examination room with the red light. "There are people out hunting all over the forest and yet no one has reported anything to the forest wardens. It's as if June Harris has vanished. If there was a body somewhere out in that area, surely someone would have smelled it by now?"

"Maybe, but the forest is vast. People are field-dressing their kills as well, and that stinks. Most people would assume the smell is from an animal." Kane removed his jacket and pulled on scrubs. "If she's up there and alive, she'd head for one of the trails, or a hunter. If she's dead, the bears could have eaten her by now and we'll be lucky to find any remains at all." He snapped on gloves. "Ready?"

Jenna smeared mentholated salve under her nose and pulled on a facemask. "Yeah." She followed him inside and the doors whooshed closed behind her.

She immediately noticed that Emily was missing but Colt Webber stood beside Wolf, ready to assist. "Morning. Where's Em?"

"Exams." Wolfe looked at her over his mask. "She seemed a little more confident this morning. She has it in the bag, I have no doubt. She worries if she fails post grad, she won't be able to study for her medical degree." He sighed. "She's a straight-A student and there's no reason she won't pass with honors. I'm not sure why she's so worried." His eyebrows rose. "On the bright side, Julie strolled through her exams without a problem, and Anna is doing just fine. They both have their heads set on carving a pumpkin with me next weekend."

Jenna nodded. "Good to know." She ignored the covered lump under the sheet on a gurney and walked to the X-rays displayed on a screen. "What do we have?"

"Apart from a bolt through the brain?" Wolfe moved to her side. "The damage you see is a good representation of the food chain in the forest." He pointed to the image. "Here there are puncture marks in the bone, made from large canines, likely a bear. The mastication, from a powerful jaw, causes pitting and scoring like we see here. See how the lines overlap?"

"Can you tell if he was dead when this happened?" Kane's brow wrinkled into a frown.

"We took samples of soil around the body and the blood loss was minimal, so no, not alive. There is evidence of lividity in the lower regions of the body, which would be normal in a corpse in a sitting position, but if he'd been alive when his femoral artery was severed, he'd be sitting in a pool of blood." Wolfe turned and uncovered the remains of Payton Harris. "Animals usually go for the soft parts, so the internal organs, genitals, would be a target, but in this case the gasoline would have kept them away. What clothes remain are soaked. It wasn't just poured over him, it was dripped over to ensure full penetration of his clothing, hair. His hands were placed inside his pockets and his gloves were still damp when we examined him. There are no defense wounds on his arms, no sign of a struggle."

"So, he just sat against the tree and allowed someone to shoot him?" Kane scratched his head. "His wife was asleep in the tent and he doesn't try to fight? That doesn't make sense."

Jenna scanned the crime scene photographs. "He was looking up when shot. Is that your conclusion, Shane?"

"Yeah, from the angle, he was staring at the man who shot him." Wolfe flicked up an image showing a simulated trajectory of the crossbow bolt. "From this I determined the shooter must be approximately six feet tall." He looked at Jenna. "From the information we have on his wife, she was five-seven. I don't think she is the shooter."

Jenna turned to stare at the mangled remains of Payton Harris. "A bear did all this?"

"Nah." Kane bent to examine the remains. "Parts have been carried away. I'd say a variety of wildlife were involved. Cats wouldn't be able to drag the body so would take a piece after the bears had left, and dogs often run off with parts. The smaller bite marks are from other critters."

"The food chain, as I mentioned." Wolfe turned to her. "The bigger predators get in first and then down the line. The limb Atohi found was carried away by a dog and belongs to Harris." He sighed. "It wasn't robbery. He had five hundred in his wallet and all his credit cards." He looked at Kane. "Possible scenario?"

"Are you asking me how I could trick a guy into sitting still while I shot a bolt into his head at close range?" Kane's eyes flashed with something Jenna had never seen before as he tipped his head toward Colt Webber. "Webber is a hunter, so maybe you should be asking him?"

Jenna glanced from one to the other and cleared her throat. "I'd try and distract him." She thought for a beat. "The time of death would add a variant. Have you figured out when he died?" She looked at Wolfe.

"Late Thursday to early Friday morning, going on rigor, decomposition, insect infestation, and taking the local conditions into account." Wolfe lifted his chin and gave her a quizzical stare. "How do you distract someone in the middle of the night?"

"From the disturbed sleeping bags, the couple were asleep in the tent." Kane was staring at his boots and then raised his head slowly and looked at Jenna. "I figure the killer knew the victim because there's no sign of a struggle in the tent or anywhere else. Maybe he made up a story about seeing a bear close by or something and woke Harris."

Inside Jenna's head the scene played out. "If he'd mentioned seeing a bear, Harris would have woken his wife." She looked at the three men. "It's more likely they sat around the fire having a drink."

"Okay, so the killer gets him outside." Webber's gaze narrowed in thought. "The first thing I'd want to do after being asleep is urinate—that's normal, right?" He cut a gaze to Jenna.

She shrugged. "As there's bears around here, would a guy be wandering off into the forest to pee?"

"Nah, it's likely he'd have headed for the closest tree." Kane leaned against the counter and folded his arms. "Forget the bear warning. I agree with Jenna he'd have woken his wife if an attack was imminent, but how did he get Harris to sit behind the tree?"

"It was a full moon, so he had an excuse to be out hunting." Webber shrugged. "Maybe he said something like, 'There's that elk I've been stalking. It's heading this way. Duck down behind that tree or it will see you. I'll take it down from here.' Or whatever."

"Yeah." Kane straightened. "Harris would have been staring at the killer waiting for him to make the shot and wham he got one straight between the eyes."

"Silent and deadly." Wolfe nodded sagely. "The sound wouldn't have woken his wife. It gave the killer time to retrieve his can of gas and soak Harris' hair and clothes. Maybe then he crawled inside the tent to retrieve their phones and woke June Harris. There are broken branches around the campsite but we can't discount bears disturbing the area after the murder. I can't say for certain there are signs of a struggle. The pine needles are so thick there are no footprints, but we know from the scratches and scat in the area bears frequent the clearing." He looked from one to the other. "Shall we get on?" He moved to the body and rolled it over onto one side. "There are no marks to indicate any injury. No bruises or contusions to make me believe he fought for his life. I found nothing unusual in his blood to indicate any drugs. I've tested for the usual substances and I'm running a full tox screen, but I don't believe we'll find anything."

Singing a tune in her head to disassociate herself from the horrific sight before her, Jenna concentrated on a paint fleck on the bench as Wolfe dissected what was left of the torso. He made comments as he went and everything not chewed on was perfectly normal. "So, he didn't die of a heart attack or similar?"

"No. He was fit and healthy, a nonsmoker from his lungs, his heart is good. I'm sure the bolt is responsible for his death. I'll be conducting a brain examination and dissection to record the damage. Do you want to stick around? It might take some time."

Sorrow for the poor young man welled up, and Jenna swallowed hard. "No, that's fine, just send me the report as usual. I've seen enough for today." She turned to Kane. "Do you have any questions before we leave?"

"Yeah, I do." He looked at Wolfe. "How far did the bolt penetrate into the tree?"

"Approximately three inches." Wolfe turned to him. "Before you ask, it was a standard aluminum bolt, twenty inches long." He sighed. "They are a popular generic brand. No fingerprints or foreign trace DNA fragments. I only found the victim's blood and tree sap."

"I'd assume a crossbow could take down game at forty yards, so to pierce the skull and the tree it must have been fired at close range to gain the maximum kinetic energy." Kane unfolded his arms and straightened. "Consider that he's shooting at a target about six inches wide, we have an expert on our hands. I searched the area for bolts, or signs of them hitting around the body. This killer pulled off a small target in the dark with pinpoint accuracy." He frowned. "He's good, damn good."

Excited, Jenna turned to him. "So if he lives locally, he'd be known for his ability. Someone that skilled would be using the practice range. We'll go talk to the owners and see if we can get a list. We'll have a starting point." She smiled behind her mask at Kane. "I knew together we'd work out this case."

"Before you head out"—Wolfe lifted a cranium saw from the trolley—"Kalo called. He's uploaded the security for the ranch onto your new phones. So, the video feed is available on demand. The cards you use to access secured areas here and at the office now include the gate at the ranch, but if you misplace your card, one call to Kalo and he'll change the access codes. There is a scanner beside the front door to the house. To gain entry, you'll need a retinal scan. Kalo has incorporated your scan, Dave's, and mine into the system. I figured as you trust both of us, in times of trouble you'd like us to be able to assist you. You don't need to set the security each time you come and go. It resets when you enter and leave. The tracker on Duke has been programmed so he won't set off the alarm if he's out doing his business. You're good to go." He tapped his pocket. "I'll keep my phone on me at all times."

Jenna laughed. "I feel safer already." She gave him a wave and headed for the door.

CHAPTER TWENTY

It was a perfect day for hunting humans. The wind had calmed some this morning, and the forest at the foot of Bear Peak was dense and shrouded in shadows. A tang of the wild hung in the air and overhead a murder of crows waited for the next chance of a meal. It was as if they anticipated his arrival in the forest. The birds either sat on the branches still and calm as if imitating black flowers, or they argued amongst themselves. Some whistled as if sending secret messages across the forest to their lookouts. At this time of year, with hunters field-dressing their kills, the crows could pick and choose their meals. Many disliked crows, but not him. They'd helped him and others like him many a time. As nature's cleaners, once a flock had feasted on a carcass, only the bones remained.

He grinned as a little before eleven-thirty Emmett and Patti Howard drove into the deserted parking lot at Bear Peak and pulled up alongside him. He jumped down from his truck and pulled his backpack, crossbow, and quiver from the back. "Right on time."

"Morning, Mr. Bolt." Patti Howard wriggled into a backpack.

He'd almost forgotten his alias and turned to her. "Call me Jerry."

"And we're Patti and Emmett." She ran her fingers through her long black hair and then pulled out a bright-orange knitted cap and scarf from the truck and put them on. "I want to stick out in the forest. Emmett has a hunting jacket with an orange stripe all around. We don't plan on any accidents happening."

Jerry nodded, but his head was making a pleasant buzzing sound and the need to get going became overwhelming. He took a deep breath; he wanted to savor the kill, enjoy every tantalizing second, but time was against him. His gaze moved over her face—her dark brown eyes, so alive now, would rest on him before she died. The thought made him tremble. Each time he killed it was as if he collected their energy deep inside him. "That's great. I wouldn't want you to get shot by a stray bullet."

He waved them ahead down a steep trail that led from the parking lot and snaked around the mountain. It went past the famous cave where many bodies had been found wrapped in plastic some years ago, and weaved around before it came to a fork. One way led right past the cocoon cave, the place chosen and rigged to enjoy the last moments of a kill. Part of him wanted to go there and look inside, but he pushed down the urge and kept going. They'd walked for ten minutes, with Patti in the lead and Emmett hanging back taking in the scenery. It was so close to perfect Jerry couldn't believe his luck. "Take the left fork, Patti. That's great, keep going."

As Patti disappeared into the forest, he pulled out his hunting knife and walked up behind Emmett. He knew just where to strike. Closer, closer, and the second Emmett stopped and turned to say something, he grabbed him by the shoulder and slid the knife in to his spine. Apart from a gasp, Emmett didn't make a sound. When Emmett's legs gave way, Jerry whispered in his ear. "There that didn't hurt for long, did it?"

Tingling with anticipation, he sheathed the knife, dragged his kill to a tree, and sat him upright. The wound had paralyzed him from the waist down and the shock had rendered him speechless. It happened many a time: some screamed for their lives, but most had a surprised expression. Their brains wouldn't allow them to believe what had happened. He pulled out a roll of duct tape and wrapped it around Emmett's mouth and head and then wrapped it around the pine tree. He needed him to watch his wife's final performance, and what a performance it would be. He'd choreographed it in his head, every move, each mouth-watering cut. Sweat ran down his back in an urgent need to get started, sticking his shirt to his skin. When Emmett's eyes lifted to his face, Jerry smiled at him. "I'm going to find Patti and then I'm going to make you both famous."

CHAPTER TWENTY-ONE

After grabbing two to-go cups of coffee from Wolfe's office, Kane followed Jenna to the Beast. She'd appeared to be off-kilter since the home invasion, and as pale as a ghost. He placed the coffee on the console and waited for Duke to come out of the bushes adjacent to the ME's office. His dog was happy to wait in Wolfe's office for as long as necessary, especially since Wolfe had added a doggy bed and food and water receptacles, but before another trip he needed to stretch his legs. Kane looked at Jenna as she added notes to the files and cleared his throat. "Is everything okay?"

"Apart from another murder victim in our town, just peachy." Jenna went back to her iPad.

Kane shrugged off her snappy reply and slipped behind the wheel. "I know that, Jenna. Do your back and head still ache? Are you okay? You're pale and the autopsy was brutal." He handed her a cup of coffee. "Here, I guess you won't feel like eating for a while?"

"Thanks. No, I couldn't look at food right now." Jenna sipped the coffee and looked at him. "I'd be fine if I could just shake the feeling that Stone is going to creep up on me." She sighed. "Even if they finish up early on the repairs, do you mind if I stay in the cottage until we catch this killer? I don't want to be in the house alone right now. I feel like my privacy has been invaded and I don't feel like shopping to replace what the intruder destroyed."

Kane pushed a strand of hair behind Jenna's ear and cupped her cheek. "You can stay as long as you like, or I'll move into the ranch house—whatever makes you feel safe. When this is over and this killer is behind bars, we'll go on a shopping trip to Helena or wherever you like and pick out some things together. I think we need to make nice memories to cover the disturbing ones."

"So, you think my house needs a man's touch, huh?" Jenna grinned at him. "You'll be wanting a man cave in the basement beside the gym next."

Kane chuckled and got out the truck to lift Duke into the back seat. "That sounds like a plan." He got behind the wheel. "Practice range first?"

"Yeah." Jenna sipped her coffee. "Then we hunt down a few suspects." She gave him a long look and then raised one eyebrow. "We should make Aunt Betty's by one. Can you survive that long?"

Kane started the engine, backed out of the parking space, and headed for the practice range. "Sure."

"Good. I'll call the office and get an update." Jenna made the call.

The drive through town was interesting. After the storm, the high wind had scattered many of the Halloween decorations into mounds of weirdness. He slowed to negotiate a pile of plastic pumpkins entangled with skeletons and a ghost piled up against the curb. A small group of townsfolk were trying unsuccessfully to drag the pile onto the sidewalk. He pulled over, jumped out, and with some effort pulled the decorations from the blacktop before returning to the truck. "That must have been some storm."

"It was noisy and windy but not a drop of rain." Jenna turned in her seat. "Even with the wind howling and lightning flashing, the intruder still managed to hit his target on my front porch. He barely missed my head a couple of times. We're looking for someone highly skilled."

Kane looked up at the sky. "From the speed those clouds are moving, I figure we're in for more bad weather. He turned to her.

"We'll find him. Like you say, a man with that skill doesn't go unnoticed."

They headed out to the range. The grasslands resembled an angry sea moving restless under the swirling wind. Dust devils rose up high in the air, mimicking mini tornadoes, and crossed the highway, leaving a coating of seeds and other particles clinging to the windshield and dulling the glossy black paint job on the Beast. In the distance the sky had darkened to a threatening line of dark gray clouds. Kane took the sideroad with the signpost directing them to the practice range. The gates sat wide open and on each side notices had been posted to direct people to the office and warn against roaming onto the ranges. If an enthusiast shot bolts or arrows, this range catered to them.

Kane pulled up outside the office, which appeared to contain a store that sold everything a person could need to join the sport. He turned to Jenna, who'd finished her call. "Any updates?"

"They haven't found June Harris, but they had a phone call from the new assistant manager at Aunt Betty's. Her name is Wendy. She recalls seeing June and Payton Harris talking to a man but can't recall the exact day. It's lucky Susie Hartwig is the manager there. She's offered to look at the CCTV tapes with her to pinpoint the time and to identify the other person." Her lips twitched into a reluctant smile. "So, darn it, Dave, we have to drop by Aunt Betty's to check it out."

Kane frowned. "So Atohi found no trace of her either?"

"Nope, and there have been hunters in the area of Bear Peak all weekend." Jenna pushed two hands through her hair and secured it with a band from around her wrist. "A woman running for her life would scream the place down. How come nobody heard her or came across her?"

"The forest is vast and the vegetation around Bear Peak is dense. Sound echoes and cats can sound like screams." Kane shrugged.

"Most of the hunters out for the weekend might not have seen the news yet. Then again, some people don't like to get involved if they believe it's a domestic." He pushed open his door. "Maybe someone here can give us a lead."

"I hope so." Jenna followed him into the office.

Behind the counter a man swirled around on a leather padded chair in front of a computer to face them. His eyes opened wide and he stood.

"What can I do for you, Sheriff and— ah, Deputy Kane, isn't it?"

Kane looked at the name bar on the man's chest. "Morning, Eric. We're wondering if you keep a record of the highest-scoring crossbow shooters on the range?"

"Do you have competitions at all?" Jenna turned to examine a bow. "I'm sure there's a hierarchy in this sport?"

"Umm." Eric looked from one to the other as if trying to decide what question to answer first. He looked at Jenna. Seniority was obviously of importance to him, and he smiled. "Indeed, we do. It's a very competitive sport but not everyone gets involved. The hunters, well, some of them can bring down a buck with one bolt at fifty yards and that's no mean feat."

Kane removed his Stetson and smoothed his hair. The recent haircut had left his neck prickly and he didn't like the distraction. He slid the hat back on and stared at the man. The shooting range was classed as private property. He had joined the shooters' club and used the rifle range and the inside gun range as well. But Eric wasn't the owner—Bill Straus worked at the rifle range. Kane wondered if Eric would be forthcoming with names of members. "Do you keep a list or can you give us the names of anyone who used the range recently and is a crack shot? We're looking for assistance in a case we're investigating."

"Well, let me see." Eric stroked his thick beard and stared into space. "There's been a few new members over the last few weeks. I recall they came in with their targets shredded—they had all shots to the head. It takes some skill to put five bolts into the same target. I recall them because they reminded me of a dart player I'd seen on TV in one of those British competitions. He placed three darts in the same place. Incredible."

"Did they come in together?" Jenna moved to the counter and gave Kane a meaningful stare.

"Nope, all three came in alone." Eric shook his head. "I told them about our competition but none were interested. They all gave the same reply that they used their skills for hunting."

"And they never crossed paths?" Jenna leaned forward onto the counter. "Are you sure?"

"They've been here at the same time but they didn't socialize." Eric shrugged. "I'm not here all the time. Buzz works here as well, so I guess they could have become friends. Two of them came by last week, on Wednesday, and I don't recall them speaking to each other. In fact, I'm pretty darn sure they didn't cross paths. I was watching them on the CCTV. They gave quite a show but they did their practice run and left." He turned to a book on his desk and flicked through it. "I keep a record of their scores beside their names. Members like progress scores and it gives me an idea of which range to send them to. You know, I like to keep the novices well away from everyone else."

Three men who practiced headshots seemed too good to be true. Kane cleared his throat. "Those members sound like the experts we've been looking for. Can we have their names?" He indicated with his chin toward Jenna. "We're both members of the Black Rock Falls Shooters Association but we use the rifle range."

"Sure, sure." Eric pored over the book. "Ah, here we are. The most recent best of the best would be Riley Adams out of Snowberry Falls, Tyson Long out of Summit Heights, and John Foster, he lives out on Pine. Adams and Long were here on the same day last week, as I mentioned, and I do still have the CCTV footage of all the ranges from last week."

"Well, if you could make us a copy I'd appreciate it." Jenna pulled a flash drive from her pocket. "We could drop by tomorrow and collect it?"

"Not a problem, Sheriff." Eric smiled at Jenna, showing a flash of a gold front tooth.

Kane offered Eric his notebook. "Could you write down the details of those men for me?"

"Sure thing." Eric dutifully copied the details from his computer and handed the notebook back to Kane.

Kane glanced at Jenna and she gave him an almost imperceptible nod. He slapped the counter and smiled at Eric. "Thanks, we'll see you tomorrow." He followed Jenna back to the Beast. "I figure that's the first time we've found a decent lead into a case from the get-go. Three possible suspects in one day. Maybe we should buy a lottery ticket."

CHAPTER TWENTY-TWO

Allowing the information to percolate into her mind, Jenna entered the names into the computer in the Beast. The MDT, or mobile digital terminal, gave her fast access to drivers' licenses and any outstanding warrants. She could access criminal records as well, but what she needed was photographs to show Wendy at Aunt Betty's Café. She allowed the machine to do its thing and then sent the results to her iPad. She looked at Kane. "No outstanding warrants, but all three have been in the system at one time or another but I can't find anything on them for the last six months."

"It might just mean they haven't been caught yet or they've all decided to go straight." Kane turned onto Main and drove slowly toward Aunt Betty's Café.

Jenna admired the Halloween displays popping up all over town. Some of the storefronts had gone all out this year. She chuckled at a table with skeletons dressed as old Wild West cowboys smoking cigars and playing cards. "Some of the decorations this year are amazing." She pointed to a circle of ghostly figures that resembled long-gone famous film stars, long hair flowing as they waved at passersby with ethereal fingers. "The girls are going to love trick-or-treating this year. Are you going with them as the Grim Reaper again?"

"Maybe." Kane flashed her a white smile. "I was thinking Frankenstein, but I'm not into masks. With the Grim Reaper costume, I just have to scowl at people. What about you?"

Jenna thought for a minute. "Not a devil this time, maybe a witch. Emily has a ton of costumes in their attic. I'll find something when we next go and see Shane." She sighed. "If we get to go with the kids this year. I hope so. It means a lot to the girls and Shane when we join in."

"I enjoy all the family stuff with Wolfe and his kids, too. I'm hoping Rio and his brother and sister will come too." Kane pulled up outside Aunt Betty's and his stomach growled so loud Duke barked. He turned to look at him. "Okay, I know, you're starving too. I'll see what leftovers Susie has put by for you."

Jenna climbed from the truck. Susie Hartwig, the manager of Aunt Betty's Café, had a soft spot for Duke and usually kept him some of the leftover meat from the previous day. She led the way into the diner and went to the counter. "Hi, Susie, is Wendy around?"

"Yes, she's in the back. I'll go get her for you." Susie gave her a bright smile and looked over the counter at Duke. "Hello, Duke. I've been waiting for you to come by." She glanced up at Kane. "We have a pot of chili on the stove and cherry pie is the special today."

"You read my mind, but we'll need to speak to Wendy before we eat." Kane had removed his hat and was moving his fingers around the rim.

Jenna shook her head. "No, Dave. You go and eat before the folks in here think there's another storm coming." She looked pointedly at his growling stomach.

"Sure thing. I'll be right back with the order." Susie hurried into the back.

Scratching her head, Jenna turned to Kane. "She didn't ask me if I wanted something to eat. I guess she must be preoccupied." She shrugged. "I'll go talk to Wendy and when Susie comes back, can you order a turkey on rye for me and I'll take the cherry pie as well?"

"Sure." Kane smiled at her. "Coffee or soda?"

Jenna blinked and turned up her face to examine him. "Soda? Since when do I drink soda at lunchtime? Are you Dave Kane or have you been taken over by an alien body snatcher?"

"I guess you'll have to wait and see." Kane ruffled her hair and laughed.

Jenna smoothed down her hair and frowned at him. "Now I'm sure it's not you."

"Woo-woo." Kane wiggled his eyebrows. "It's Halloween, go with the flow."

It seemed to Jenna that Kane always tried to break the trauma of visiting a murder scene or an autopsy with his brand of often black humor. It was his way of de-stressing, and she'd grown to appreciate it. After a horrific day, Kane had turned it around to some type of normal. Whatever *normal* was in Black Rock Falls.

Jenna waited for Wendy to come to the counter and introduced herself to the bubbly blonde-haired woman. "I'm following up on the call you made to the hotline. Did you find any CCTV footage of the man?"

"I sure did, and it's set up and ready for you in the office." Wendy smiled. "This way." She headed into the back.

"Great!" Jenna followed her into a neat office and peered at the screen showing people enjoying their meals inside the dining area.

"I'll get it up for you." Wendy quickly accessed a file. "I copied it onto a separate file so I could find it quickly. Here you go."

Seated at the desk, Jenna viewed the footage of the couple speaking to a man the previous Thursday. She stared at the man in the footage and a freezing cold trickle slid down her spine. The height, black Stetson, and long black slicker made her hand shake. He was a match for the man she'd seen in her yard. Drawing on her professional mask to hide her anxiety from Wendy, she zoomed in on the man's face, but as if he knew someone was filming him, he kept his back to the camera or pulled his hat down over his eyes. One side shot was all she had to go on. She pulled out her phone, accessed the image files, displayed a few random headshots of other men, and mixed in the three suspects. She handed the phone to Wendy. "Do you recognize the man from any of these images?"

"Yeah, I spoke to him. He's a Montanan by his accent and I don't recall seeing him in here before, but that's him for sure." Wendy pointed to Riley Adams out of Snowberry Falls.

Jenna held her breath. This had to be too good to be true. She had a match for one of the men singled out at the practice range. She fumbled inside her jacket for one of the empty flash drives she carried in her pocket and handed it to Wendy. "Could you make me a copy, please? I'll clear it with Susie." She stood. "I'll go and grab a statement book from Deputy Kane. I'll be back in a minute."

Breathless with exuberance at her discovery, she hurried through the busy lunchtime diners to the table at the back beside the window. Susie always kept a RESERVED sign on the table for the use of the sheriff's department. When Kane looked up from his bowl of chili, she grinned at him and lowered her voice to just above a whisper. "We have a suspect." She reached for the folder on the table. "I'll get a statement."

"Find what you needed?" Susie came up behind her carrying a pot of coffee.

Jenna straightened. "Yeah, I've found some useful information. I'll just need a statement from Wendy and if you could give us permission to copy some of your CCTV footage, I'd appreciate it."

"Anything I can do to help, you only have to ask." Susie placed the coffee pot on the table and looked at Kane. "I'll fill out the paperwork now if you have it with you."

"Yes, ma'am." Kane pulled a notepad out of the folder and handed it to her. He glanced up at Jenna. "I'll hunt down the suspect's whereabouts while you eat."

It didn't take Jenna too long to get the statement. She thanked Wendy and headed back to Kane. She handed him the statement and dropped into a chair. "We have a positive ID for Riley Adams out of Snowberry Falls. Wendy picked him out of the three guys from the practice range and another three random images I showed her." She filled a cup from the pot on the table and added the fixings. "From the CCTV footage, he was sitting close by, then stood and spoke to them. It looks like Payton Harris asked him to join them. They talked for some time and the couple appeared animated after he left, as if he'd given them some good news."

"They're out of Buffalo Ridge, so about two hours' drive from town." Kane pushed away his empty bowl and sipped his coffee. "Close enough not to stay in a motel, if they planned on camping in the forest." He smiled as Susie came back, bringing Jenna's sandwich and two wedges of cherry pie. "Oh my, that pie looks incredible." He lifted the plate to his nose and sniffed. A look of bliss came over his face and he looked at Susie. "I'd like one pie to go as well, please."

"I have individual pies as well, fresh out the oven." Susie grinned down at him. "Cherry and peach."

"Six of each. I'll store them in my freezer." He looked at Jenna. "You can never have too many pies."

Jenna rolled her eyes and laughed. "Obviously." She waited for Susie to walk away. "We need to find Riley Adams today. I might call Bobby Kalo and see if he can dig up any dirt on him. He can get into files we don't have access to. It might save time."

"As he's already involved, we might as well save the grunt work." Kane bent to pat Duke on the head; as a police dog, he was allowed in the café.

Jenna made the call. "Yeah, we have an address from his driver's license but at this time of the day, he's likely working somewhere. Can you hunt him down for me, please?"

"Sure, it's as quiet as a grave in here today." Kalo tapped away at his keyboard.

"Thanks." Jenna put the phone on speaker and ate her sandwich. About five minutes later, Kalo came back on the line. She took the phone off speaker and listened with interest.

"I found him. Oh, you're gonna love this. He was arrested in Blackwater five years ago. Apparently, he shot and killed a guy named Jonathan Lamb. He was released four months ago from the Black Rock Falls County Jail after an appeal reduced his manslaughter conviction to a misdemeanor. He is a nurse at an old folks' home in Black Rock Falls by the name of Sunset Valley. Hmm, interesting. He wasn't on duty Thursday through Monday."

"That's just what we need." Jenna took down the details Kalo supplied and disconnected. She looked up at Kane and brought him up to speed. "I have the address of where he's working. Kalo even accessed the old folks' home computer and found the staff schedule. Guess what? Riley Adams wasn't on duty Thursday through Monday." She pushed the notebook toward Kane. "This all seems too good to be true."

"It sure does." Kane finished his coffee and leaned back in the chair, observing her with a frown. "It's almost as if he's being framed for the murder. When things look too good to be true, they usually are."

CHAPTER TWENTY-THREE

Kane wrinkled his nose at the less-than-fresh smell oozing from the Sunset Valley nursing home, leaned on the counter, and stared at the receptionist. He'd asked to speak to Riley Adams and received a hostile reply, for what reason he had no idea. He'd been pleasant enough and Jenna had smiled at the pinched-faced, thin-lipped woman with the severe haircut. It seemed she had opted out of visiting the beauty parlor and slapped a bowl on her head and cut around it. "Ma'am, you are obliged to inform Mr. Adams we're here. This is a matter for the sheriff's department. Now please get on the phone and ask him to come out and speak to us, or we'll go and look for him ourselves."

"I'm not required to chase down employees." The woman, with the name tag Yvonne, glared at him with beady eyes.

"Well, unless you find someone who can find Mr. Adams for us without delay"—Jenna removed the cuffs from her belt and dropped them on the counter—"I'll arrest you for interfering with an investigation." She gave her a look to freeze Black Rock Falls Lake and tapped the cuffs on the counter.

"Oh, very well." Yvonne's mouth puckered into a tight pout, showing deep lines where the lipstick had bled into the wrinkles. She gave a grunt of displeasure and picked up the phone. After a few moments, she turned her attention to Jenna. "He'll be right out." She waved toward a door. "You can wait in there."

"When did he start work today?" Jenna stood her ground.

"His shift started at eleven." Yvonne wrinkled her nose as if she'd smelled something bad. "Is that all?"

"For now." Jenna walked away in the direction of the waiting room.

Kane followed Jenna into the clinical, white, tile-lined room with a few plastic chairs against one wall. "Don't put me in here when I'm old. Just pack me for bear, take me out to the forest, and dump me. I'll take my chances."

"Me either." Jenna's gaze narrowed. "How come this place hasn't come under Mayor Petersham's latest round of inspections? He's been clamping down on any nursing homes not up to standard with their care." She peered through the glass door at one end of the room. "Look at that poor soul."

Kane moved to her side. An orderly had one hand on the back of the shirt of an elderly man, pulling it tight under his arms. The old man's joints moved as if he had the uncoordinated limbs of a wooden puppet, and the man leading him was using his shirt like strings to guide him. The old man had a tuft of red hair in the middle of a bald head and Kane had a flashback of an image of the Howdy Doody marionette his father kept in a display case in his office. He snorted in disgust. "The elderly deserve dignity. That's inhuman treatment." He pushed through the glass door and in three strides had reached the orderly. "Where are you taking him?"

"Back to his room." The orderly smirked at him. "He needs his exercise."

Kane nodded and looked at the old man. "Do you know the way to your room, sir?"

"Yeah, down the hall, first on the left." He looked up at Kane. "You planning on arresting someone, Deputy?"

Kane brushed the orderly's hand away and slid his arm around the man to support his weight. "Maybe. Can you walk okay?"

"Sure can, unless that jerk is pulling me off my feet." He headed down the hallway.

Kane looked at the orderly. "Come with us."

After he'd settled the man in his chair, he gave him his card. "I'm Dave Kane. You call me if they rough you up again and I'll come by and have a little talk to them."

"Seymore Huggins." The old man offered a pale, thin hand and smiled at him. "Thank you, Deputy Kane."

Kane took the old man's hand and shook it gently. "Tell your friends in here as well." He fished a few more cards from his pocket and handed them to him. "Any time, day or night."

"I won't forget." Mr. Huggins ran his fingers over the cards. "Take care of yourself, son."

Anger simmering just below the surface, Kane walked into the hallway. The orderly was waiting obediently and still had the stupid grin on his face. He walked up to him, grabbed the back of his T-shirt, lifted him onto the tips of his toes, and marched him along the hallway.

"Hey, man. You're hurting me." The orderly flapped his arms, trying to free himself. "Put me down."

Kane dropped him at the end of the hallway. "What's your name?"

"Wayne Dimple." Dimple rubbed under his arms. The smile had vanished.

Kane straightened to his full six-five and looked down his nose at the jerk. "Well, Dimple, now you know how it feels, I'll expect you to treat the residents with respect. I'll be making spot checks from now on and if you mistreat anyone again, I'll throw you in jail and toss away the key. We have laws in this county to deal with clowns like you." He poked a finger into the man's shoulder. "Have I made myself clear or do you require further instruction?"

"I understand." Dimple's face had turned beet red.

"Good." Kane turned on his heel and walked back to where Jenna was speaking to a tall man he recognized as Riley Adams. The man was standing far too close to her and, by the look on Jenna's face, something about this guy had spooked her big time.

In Jenna's hand he could make out the images of Payton Harris and his wife displayed on the iPad. He moved in closer and listened to the conversation.

"Did you know June and Payton Harris from before, or did you first meet them at Aunt Betty's Café?" Jenna's eyes darted to him and returned to Adams' face. "From the CCTV feed you seem pretty friendly."

"No, not from before." Adams leaned one shoulder against the wall and took a nonchalant pose. "They were sitting at the table next to me and I overheard their conversation. June had her heart set on hiking up to the top of Bear Peak and visiting the falls, but she was concerned about them going alone into the mountains. They didn't have a satellite phone and as I was planning on heading that way to do some hunting, I offered to go along, seeing as I know that trail, and I offered to show them the way."

"Can you give me a timeline?" Jenna pushed her tablet under one arm and took out her notepad.

"Look." Adams straightened. "I heard the news about June going missing. I'd have called the hotline if I'd had any information. She was a nice person."

"'Was' a nice person?" Jenna narrowed her gaze on him. "Is there something you're not telling me, Mr. Adams?"

"Hey, lower your hackles." Adams flicked a glance over Kane and rolled his shoulders. "I met them in Aunt Betty's on Thursday morning. I grabbed my gear and they followed me to the forest. We left our vehicles there and hiked up to a spot close to the falls. We rested there for a spell and then I showed them the trail to a campsite about a half mile away. If you know the area, there's a clearing with a firepit about twenty yards from the river, the one fed by the runoff from the mountain? It's low at this time of year. I left them there and hiked to a hunting area about a mile west. I came back down that night and went home."

Unconvinced, Kane took in Adams' confident pose and the way he stood inside Jenna's personal space. It was unusual behavior to act that way during an interview with a law enforcement officer. Most people would be a little nervous, even the innocent ones. He took a step closer to Jenna, and the action made Adams take a step back. *Good, I'm intimidating him.* "What time did you last see June and Payton Harris?"

"Maybe around two." Adams shrugged. "I'm not sure. They insisted they could find their way back to their pickup. They wanted a romantic night in the mountains, so I let them be." He looked directly at Jenna. "Women like that, don't they? The isolation and fear of being eaten by bears must be an aphrodisiac or something." He chuckled.

"Well, I figure you shouldn't include all women in that statement." Jenna gave him a stony stare. "Or men. Sleeping on hard ground in the freezing cold isn't everyone's idea of fun."

"You really need to loosen up, Sheriff." Adams pushed a hand through his hair. "Being so uptight isn't healthy."

When Jenna snorted in disgust, Kane spotted the triumphant glint in Adams' eyes. He had enjoyed making her angry and no doubt was trying to push her buttons. He was so smooth, so confident, and almost too good to be true. Firing a barrage of questions at him might cause a chink in his armor. "Where exactly did you park?"

"A short way past the forest warden's check station on Stanton Road." Adams pushed his hands into his pockets; slight irritation showed but he had it under control and soon slid back into a confident pose.

It was at times like these that Kane appreciated his height and body bulk. Adams was a strong guy, athletic in build, and had the pleasant features and confidence of a serial killer. He kept eye contact and leaned a little closer. He wanted to see just how far he could push him. Most people would be either annoyed or shaking in their boots by now. "What is your favorite weapon of choice?"

"I can't decide between a rifle and crossbow. They both have their appeal." Adams held his gaze and his lips twitched into a smirk. "I was hunting elk to fill my freezer. I only hunt game for food, Deputy."

"And what weapon were you carrying on Thursday?" Jenna was making copious notes and looked up at him.

"*Weapons,* Sheriff." Adams gave her a slow, confident smile. "I never go into the forest without my sidearm, but I was carrying a crossbow that day."

"I noticed you were wearing a slicker in Aunt Betty's. Do you usually wear a slicker in the mountains when hunting? I don't recall seeing any hunter orange on it."

"I wasn't big-game hunting, ma'am." Adams rolled his eyes. "It gets wet and cold up there, and yes, I wear my slicker most times when rain or storms are forecast."

"So, did you bag an elk?" Jenna's eyes narrowed.

"Nope, can't say that I did." Adams crossed his arms over his chest. "I didn't run into anyone, nor did I visit the check station. I should have, but I wanted to get the Harrises on the trail."

"Okay, ah… do you work here full time?" Jenna held his gaze.

"I work my shifts." Adams sighed. "If I do a double, I usually have the next day free. I didn't work on Thursday."

Kane cleared his throat. "Did you work on Sunday night?"

"Nope." Adams looked at him. "I was at home during the storm. It's too dangerous to be out in a dry storm with the lightning and all."

"Can anyone verify your whereabouts on Sunday night through Monday morning?" Jenna lifted her chin with a determined expression.

"I dropped by Aunt Betty's for breakfast and collected some supplies from the general store on Monday." He shrugged. "I'm sure they'll remember me and you'll have the CCTV footage to verify I was in the diner. Won't you, Sheriff?"

"Yeah. I'll be checking out your story." Jenna looked down at his shoes. "What size shoes do you wear?"

"You want my shoe size?" Adams grinned. "Now you're getting personal but hey, I'm easy to get along with, Sheriff. Size twelve."

"Size twelve, huh?" Jenna exchanged a knowing look with Kane and then turned back to Adams. "Well, seeing as you are the last person to see the couple, I'm taking you in for questioning over the death of Payton Harris." Jenna straightened and read him his rights.

"Really?" Adams laughed at her. "I'm a nurse. I *help* people, no one in their right mind will believe I'm involved in a murder."

They always make a mistake. No one had mentioned murder and most people who'd befriended the couple would be shocked to hear of Payton Harris' death. Unless they already knew. Kane took Adams' arm and led him from the building, but something gnawed at his gut. The confident swagger hadn't receded. He ground his back teeth. There had to be another side to Riley Adams, and he figured it was as dark as the entrance to hell.

CHAPTER TWENTY-FOUR

It was a little after three by the time Jenna had secured Riley Adams into an interview room. She wanted to go over his story again but he'd lawyered up and, of course, he'd insisted on her arch nemesis, Samuel J Cross, to represent him. The man made Carter look sophisticated. With his straight off the ranch style dress and long hair tied in a ponytail, battered hat, and scuffed cowboy boots, Sam Cross was the opposite of any lawyer she'd ever met but oh boy, was he smart. After Jenna had waited the obligatory time his secretary seemed to have made mandatory, she winced as Cross picked up the call and addressed her with an overly familiar tone. She certainly did not regard him as a friend.

"Hi, Jenna. I was wondering when I'd have the pleasure of sparring with you again. Who do we have this time?" Cross tapped away at his keyboard as if he wasn't really interested in what she had to say.

Drawing on her mask of professionalism, Jenna referred to her notes. "We've brought in Riley Adams out of Snowberry Way for questioning over the murder of Payton Harris. We found Harris' body close to Bear Peak. TOD is estimated on Thursday night or Friday morning. Adams was the last person to see him and his wife, June, alive. June is still missing. I also saw a man in my yard on Sunday night matching Adams' description. My house was shot up with a crossbow and I suffered a home invasion over a period of some hours. Deputy Kane is handling that case to avoid a conflict of interest. Mr. Adams has stated that he is a client of yours."

"He is indeed, Jenna." The tapping at the keyboard stopped abruptly. *"Have you questioned him?"*

Jenna smiled to herself. "Yes, we did ask him a few questions at his workplace about the Harris case, not the home invasion, and he didn't object or ask for a lawyer. From his replies and footage of him with the couple in Aunt Betty's Café, I decided to bring him in for questioning."

"Did you read him his rights before transporting him?" Cross sounded serious.

The hairs on the back of Jenna's neck rose. "I do things by the book, Mr. Cross. Of course, I did, and when we arrived here, he asked for you. There's been no delay in contacting you. When can you speak to your client?"

"I'll be there a little after five." Cross disconnected.

Jenna stared at her phone. "Why is calling you like having a root canal?"

"Problem?" Kane dropped into the chair in front of her desk.

"Sam Cross." Jenna pulled a face. "He covers his rudeness in such a polite way it really gets under my skin." She rubbed her temples. "The circumstantial evidence we have on Adams is enough to convict him and yet Cross will find a way to get him off the charge."

"He's a very good defense attorney." Kane held up both hands. "Don't look at me like that, Jenna. To get the best of you, he must be good at what he does."

Jenna peered at him from beneath her bangs. "Give me some good news."

"Rio and Rowley found Payton Harris' truck just where Adams said it would be. We're waiting for a tow truck to take it to Wolfe for forensic examination but unless something happened to them inside the pickup, there won't be anything we can use." Kane stood and went to the coffee machine, poured two cups, added the fixings, and gave her one. "I've been writing up an application for search warrants for Adams' truck and residence. As you say, the circumstantial evidence is good. I also presented one for the home invasion and used the evidence we've collected. That might be successful, as we have a man who fits the description and a match on the boot size."

Jenna thought for a beat. "How are we going at locating June and Payton Harris' next of kin? If we find them, they'll be able to give us a close relative for June. We need to know if the ear left on my porch post belongs to our missing woman."

"Rowley and Rio are working on it now." Kane sat back in the chair and stared at his iPad. "I'll print up the search warrant applications and head over to the courthouse." He looked across the desk at her. "If we discover the ear belongs to June Harris and you're convinced Adams is the possible killer and the guy who trashed your house, you'll need to take a step back from the investigation. You know Cross, and he'll play any advantage he can find, and this screams conflict of interest."

As the printer hummed into action, Jenna leaned back in her seat, mind spinning. She needed to be involved and not sitting on the sideline, but she'd already decided her course of action. She nodded slowly. "Yeah, I am aware of the situation but all this"—she waved a hand toward the few notes Rio had added to the whiteboard in her new office—"isn't sitting right with me. There are too many coincidences with the James Stone murders. Adams is so darn sure of himself he must have a trick up his sleeve. It's as if the murder was planned to keep me out of the investigation. James Stone was my case but Adams knows by invading my home, I can't be involved in the murder investigation. Problem is, Adams doesn't seem smart enough to have orchestrated this alone, I'm convinced Stone is behind it. Somehow, some way, he's influenced Adams to kill for him." She blew out a long breath and stared at Kane. "I bet he's just waiting for the reports to hit the news so he can drool over them, as if he'd murdered the victim himself. We must keep the home invasion from the press, because as sure as hell, I don't want Stone gloating over the notion that he's gotten away with scaring me."

"I'm concerned you've connected this murder with Stone." Kane sipped his coffee and eyed her intently over the rim. "Wolfe has already explained that the cases are different. Yes, maybe a copycat, but if Adams is copying Stone, he missed several pertinent clues. The paralyzing of the male victim, the mutilation of the woman, are all very important parts of the scene that are missing." He blew over the cup, making steam curl around him. "If Stone had communicated with Adams, why would he leave out what he'd consider the best parts of the kill? The stabbing or shot to the spine was his signature, not just the bolt to the head of the man or soaking him with gas. Those two things could have been leaked by the people who found the victims. The spinal injury only came to light during the autopsy. It was a crucial part of the evidence."

Jenna chewed on her bottom lip and thought it through. "True, and no doubt paralyzing his victim and making him watch the love of his life tortured would be a highlight of the kill." She leaned back and stared at the ceiling and then lowered her attention back to Kane. "You know, Dave, I know you go on gut instinct so many times and you're usually right. My intuition, or whatever you call it, is screaming at me that James Stone has a hand in this murder and the home invasion. I know home invasion isn't his style but by scaring me, I figure he believes he is regaining control. No matter how you try and convince me otherwise, my life is on the line, and it's only a matter of time before he shows his hand."

CHAPTER TWENTY-FIVE

Deputy Jake Rowley smiled as he disconnected from his wife Sandy's call. She'd been for her regular prenatal checkup at the doctor's, and both she and the twins were doing just fine. They'd hoped for a Christmas delivery but the babies were due to arrive late in January, right in the dead of winter. He went back to check the search results from the many databases he'd been checking since coming back from hunting down Payton Harris' vehicle. At last he'd found a match, with current details. He picked up the phone and called the Buffalo Ridge Sheriff's Department and explained the situation. As luck would have it, the sheriff knew Payton Harris and his family. "I'd appreciate if you'd inform them about Payton's death, and I'll need a list of June's family members as well. We'll need a close blood relative to supply a DNA sample ASAP. Her mother would be the best person to ask. I'm sure you have a doctor in town that could handle a swab for us?"

"No need. I have DNA collection kits here. I'll get you one from her mother this afternoon." The sheriff sighed. *"Where do you want me to send it?"*

Rowley opened a book on his desk and flipped through the pages. "I'll message you the address of the ME's office. You'll need to send it by an express pathology collection courier. Send the bill to the ME's office here in Black Rock Falls."

"Sure. This is bad business. They're a lovely couple." The sheriff took a long breath as if drawing on a cigarette. *"I hope they find June alive."*

Rowley nodded even though the sheriff couldn't see him. "Same. We have people out searching the forests and lakes in case she is still out there, but it's been four days since anyone laid eyes on her, so it's not looking good." He cleared his throat. "I'll send you the ME's phone number as well. The next of kin will want to contact him about the collection of the remains." He ran a hand through his hair. "Thanks for your help."

"It's all in a day's work." The sheriff disconnected.

After Rowley sent the messages, his phone buzzed. It was Deputy Zac Rio. "Yeah."

"I have something." Zac sounded excited. "Come take a look."

Rowley headed out of Sheriff Alton's old office and went to Rio's desk. His partner was scrolling through images he'd taken on their trip to and from the crime scene. After finding Harris' vehicle, they'd arranged for it to be towed to the ME's office and then decided to view the crime scene. They'd taken the track most likely traveled by June and Payton Harris to the campsite. They'd split up and searched all around. He'd found nothing of great interest along the way. The odd energy bar wrapper tossed onto the forest floor without thought of the environment had caught his eye, but Rio had a different tilt on things and had gone deep into the forest, coming back with soil samples. He stared over Rio's shoulder at the images. "Did you find anything interesting?"

"Maybe." Rio scrolled through the images and stopped. "When we were approaching the campsite, I noticed a few holes in the tree trunks. Not a lot but the odd few, plus in some places the forest floor had been disturbed."

Rowley shrugged. "If they'd been of consequence, Wolfe would have noted them in the crime scene report."

"Yeah, but these are in an area up to fifty yards from the campsite. On the opposite side of the river. It was a hunch. I looked in the area just over where the river flows under the rock formation. It looked disturbed, so I took some images and walked around some." Rio turned to look up at him. "I have the ability to process all the information I see at once. It's like seeing a jigsaw puzzle come together." He pointed at the screen. "These marks on the trees and ground are progressive. They move away from the crime scene and are spaced almost uniformly. The hunter was collecting his arrows or bolts as he went."

"Okay." Rowley looked closer. "I can see that, so why is that unusual? Bolts are expensive and most hunters retrieve them."

"At first I thought the person doing this was a bad shot, now I'm thinking he was herding something to a better place to kill it." He shrugged. "Do hunters do that?"

Rowley shook his head. "No, they'd make the shot before the animal moved away. What else did you find?"

"I found what could have been blood." Rio leaned back in his chair and smiled. "That's the sample we dropped into Wolfe. He called before and verified it's human blood. Right now, he's running it against the ear found at the sheriff's ranch. If it's a match, we'll have to wait for a positive ID on June Harris, but we'll know someone was hunting a human up there and injured them." He looked up at Rowley. "I think we need to talk to Jenna."

Rowley nodded. "Let's go."

They headed up the staircase leading to Jenna's new office. The second floor now housed the evidence room and locker rooms with showers, and toilets. It added a new level of security for the team. Rowley knocked on Jenna's door. "Rio has information."

"If it's about the break-in at my ranch, you'll need to speak to Kane." Jenna dropped a pen into the old chipped mug with WELCOME TO HAWAII on the side and looked up at him. "If it's about the Harris murder, you can speak to me but if we discover that Riley Adams is involved in both cases, I'll have to stand down and let Kane take the lead." She leaned back in her chair. "He should be back soon. He's chasing down search warrants for the suspect we have in custody."

"It's more about June Harris." Rio explained his theory. "I figure we need to concentrate the search from the campsite back up to Bear Peak. From what I could surmise, the blood seemed to be heading in that direction. We really need an experienced tracker to take a look at the evidence I found and go from there."

"Hmm, interesting." Jenna stared at him. "Kane and Atohi Black-hawk took the dogs and lost June Harris' trail at the edge of the river. Both are excellent trackers. Where exactly did you find the blood?" She raised a dark eyebrow. "I hope you marked everything clearly?"

"Yes, ma'am." Rio went to the whiteboard and drew a map of the forest trails with amazing accuracy. "I found it here. I figure if a tracker heads from here in the general direction, he might pick up a trail. I went as far as I could see any blood spots and then it just stopped. I didn't push on in case I destroyed evidence."

"Could you smell anything?" Jenna drummed her fingers on the desktop. "If there was a corpse close by, you'd smell it."

"Nope. I called out but heard nothing." Rio passed her his iPad. "These are the images I took of the scene. It's not much to go on, but as it's human blood, it might be significant."

"Good work." Jenna stood and, using her phone, took a photograph of the map. "The last report I had from search and rescue and the other teams is they found no trace of her. They've been concentrating along the trails and have been searching the rivers and lakes as well, in case she fell into the water somewhere. I'll contact Atohi and if he's available, I'll need you both to head up there with him first thing in the morning."

Rowley shuffled his feet. They had a suspect in custody and someone would be needed to stay with him. "What about Adams?"

"Sam Cross will be here at five, and knowing him, he'll have him out by six, but I've asked Deputy Walters if he's willing to come in from six to midnight to watch our suspect should we need to keep him overnight, and I have a relief deputy on standby from Louan for the second shift. I'll be here to take over by seven if the need arises." She looked from one to the other. "There's nothing to keep you back. Head off home at five and I'll see you in the morning." She reached for her phone and then looked at Rowley. "How is Sandy?"

Rowley smiled at her. "Everything is going along just fine. The doctor says to expect the babies the end of January." He laughed. "I hope she doesn't decide to have them in the middle of a blizzard."

"Me too." Jenna chuckled. "Unfortunately, when it comes to babies arriving, when they've made up their minds it's time, their moms don't have much choice."

CHAPTER TWENTY-SIX

The case Jenna's team had compiled against Riley Adams gained momentum the moment Kane walked into her office with the search warrants. She stood and took them from him, scanning the pages. "Oh, you have gotten everything you asked for. This is amazing." She smiled up at him. "I figure Wolfe will want to be on scene. I'll give him a call. As I need to keep a low profile in this case, I'll give you the pleasure of serving them on Adams."

"Maybe they'll wipe the smile off his face." Kane collected the documents from her and tapped them into a neat pile. "I'll give them to him when his lawyer gets here."

"I hope this is our guy. I guess at some point in our murder investigations we're due for a break." Jenna leaned against her desk. "Rowley and Rio discovered evidence of a possible struggle some ways from the murder scene." She filled him in with the details. "Wolfe is running the DNA from the ear attached to my house against the blood Rio found. I've contacted Atohi and he'll get a group of trackers together to hunt down June Harris. He's meeting Rowley and Rio at first light out at Bear Peak."

The phone on Jenna's desk buzzed and she lifted the receiver. "Sheriff Alton."

"It's Maggie from the front counter. Sam Cross has arrived. Where do you want me to send him?"

Jenna glanced at Kane. "Just a second. He's early." She covered the mouthpiece. "Do you want to take Sam Cross to the interview room? You'll need to be on hand to interview Adams. I'll send Rio to meet Wolfe and do the search. I'd rather not hold up Rowley this afternoon, he should get home to Sandy."

"Not a problem." Kane looked at her. "I hope Cross won't cause a problem."

"It's only me he has trouble with." Jenna uncovered the phone to speak to Maggie. "Kane is on his way. Thanks Maggie." She put down the phone and chewed on her bottom lip. "I'm out of things to do. I've updated the files. If you don't need me, I might drop by Marvelous Cookies. I've been itching to see inside. Maggie has been telling everyone how great they are. The shop is down the alleyway beside the general store. It's been made to look like a store from the eighteenth century. I figure you'll want a box of their finest?"

"I sure will, but not many can make chocolate chip cookies like you, Jenna." Kane smiled at her, finished his coffee, and stood. "As it's getting late, I wonder if you could do something for me, as you're heading downtown?"

Jenna nodded. "Of course, what is it?"

"I ordered a box of gun cleaning patches and they called to tell me they'd arrived." He sighed. "The gun supplies store will be closed before we leave here tonight. Could you go by and get them for me? I paid for them already."

"Not a problem." Jenna pushed to her feet. "I'll go now. I'll be back in twenty minutes max." She grabbed her jacket, followed him out the door and down the stairs. She nodded at Sam Cross waiting at the counter. "Sorry to keep you waiting. Deputy Kane will take you to your client."

When Kane headed to the interview room with Sam Cross, Jenna hunted down Zac Rio. "I have to go out for a few minutes. Kane has a search warrant for Riley Adams' home and vehicle. Contact Wolfe and see if he will go with you to conduct the search. Get a copy of the paperwork from Kane and head out there as soon as possible. Adams lives out Snowberry Way but his truck is parked out front of the Sunset Valley nursing home. Adams' keys are in the property room." She sighed. "If Wolfe can't go with you, ask Colt Webber. You know the drill: glove up, take photographs, bag all evidence."

"Yes, ma'am." Rio picked up his phone.

Jenna had headed out the door pulling on her jacket when a bark came from behind her. She turned to see Duke looking at her expectantly. "Okay, come on." She hurried out the door.

She headed down Main with Duke on her heels. The town was unusually quiet. Another storm had been forecast for later and perhaps people had made their way home earlier than usual. A few people moved along the sidewalk, like her bundled up against the oncoming chill of night. Hurrying along, she admired the Halloween decorations filling the storefronts. Garlands of plastic pumpkins had been strung between the lampposts and gave the town a festive look. The afternoon was growing late, and mist poured from the river to overflow through town like a swirling snake. It seemed almost alive, a strange white beast of the night, changing into shapes and bending the imagination. It billowed toward Jenna as a vehicle drove through it, sending it toward her in great waves of white diaphanous creepiness.

The mist had added a surreal sensation to Halloween every year since she'd arrived in town. It was never just one night of celebration in Black Rock Falls. Decorations started to appear two weeks or more before October 31, and this year they had taken on a new level of bizarre. A shiver went down her spine at the overly realistic corpses sitting in chairs in people's front yards and the grinning skeletons in various stages of dismemberment. It would seem that macabre had become the new normal.

After everything she'd seen since moving to Black Rock Falls, she would have thought her skin would have thickened considerably and she'd become immune to the horrors of murder and mayhem, but in truth, she'd never get used to it and she still believed in ghosts. She glanced down at Duke, glad to have his company as she made her way to the gun supplies store. She moved inside, surprised to see the store almost empty, and hurried to the counter. "Hi, you have an order for Dave Kane?"

"Sure thing, he said he'd be by this afternoon, Sheriff." The man behind the counter was elderly, with weather-beaten, leathery skin and a shock of white hair. His dark brown eyes twinkled at her. "It's quiet this afternoon. Strange for this time of the year. Most are out looking at the decorations. I figure it's the storm warning. Those dry storms are dangerous." He took a packet from behind the counter, slid it into a shopping bag, and handed it to her. "There you go."

Jenna took the bag and smiled at him. "Thank you." She headed out of the store. "Come on, Duke, stay close now. I don't want to lose you in the mist."

She walked two blocks down Main, crossing twice before she came to the alleyway beside the general store. Everything possible had been done to create an old-world atmosphere, right down to cobblestones and a replica of a gaslit street lamp. The store's round windows displayed the treats within, not just cookies of every shape, flavor, and size, but also enough cakes and muffins to keep a smile on Kane's face for life. She chuckled and, after telling Duke to sit outside, pushed open the door. A bell tinkled above her head and it was as if she'd walked back in time. Even the woman serving behind the counter had dressed the part. A dust cap covered a mass of brown curls, and her dress, straight out of the eighteenth century, brushed the floor when she walked.

Jenna nodded at her and perused the display. The cabinets still had a few cakes on the glass shelves, but the remaining cookies came wrapped or in decorative tins. She selected an assortment of cakes and took three packs of cookies. With them safely in the bag with Kane's parcel, she pushed open the door. As she stepped outside, Duke made a whining sound. "You can have a cookie when we get back to the office."

A thick white blanket of fog had risen to her knees, almost obscuring the dog. In the short time she'd been inside the store, everything had changed. All around her buildings cast deep shadows, blocking the late afternoon sun, and concealing the far end of the alleyway joining Main to Maple. From between the buildings, the remaining beams of watery light skipped over the ever-moving band of water vapor, creating strange ethereal shapes. When Duke whined again, she patted her leg. "Let's go. Come on, boy."

Before she could take a step, a movement deep in the alleyway swirled the mist around her, sending a surge of ghostly dancers in her direction. Every hair on her body stood to attention as the figure of a man, wearing a cowboy hat and a slicker, emerged from the gloom. The air seemed to distort as the mist curled around him. Jenna's hand went to her waist to grab her Maglite but came up empty. She'd left her heavy, duty belt back at the office, opting for a shoulder holster for the short trip to the store. Without hesitation, she slid her hand inside her jacket and closed her palm around the handle of her Glock. Heart thundering in her chest, she peered into the distorted alleyway, trying to make sense of what was in front of her. A hint of a breeze brushed her cheek like the ice-cold touch of a corpse as she stared at the tall figure. He stood silent, feet apart and back straight like a gunslinger from the old west as if he was planning on drawing down on her. Jenna swallowed hard. Was he really there or was her mind playing tricks on her? As the mist poured over him, almost burying him from sight, he seemed to dissolve and then become whole again. Could he be an illusion, or a figment of her overactive imagination?

Duke pressed against her leg and she reached down to pat him, glad of the solid, warm strength of him. He trembled under her fingers, then a rumble went through his chest, his hackles raised, and every muscle became taut and ready to fight. A wave of uncertainty gripped her and she dragged her eyes away from the man to glance down at him. "You see him too, don't you? Is that the same man that was in my yard, or is he locked up in an interview room back at the office?"

Heart pounding, Jenna rested one hand on her weapon and peered back into the darkness, but the man had vanished, dissipating into the breeze like a puff of smoke. Putting her faith in her Glock, she placed the bag on the ground and moved deeper into the alleyway but stopped when dumpsters at the far end obscured her view. She stood listening, but not a breath of sound came from the darkness. She held her weapon steady in both hands. "This is Sheriff Alton. Come out and show yourself."

Nothing.

The mist moved, appearing to mimic the swish of a slicker, but the shadows had swallowed the man, imaginary or not. Backing toward the cookie store, she noticed that the owner had turned the sign on the door to Closed. She swallowed the sudden rush of fear tightening her gut. She collected the bag and continued to back down the alleyway. As she stepped back onto Main, laughter, deep and sinister, carried on the night air.

CHAPTER TWENTY-SEVEN

Kane waited patiently in the interview room for Sam Cross to read through the search warrants. The lawyer said nothing, only raised his eyebrows once or twice, gave Kane a nod, and then passed the documents to his client, Riley Adams. Kane took his copies and stepped outside to hand them to Deputy Rio. "Wolfe and his team will do a forensic sweep of the house and vehicle. You'll need to record the search and update the files before you head home tonight."

"Sure, I have my equipment in my truck." Rio took the documents and dangled a set of keys from his fingertips. "I have Adams' keys. It will be too dark by the time we search the house to work on the vehicle. Wolfe said he'd be taking the truck to his office and he'll get to it later this evening. Do you want me to remain with him during the vehicle search?"

Kane shook his head. "It's not necessary. Colt Webber is a badge-holding deputy and he'll be able to capture the scene. Wolfe was at one time too, but he was a little overqualified for this office."

"I can imagine." Rio's eyebrows met in the middle in a frown. "Why didn't he get an ME's job at the time?"

If only he knew. Kane took a casual pose and leaned a shoulder against the wall. "He's Black Rock Falls' first medical examiner; we had the undertaker examining the bodies before Wolfe arrived, but then the murders were few and very far between. Wolfe was waiting for his license to be approved. He came from a different state and then of course he had to set up shop. In the meantime, he worked here. That's why we're all such a tight knit team—we've all known each other from the get-go."

"I see." Rio looked at the papers in his hands. "I'd better get going, I'm meeting Wolfe on Stanton, in ten minutes." He looked at Kane. "Will Jenna be waiting for my report?"

"Yeah." Kane straightened. "We'll be here. I have a feeling Adams might be staying overnight, at least for questioning. It seems an open-and-shut case right now."

"Okay, then I'll see you later." Rio hurried down the hallway.

Kane waited outside the interview room. He could watch through the two-way mirror but had no idea how the interview was going. The desk was set to allow lawyers and their clients to have their backs to the mirror. The idea of observing was a safety issue. With the number of serial killers he'd dealt with since arriving in town, standing outside the interview room was a priority. Surprisingly, Sam Cross didn't take long at all and pressed the button on the table to notify Kane he was ready to either leave or allow him to interview his client.

After scanning his card, Kane opened the door and looked at Cross. "Is your client ready to talk?"

"Yeah." Cross leaned back in his chair and tipped back his Stetson. "Mr. Adams doesn't have anything to hide. Ask away."

Kane picked up his iPad from a hall table and went inside the room. He sat down, pulled a book out of the desk drawer, and then started the recorder. After announcing the date, time, and who was present, he took out his pen and looked at Adams. "From our previous chat at the Sunset Valley nursing home, where you work as a nurse, you mentioned you'd met June and Payton Harris. Could you explain how you met them and how you came to be with them in Stanton Forest the day Payton Harris was murdered."

"One moment." Cross leaned forward and rested his hands on the table. "The time of death of the victim has been established as Thursday night to the early hours of Friday morning. Is that correct?"

Kane scrolled through Wolfe's findings from Payton Harris' autopsy and nodded. "Yeah, the TOD is always an estimate. I'm sure you know that?"

"I do indeed, but from the information you gave me about the previous… ah… as you put it 'chat' with my client, you would be aware he left Stanton Forest before dark on Thursday night, so he couldn't have been in the forest at the time Payton Harris was murdered."

Wanting to roll his eyes, Kane leaned back in his chair and called on his patience. "The question was, 'How did your client come to be with June and Payton Harris in Stanton Forest the day Payton Harris was murdered?' I didn't specify the time."

"Okay, go on." Cross turned to Adams. "Just tell him what you told me."

"Like I told the sheriff. I overheard them saying they were heading for the falls out of Bear Peak and needed a guide. I told them I wasn't a guide and official guides around these parts are licensed, but I told them I planned to head up that way and would be happy for them to tag along." He rested his elbows on the arms of the chair and linked his fingers. "I took them the most straightforward way and even gave them a map so they didn't get lost on the way back."

The crime scene tumbled through Kane's mind. They'd searched all over and they never found a map of any description. "What kind of map did you give them? Was it a handwritten one?"

"Yeah, and they followed it just fine on the way to the clearing." Adams shrugged. "I don't know what happened to them after I left them in the forest."

"Do you own a crossbow?" Kane stared at his notes. He expected a pause or something, but Adams owned up immediately.

"Yeah, I own a couple of them and I'm a darn good shot too." Adams gave him a smug smile. "I like the stealth of it in the forest. It's great for hunting. Why?"

Kane looked up at him but ignored his question. He wanted to see a reaction. "Do you know or have you heard of James Stone?"

He caught a flicker in Adams' eyes, but then he steepled his fingers and stared at Kane in a display of overconfidence. He noticed the frown on Cross' face. He hadn't missed his client's action. Like investigators, lawyers used body language to select jurors, and steepling fingers signaled a person was not only overconfident but believed they had the upper hand.

Kane held Adams' gaze. "Well?"

"Anyone from Black Rock Falls would know the name James Stone. He was the lawyer in town for some years before he went bad." Adams' lips twitched into a smirk. "I'm sure if you asked anyone living here at the time, they'd have heard of him, too."

"Stone is in the county jail and you spent time in the same prison." Kane eyeballed him. "I hear he has quite a reputation in there."

"Does he now?" Adams barked a laugh. "Have you ever visited county? They keep the maximum-security inmates in a different building to the general population. Same with the kid killers and the freaks. They have their own space where they can discuss all the nasty details and relive the kills. They love it in there, don't you know?"

"Really? I'll have to tell the warden." After glancing at his notes, Kane took the questioning in a different direction in an effort to unsettle Adams. "Tell me about Jonathan Lamb. How did that incident go down?"

"My client isn't here to discuss a case that has already been dealt with by the courts." Cross moved papers around in his file. "Find another question."

Unable to resist, Kane leaned forward. "It's a relevant question." He turned his attention to Adams. "You shot and killed Mr. Lamb with a crossbow. Did you accidently shoot Payton Harris as well?"

"Payton was shot with a crossbow?" Adams opened his hands wide again, demonstrating he had nothing to hide. "I didn't shoot him accidentally, like I did Johnny. I wasn't in the forest at the time Payton was killed. I came down before sunset."

"Yet nobody saw you and you met no one in town, when it's close to Halloween and the streets are busy. You didn't drop by the forest warden's station either." Kane stared at him. "For a seasoned hunter, you don't seem to be following the rules. Is your hunting permit up to date?"

"Enough." Cross pushed to his feet. "My client won an appeal, which reduced his manslaughter conviction to a misdemeanor. He already spent time in jail for a crime he didn't commit. Are you trying to railroad him, Deputy Kane?"

"The evidence against him is substantial and I'll be holding him here until the completion of the search warrants." Kane stood. "June Harris is still missing and Mr. Adams is the last person to have seen the couple alive. Then we have the invasion of Sheriff Alton's ranch. A man fitting his description was seen at the premises, a man with size-twelve shoes, same as your client. Mr. Adams has admitted meeting June and Payton Harris at Aunt Betty's Café, and we have him on CCTV wearing the same outfit. Your client cannot sufficiently account for his whereabouts at the time of both crimes; he has no alibis." He kept his gaze on Cross. "I'll be presenting all our evidence to the DA and will be seeking an arrest warrant." He turned to Adams. "Is there anything you have to say on record before I conclude this interview?"

"Nope." Adams shrugged. "You won't find anything in my truck or home. June and Payton never went near them. You're wasting your time. I'm innocent."

Kane nodded. "Very well. The interview is concluded." He gave the time and date, switched off the recording device, and turned to Cross. "Do you want more time with your client?"

"No." Cross looked at Adams. "Deputy Kane is within his rights to hold you for questioning. I'll do whatever I can to have you released. Hang in there."

After swiping his card to let Sam Cross from the interview room. Kane dropped his iPad and notebook on the table in the hallway and held the door open for Adams. "I'll take you down to the cells. I'll arrange a meal for you. Do you have any food allergies?"

"Nope. How long is this going to take?" Adams wasn't backing down. "I have a job. I'll need to call in and have them find a replacement for my shift."

"I'll call the nursing home and tell them you've been detained." Kane waved him down a set of stairs leading to the cells. "Do you have any livestock that needs tending?"

"Nope." Adams moved into the cell and turned and looked at Kane. "I admire your tenacity, Deputy, and I know you and the sheriff have this big reputation for hunting down the bad guys, but if you try and pin this on me, you won't win. You see, I never lose."

Kane snorted. "Really, that's funny coming from a guy who spent time in county."

"Yeah, but I'm out now." Adams sneered at him. "Things usually turn around in my favor."

As the gate slid shut, Kane stared at him. "Not this time."

CHAPTER TWENTY-EIGHT

Nerves on edge and holding her weapon high, Jenna backed out of the alleyway, relieved to be under the street lights. As she turned, an elderly couple stopped and raised their hands. She stared at their alarmed expressions and quickly holstered her weapon. "I'm so sorry to alarm you. I thought I heard something, but everything is fine." She waved them past her and they hurried on their way.

She glanced down at Duke, who was still staring down the alleyway. "So, it wasn't my imagination, you saw him too."

Her phone chimed, startling her already shattered nerves, but it was Kane's ringtone and she juggled the bags and accepted his call. "Yeah, Dave, what's up?"

"Nothing to worry about. We're keeping Adams overnight. I've ordered a meal for him from Aunt Betty's. If you're close by, can you grab it on your way home?" He paused a beat. *"You sound a little uptight, is everything okay?"*

"Not really." Jenna sucked in a deep breath to steady her nerves. "There was a man in the alleyway dressed the same as the intruder on my ranch. I know you think I get this way around Halloween, but Duke was whining and he had his hackles up. He must have seen him too."

"Maybe." Kane didn't sound convinced. *"Duke would be on alert if you're spooked too. I figure he'd bark if he could see a threat. Did you do a search?"*

A cold chill spilled over Jenna the second she glanced back down the dark alleyway. It would seem the decorative gaslight was little more than a prop. "I didn't have a flashlight. I left my duty belt in the office." She needed to explain what had spooked her. "I had no idea what I was facing, Dave, and with only Duke for backup, I called out and walked some way down the alleyway pointing my weapon. I didn't see anyone. It was as if the man had vanished like smoke."

"Could you ID him if you saw him again?"

Jenna chewed on her bottom lip. "The mist has rolled in off the river and I couldn't see him clearly, but he sure looked like Adams, the same hat and slicker." She took a deep breath and started toward Aunt Betty's cheerful fluorescent lights. "Then as I got to the end of the alley, I swear I heard someone laughing."

"How far are you from Aunt Betty's?" The sound of footsteps on tile came through the speaker. Kane was on the move.

Jenna crossed the road at the end of the block. Main Street looked strangely empty and the mist only added to the eeriness of the macabre decorations. It was so quiet, not a vehicle in sight, and apart from the old couple, the sidewalk was empty. It had become full dark since she left the alleyway. "I'm passing the gun store now."

"Wait outside Aunt Betty's. I'll be there in five." Kane disconnected before she could reply.

People spilled out of Aunt Betty's chatting, and it seemed as if the sound had been turned back on. They hurried to parked vehicles and their headlights cut through the mist as they headed down Main. As she reached the entrance, she could hear the roar of the Beast's engine and she couldn't push down the surge of relief at seeing Kane's truck appear out of the gloom and pull in to the curb outside Aunt Betty's Café. She quickened her pace and pulled open the door to dump her bags inside. "You didn't have to rush out. I'm fine."

"I know you are." Kane smiled at her. "I figured someone else walking down that alleyway might not be so fine if someone is hanging out down there. It might just be a Halloween prank but I think we should go look."

Jenna bundled Duke into the back of the truck, attached his harness, and then climbed in the front. "Sure. I didn't think it could be a prank. After the break-in, my nerves are on edge."

"Well, all the better if we put your mind at rest." Kane turned the Beast away from the curb and drove to the entrance of the alleyway. "This one?"

Jenna nodded. "Yeah." She climbed out and drew her weapon.

"Okay, let's see if anyone is down here." Kane aimed his flashlight down the alleyway. "That street light is out." He pointed the light at the glass. "It's broken. So, it's been vandalized on purpose." He headed into the darkness, his light illuminating the line of three dumpsters ahead.

"I saw him down there near the dumpsters." Jenna followed close behind. "The mist and the shafts of sunlight made it difficult to see him."

"There's no one here now." Kane lowered the flashlight to the ground. "There are a ton of footprints. No doubt people from the stores are in and out all day dumping their garbage. There's nothing here we can use to identify anyone." He turned to look at her. "This doesn't mean someone wasn't here trying to frighten you, but if it was the same person who broke into your house, how would they know you were here?"

Suddenly cold, Jenna looked at him. "They're watching me, or followed me from the office and slipped by when I was in the store." She shook her head. "I saw him, Dave. I'm not going crazy."

"I believe you." He took her hand. "You're freezing. We're going to be stuck in town for a while. I've called in the night shift you arranged to stay with Adams but we'll be late getting home. Maggie is staying back, so we might as well grab a bite to eat as we have to stop by Aunt Betty's to collect Adams' meal." He led her back to Main and they climbed into the truck. "I want to discuss the interview with Adams. I'm convinced he killed Payton Harris. He has the overconfident attitude of so many serial killers we've interviewed. The only problem I have is he is admitting to everything."

Astonished, Jenna turned to him. "He admitted to killing Harris?"

"Nope, but everything else. Including meeting the couple in Aunt Betty's and taking them into the forest. He took them to an isolated area and supposedly left them there to find their way home in the morning." Kane raised an eyebrow. "What sensible person does that to an out-of-towner? He uses a crossbow and admits to being a good shot. He knows about James Stone and was in the same jail for a time. He didn't admit to meeting him, though; he said he was in a different part of the jail. We don't know if Stone's story influenced him or if he found out how Stone killed his victims through prison scuttlebutt." He pulled to the curb outside Aunt Betty's. "It's as if he admitted being with the couple all the time but just left out killing Payton Harris. Then we have his conviction of the supposedly accidental shooting of another man. I'll check that out when we get to Aunt Betty's. If Adams shot him in the head with a crossbow, I think we have enough circumstantial evidence for the DA to charge him with murder."

After eating a quick meal, Jenna collected the sandwiches and a to-go cup of coffee for Riley Adams and they headed back to the office. While Kane delivered the prisoner his meal, Jenna correlated the evidence to present to the DA for an arrest warrant for Adams. She glanced up at a knock on the door. "Ah, Zac, what do you have for me?"

"Nothing much, I'm afraid." Deputy Rio stood hat in hands just inside the door. "We have his quiver and Wolfe has identified small fragments of wood on them that could be from the holes in the trees I noticed in the forest."

Jenna straightened in her chair. "Or from my house. He did make the effort of removing most of the bolts before he left. If Wolfe finds a match to my house, it will be all we need. I'd say the pine trees in Stanton Forest will all come back as the same species but not the interior of my home." She pushed both hands through her hair. "Nothing else?"

"Not in the house." Rio smiled. "We went over that place with a fine-tooth comb, vacuumed the carpets, checked for any trophies, took his dirty laundry and a pair of his boots. Wolfe will check everything back at the lab but the tests he did on scene didn't show anything of interest. It looks clean. The vehicle is immaculate, I figure he had it cleaned this morning, but Wolfe will do a forensic sweep as soon as possible."

"Okay, thanks." Jenna stood, collected the documents from the printer, and tapped them into a neat pile. She turned back to Rio. "What's your take on Adams?"

"The evidence points to him." Rio shrugged. "It would be a slam dunk if we had some physical evidence." An expression of remorse crossed his face. "I've been checking in all day with search and rescue as you asked. It's as if June Harris has disappeared without a trace." He rubbed his chin. "I hope Blackhawk is as good as you say and he can track her from the marks I found in the trees. I'm convinced the blood in the forest belongs to her."

Jenna nodded. "He's the best tracker I know, and we should have an answer on the blood you found this evening. I know Wolfe set up the DNA sequencing machine before he left with you but that's to see if it's a match for the ear we found at my ranch. He's still waiting for a DNA comparison from a close relative of June Harris." She smiled at him. "Go home and get some rest. You've an early start in the morning."

"I will, thank you." Rio turned and headed down the steps.

A few moments later, Kane walked into the office with his phone pressed to one ear. He glanced at Jenna. "One moment, I'll ask Jenna." He muted his phone. "I have caught the DA at his office, he'll wait for the paperwork on Harris and go over it at home tonight if it's ready?"

Jenna slid the documents from the printer into a folder. "Yes, everything is here. We'll update him if any forensic evidence comes to light overnight."

She listened as Kane relayed the details. When he disconnected, she handed him the document. "You'll have to run through this with him."

"I already have over the phone." Kane grabbed his coat from a peg behind the door and shrugged into it. "I'll take this to him now." He picked up the folder. "Oh, by the way, I sent Maggie home when the night shift arrived."

Exhausted, Jenna stood and walked around the desk. "Thank goodness. I'll grab my coat. We can drive over to the DA's office and then head straight home. It's been a long day." She looked down at Duke curled up in his basket, eyes tight shut. "Even Duke is tuckered out."

"He doesn't need an excuse." Kane chuckled and collected the bag from the gun store. He peered inside. "Mmm, cookies." He looked at Jenna. "Did you buy these for me?"

Jenna followed him down the stairs. "Yeah, and I have cakes too, but after seeing the man in the alleyway, they slipped my mind." She tapped him on the shoulder. "I hope you have hot chocolate to go with the cookies?"

"Sure." Kane headed for the front door. "I'll make you some as soon as we get home." He glanced at his phone. "I hope this new phone opens the gate, or we'll be sleeping in the truck."

CHAPTER TWENTY-NINE

Wednesday

Wind buffeted the cottage and rattled the windows, but it was Kane whistling a tune that woke Jenna on Wednesday morning. She peered from under the blankets to the light streaming from the hallway across her bedroom floor and listened to Kane clattering around in the kitchen. She turned to look at the clock on the bedside table. It was almost six, and by this time Kane had probably already tended the horses. She moved and Pumpkin, her black cat, stretched and rolled onto her back with four feet raised and front paws kneading the air. Cats seemed to stretch from the tip of their tails to the ends of their claws, and watching her fascinated Jenna. Pumpkin had arrived at the cottage when they returned home, tail held high and complaining bitterly about being left alone with strangers.

They'd been stopped at the gate, their creds scrutinized, and escorted to the cottage. The ranch resembled a building site crossed with a scouts' jamboree. Tents and the smell of cooking greeted them the moment they climbed out of the Beast. The noise of men working went long into the night. To Jenna's surprise, the horses had been tended, too, and the stables were spotless. She'd wanted to enter her house and see what progress had been made during her absence but had been prevented by the guard at her front door saying it was too dangerous to go inside. The smell of paint spilled from the house, and through the open door she could see men working in organized chaos.

She sat up and shivered. There was a chill in the air, which was unusual, as Kane usually kept the heat turned up. She dropped her legs over the edge of the bed and pushed her feet into her slippers. Pulling on her coat as she walked because she'd left most of her clothes at the house in her rush to escape, she headed for the kitchen. "Morning."

"Hey." Kane flashed a white smile at her. "I've just put on the coffee. You could've taken your time this morning, everything is done. "I had help with the horses this morning; in fact, I hardly did a thing. The team Wolfe organized to repair the house is doing just about everything." He frowned. "You look kinda lost, Jenna. Is your back still sore? Come here." He walked toward her and pulled her against him, enclosing her in a bear hug.

Jenna sighed. "Back is a little stiff but I'll be fine." She looked up at him. "I hope we find June Harris today. I've thrown every resource out there to hunt her down. It's like looking for a needle in a haystack." She glanced out the window at her ranch. "Look at the state of my house. I hate the thought that someone trashed my home."

"It will be as good as new soon." Kane rubbed her back. "No one is going to get on the ranch again. You'll be safe once the upgrades are finished."

"Maybe, but that doesn't account for seeing a similar man in the alleyway last night." Jenna chewed on her bottom lip. "It might have been a harmless prank, but it gave me the jitters. I mean how would anyone know about the intruder at the ranch? How come the man I saw was identical?"

"I don't know, but most of the men wear cowboy hats in town and it was dark and misty." Kane shrugged. "You've been through a traumatic event and seeing a guy in the alleyway would naturally spook anyone in the same situation. You know we have Adams in custody, so it couldn't have been him. Try not to worry, it's all going to be a distant memory soon." He rubbed her back.

It would be hard to forget someone invading her home and trying to kill her. She'd been on edge the moment she stepped back on the ranch. Jenna rested her face on Kane's chest and nestled against him. She'd missed human contact in the time before Kane arrived in Black Rock Falls. It had been a very lonely time for her, with no friends and trying to act normally when everything she'd ever known had been snatched away from her. At the time, she hungered for justice and never fully realized that being a witness against a drug cartel boss meant her job as a DEA agent and life as she once knew it would be over. Both she and Kane had ghosts in their pasts, and the hugs had been the small comfort that had kept them both sane when everything around them had suddenly gone crazy. "It will be if the DA charges Adams with the murder of Payton Harris and the home invasion, but we still have to find June."

"True." Kane sighed and rested his chin on the top of her head. "After all this time, if she's injured, she wouldn't have made it through the night in the forest. If she didn't die from exposure the wildlife would have killed her."

Jenna nodded. "Yeah, but if she got away, there's still a chance Atohi might be able to track her. One thing is for sure, from what Wolfe reported last night, she didn't go anywhere near Adams' house or truck." She stepped away and looked up at him. "I hope the Buffalo Ridge sheriff hunts down a close relative of June Harris today. Now we know the blood in the forest and the ear attached to my porch match, I need to know if it's her or not." She pushed her hands into the pockets of her coat. "Wolfe worked late last night to get the results for us, we should get a confirmation soon."

"Search and rescue and volunteers have been all over the forest, every hunter that passes through the forest warden's station has been notified she's missing." Kane hooked his thumbs into the front pockets of his jeans and shrugged. "Unless we can get Adams to talk, I doubt we'll find her. If he killed her, he could have stashed her body anywhere. Not that it makes sense, leaving her husband in the forest in plain sight and hiding her, but I have the feeling he's playing with us. I've seen overconfident psychopaths before, but if I'm reading him all wrong and he is as innocent as he claims, I'll need to be retrained."

Jenna nodded. "Then I will too. He ticks all the boxes for me. I hope the DA decides if he's going to charge him soon. Once we have Adams in county, we can concentrate on finding June Harris." She waved a hand behind her. "I'll go take a shower. I'd like to head into the office as early as possible. I want to speak to search and rescue and then get out another media release. We need to keep the townspeople aware she is still missing."

CHAPTER THIRTY

Cold seeped through Deputy Zac Rio's clothes as he stepped from the truck. Each freezing breath sent clouds of steam into the pristine alpine air. The forest smelled like the inside of a freezer with an over fragrance of pine and damp leaves. His first winter in Montana would be a challenge. He glanced at Rowley beside him, rugged up and wearing a liquid Kevlar vest under his jacket. He frowned. "I'm cold already. My blood is thinner than yours. I'm going to suffer over winter."

"Yeah, we could find snow this high, and winter seems to be coming earlier each year and lasting longer. The sheriff had an idea you might need some extra clothing." Rowley indicated with his thumb to the back of his truck. "Your winter gear was delivered yesterday. It's in the back of my truck, I grabbed it when I arrived for you."

Surprised, Rio lifted his eyebrows. "The sheriff didn't mention anything to me."

"She's kinda busy right now." Rowley smiled at him. "I completed the order when you arrived. We get new jackets, gloves, and extra boots every year. Wear the vest—it will help keep you warm."

"Sure." Rio opened the hatch to Rowley's truck and noticed the brown paper wrapped packages, some with his name on them and the others with Rowley's. He went through them, found his vest and a fine thick jacket with a hood, numerous pairs of gloves, and woolen hats, along with boots, pants, and shirts. "Wow! She went all out."

"We do a ton of work in the snow and the winters here are long." Rowley collected his rifle and checked the load. "Our department gets a generous allowance from the town council and since Black Rock Falls has become a tourist destination, there is more money in the budget." He pulled on his gloves. "The tech comes through the ME's office, so I assume Wolfe gets a substantial amount to run his office as well."

Rio touched the tiny in-ear wireless com he'd been given. "I've only seen the FBI with these coms."

"Yeah, we get the new devices because we have so many serial killers in the county." Rowley frowned. "Well, that was Wolfe's explanation." He looked over Rio's shoulder. "Ah, here's Atohi."

After going through his findings from his last visit to the mountain, the blood, and the fact it belonged to the person who'd lost an ear, Zac waited for Blackhawk to scan the images he'd taken of the scene. "What do you think?"

"I think that's not enough blood for a severed ear." Blackhawk lifted his gaze to him. "You've worked in the big city, surely you've seen what happens if an ear is sliced let alone removed from the head." He stared at the images again. "This is no more than a small cut or perhaps an injury from a crossbow bolt. If the bolt passed through the skin of the arm or leg or more likely became lodged in a person, I'd expect a small amount of blood. It's a puncture wound and, from this, it didn't hit an artery."

"Yeah, but people rarely use a crossbow in the city." Zac shrugged into the new jacket, noting how it slipped over the liquid Kevlar vest without a problem. He liked the new lightweight body armor and thought it was only available to black ops and the like. "I've seen through and through wounds from a twenty-two hardly bleed, so it could be the same."

"It is." Blackhawk rolled his eyes and shook his head. "We're wasting time leaving from here." He motioned to the images. "I know this part of the forest. I can see Bear Peak in the background.

If we drive there, we can come down the rockface and follow the likely trails back to that area." He pointed to another shot of the scene. "Where the bushes are flattened and the ground disturbed, if the woman had run away, there'd be more signs. I figure the person who hurt her carried her over one shoulder."

"So, we should assume he knocked her out first?" Rowley's mouth tightened into a grimace. "If he's carrying a crossbow, moving through the forest would be difficult enough without a squirming woman."

"Yeah, that makes sense." Atohi waved them into the truck. "It also means she may still be alive. Let's go."

The bumpy drive along a small overgrown road didn't take long. The parking lot had a line of old cabins set to one side. The place looked deserted and unkempt, apart from a late-model SUV parked on one end. Rio turned to Rowley. "What happened to this place?"

"Murder." Rowley shrugged. "Bear Peak seems to be a great place to dump bodies or keep little girls prisoner." He indicated to the SUV. "It obviously didn't bother those people. They're out of town plates, probably tourists hunting down a thrill."

"It's not a good place for sightseers." Blackhawk grimaced. "There are many spirits trapped in this part of the forest. Many hear voices, children crying, or the screams of the dying." He climbed from the truck and waved a hand at the trees. "The spirits that walk this part of the forest are revengeful and seek justice. Many will never find the peace they seek."

A shiver crept up Rio's back like the stroke of a frozen finger. He wiggled his shoulders and peered into the dense forest, pushing away the sudden feeling of foreboding. Dark shadows and filtered, watery sunlight greeted him as he followed Blackhawk and Rowley down a mountain path and into the trees. He had the awful urge to keep looking over one shoulder; the forest had closed in around him, and not being claustrophobic had suddenly become a huge bonus. Ahead of him Blackhawk and Rowley moved silently, the deep layer of pine needles muffling their footsteps. Above, a pale-blue sky peeked through the pine branches in small patches of normality, but all around him the dark shadows could not be trusted. Anything could be in the darkness, waiting to pounce. He sniffed the air. Bears were still filling their bellies for their winter hibernation but as the wind was blowing toward the men, the smell of one close would be recognizable.

They trudged on, moving down the slope of the mountainside, and soon the roar of the falls broke the eerie silence, only to be replaced by a thick fog of water vapor. As shafts of light hit the branches, the drops of water looked like a mantle of diamonds, each with its own rainbow. The sight amazed Rio, but the drips of freezing water splashing his face with every step did not.

"Wait up." Blackhawk stopped where the trail split into three. He bent and lifted a wrapper from an energy bar from the ground and waved it at them. "This is fresh. Someone has been here recently." He peered down the three choices, checking the ground and vegetation. "This way."

Rio followed for another hundred yards or so, weaving in and out of the shadows along a narrow path. A stink came on the air and he pulled up his scarf to cover his nose. "What's that smell?"

"We'll find out soon. Look above. The crows wait and an eagle circles waiting for us to leave. Something has disturbed them. We'll need to step softly and stay alert." Blackhawk glanced behind him. "Have that rifle ready, Jake."

"I'm on it." Rowley shouldered his weapon and moved forward at a slow pace.

As they rounded the next bend ahead of him, choked by the unmistakable stink of death, Rio braced himself. Human or animal, the smell was the same. He followed, glancing this way and that, peering into the dark, misty shadows. When both men stopped abruptly, every hair on Rio's body stood to attention. He edged toward them down the narrow trail, but his friends had blocked his view. "What's up?"

"Oh, Jesus." Rowley's hand went to his mouth and his face drained of color.

Pushing past him, Rio peered into a small clearing and stopped mid-stride. His mind had trouble comprehending the graphic sight before him. He had to force himself to stand and scan the area. The carnage and total disregard for human dignity sickened him, and his hand trembled as he reached for his satellite phone. The men beside him stood grim faced and silent. Neither moved; they stared transfixed on the unimaginable horror before them. Someone had to do something. When Rowley turned and spewed into the bushes, he stared at Blackhawk's blank expression. "I'll call it in." He checked the time for his report. It was a little after nine.

"I'll head back. Tell Jenna I'll meet her in the parking lot and guide her here." Blackhawk gave him a long look. "Keep a tree to your back, this crazy man might still be around."

"Sure, thanks." Rio turned away, walking a few paces back down the trail to get some distance from the scene. He needed to breathe but his throat was tight and his heart pounded in his chest so fast his head spun. He called the sheriff. "It's Rio, ma'am. We have two mutilated bodies, near Bear Peak. We found a late model SUV in the Bear Peak parking lot. It might belong to this couple. We'll secure the area. Blackhawk will meet you at the Bear Peak parking lot and guide you here, but I'll send the coordinates.

"Remain on scene until we get there. I'm waiting for Sam Cross to arrive, and as soon as I've spoken to him, we'll be on our way. Dave's here, I'll ask him to inform Wolfe." Jenna's professional demeanor impressed him. *"Is it a bear attack?"*

Rio shook his head. "Not unless they've started using crossbows in this part of the forest."

CHAPTER THIRTY-ONE

It was difficult for Jenna not to be intimidated by Sam Cross, especially when the lawyer pressed his knuckles into her desk and glared at her. Refusing to be bullied, she drew in a breath through her nose and eyeballed him. Her position as sheriff made her the chief law enforcement officer of Black Rock Falls County, and it was obvious she needed to remind him. The time had come to stand her ground and to stop allowing a defense lawyer to walk all over her. She often wondered if he acted this way because he liked to throw his weight around and look important, but of late his demeaning attitude toward her had become personal. She needed to put a stop to it—and now. "In case it slipped your mind, we are both officers of the court. My job is to apprehend suspects and present evidence in a crime to the DA. He decides if the evidence is enough to proceed. It's not within my power to issue an arrest warrant on circumstantial evidence and you darn well know it." She lifted her chin, refusing to give him the upper hand. "The DA believes we have a case, and your client will be taken to county." She didn't break her stare at his angry face. "I'm sure you know the drill, Mr. Cross. There'll be a bail hearing in the morning, which we're opposing."

"Like I said before." Cross tipped back his Stetson and shook his head in disbelief. "Hold off with serving the arrest warrant until you have more information on the bodies in the forest. If the TOD is over the period my client was in your custody, it proves his innocence." He straightened.

Jenna hadn't known he'd been outside her office door when she'd informed Kane about Rio's call, and of course Sam Cross had overheard the conversation and her plans to leave to examine the crime scene. She shook her head. "That's not going to happen. At this time, we have no idea what my deputies have found in the forest. Until the ME has examined the remains and the scene, there's no reason to delay the serving of the arrest warrant. I'd be negligent in my duty not to do so. I can't just hold your client indefinitely, and if I didn't carry out my duties to the letter, as sure as hell you'd find a loophole somewhere to have him released." She sucked in a deep breath. "Of course, should evidence come to light that exonerates your client, you'll be the first to know and can take the appropriate steps at that time. Right now, the DA has decided he wants Riley Adams where we can keep an eye on him."

"I'm going to petition the DA for a stay on the warrant until the ME has examined the remains." Cross pushed his hands into the back pockets of his jeans and stared at the ceiling as if wishing for divine intervention. He let out a long sigh. "This is a reasonable request. You could be holding the wrong man and have a killer out there."

Jenna stood at the sight of Kane at the doorway. "Do what you must, but I have a crime scene to secure. If you'll excuse me?"

When Cross turned on his heel and brushed past Kane without another word, Jenna stared after him. She looked at Kane. "From now on, when we're discussing a case, we close the door. He overheard my call from Rio and now wants to put a hold on the arrest warrant for Adams."

"Well, he'll have to take it up with the DA." Kane shrugged. "I already served the warrant and Adams is on his way to county. It's out of our hands and we have more important things to deal with today." He grabbed Jenna's jacket from one of the pegs behind her door and tossed it to her. "Put this on. Rowley just called; it's freezing in the mountains." He shrugged into his coat. "Wolfe will meet us at the parking lot at Bear Peak along with Atohi. I've already packed our backpacks and we're ready to leave."

"I'm ready." Jenna slipped her Glock into the holster on her duty belt, inserted the earpiece of her com, and pulled a woolen cap over her head. She slipped on her thick winter jacket and pulled up the hood. "Let's go." She glanced down at Duke. "Is Duke coming?"

"Sure." Kane whistled his dog. "His coat is in the Beast." He led the way down the stairs.

The cool breeze smelled of the first snow and brought with it a reminder that winter wasn't too far away. The sun usually sat in a blue sky that went on forever, but this morning low cloud cover had diluted its warmth. She glanced down Main, taking in the mass of decorations. As people walked by the displays, they triggered the sounds of wailing and howls. Motion-sensing automatons came to life, some so real they made her heart race. At times, because of the horrific memories of the past, her mind superimposed crime scenes over the displays and she had to visit the macabre scenes to convince herself they were fake. Why did Halloween bring out the crazy people? It had been a happy time when she was a child with the trick-or-treating, outrageous costumes, and laughter. Of late, the poisoned candy everyone was wary of had been replaced by psychopaths roaming Black Rock Falls. Would this be the new normal for her town from now on?

She climbed into the truck and looked at Kane. "I hope you brought the mentholated salve. From what Rio said, I figure we're going to need it."

"I have, but Wolfe will have some anyway." Kane turned onto Stanton and accelerated. "You know, Sam Cross had no right to be on your office floor without permission. If he'd spoken to Maggie, she'd have given us the heads-up he was on his way." His attention remained fixed on the road ahead as they shot past an eighteen-wheeler. "He only acts that way with you. During my interview with Adams, he was like a normal annoying lawyer. I'm not sure of his endgame—defense lawyers usually want us to cooperate with them and he's sure making an enemy out of you."

Jenna stared at the forest flying by and caught sight of a herd of deer moving through the trees to lower ground, their coats glistening in the shafts of dappled light. Again, the beauty of the forest had been sullied by murder. She sighed. "He's good at his job but I just need to be better at mine. Since he allowed a killer to walk from my custody, I make doubly sure we don't leave any loopholes for him to exploit." She turned in her seat to look at him. "The problem is, I do have concerns about the Adams case. It all seemed too good to be true. The evidence pointed to Adams without a doubt, but now we have another murder in the same area of Stanton Forest using a crossbow. If it happened while Adams was in our custody, we'll have accused an innocent man."

"He had plenty of time to kill, clean up, and get to the nursing home. You have to admit two murder scenes with evidence of a crossbow as the weapon is too much of a coincidence." Kane flicked her a glance as they took the turn off the highway to Bear Peak. "The time of death is going to be crucial." He frowned. "With the temperature dropping so fast, I don't envy Wolfe's task. The entire case will hinge on the timeline we have for Adams."

As they pulled up beside Rowley's truck, Jenna ran the plates of the late-model SUV. She waited for the response and looked at Kane. "The truck belongs to Emmett Howard out of Sleepy Creek. He is married to Patricia and they are in their late twenties." She downloaded the details and license images to her phone. She pulled the satellite sleeve out of her pocket and secured it to her phone. "Will our coms work so close to the mountain?"

"Sure." Kane gave her a slow smile. "These are way past our paygrade when it comes to technology. I'm not sure how Wolfe obtained them. The satellite network for these covers the entire world. These little earpieces are top secret, and up to this year the technology was intended for aircraft. They receive and transmit to everyone in our team at the same time. Only bad electrical storms or dense cloud cover will affect them." He pushed on his earpiece. "Wolfe, what's your ETA?"

"Two minutes." Wolfe's voice came in loud and clear.

Jenna smiled at Kane. "Wow!" She turned as Blackhawk emerged from the trail. "Atohi has arrived." She turned to him. "How far is it from here?"

"Twenty minutes." Atohi went to his truck and took out a bottle of water. He drank and then turned to Jenna. "I've seen bears be kinder to a person than what I've seen today." He shook his head. "There seems to be no end to man's cruelty."

A white van rumbled into the parking lot and Wolfe and Colt Webber climbed out. Jenna frowned. "Isn't Em coming?"

"Nope." Wolfe opened the back of the van and pulled out stretchers and his bag. "She has another exam today. This is the last one. She's a little apprehensive and I think her place in medical college is secure, but waiting to see if she qualifies is always a worry. Black Rock Falls Medical College has pushed the bar pretty high, but with the internship she did with me and a good undergraduate degree, she should be okay."

Jenna nodded. "I'm sure she'll sail through." She pulled on her backpack. "What do you have for me to carry?"

Once they were all set, they followed Blackhawk down the mountain and onto the trail. She moved up beside him. "What's your take on the scene?"

"Someone used a crossbow to shoot two people and then went crazy with an ax or maybe knives." Blackhawk kept his gaze straight ahead, but she could see his Adam's apple move as he swallowed. "I've never seen anything like it before, it's… indescribable."

CHAPTER THIRTY-TWO

Walking beside Kane, Wolfe noted the way his friend kept up a constant scan of the forest as if expecting an attack. He kept his voice low. "Do you sense someone is watching us?"

"The forest is too quiet." Kane peered into the canopy. "The animals seem to know if there's another bad storm coming, or if there's a bear hanging around. The birds usually warn of a problem and stay quiet when a storm is coming. This feels different, unless it's the smell." He pointed upward. "Crows are scavengers and yet they're sticking to the trees. The stink from the crime scene has attracted them but something is keeping them up there. They're not stupid and won't feed if there's danger."

Wolfe looked ahead at Blackhawk. "I don't think Atohi would walk into danger either. He knows the forest in all its moods." He raised his voice. "How much further?"

"It's about twenty yards around the next bend." Blackhawk looked troubled. "You should all prepare your minds for a shock." He nodded and turned back down the trail.

The smell was getting bad. Wolfe held up a hand. "Hey, hold up, everyone. We should stop here and suit up. I don't want anyone stepping inside the perimeters of the crime scene before I've taken a look." He dropped his end of the stretcher and placed his bag on the floor. After pulling out masks, gloves, and coveralls for Kane, Jenna, and Webber, he pulled on his gear. "From all accounts this murder is nasty. If anyone feels the need to puke, keep it well away from the scene. If you feel sick, walk away. We don't need people passing out."

"That bad, huh?" Jenna raised both eyebrows. "It would seem Rio gave you a little more information than he did me."

Wolfe nodded. "I called him for details, Jenna. I needed to know what to bring with me. I can't just bring a forensics kit and hope for the best."

"It's just ahead around the next bend." Blackhawk turned to look at him.

"Okay." Jenna climbed into coveralls and rolled up the legs. "I'm good to go." She snapped a facemask in place and spoke through her com. "Rowley, we're coming up to your position now."

In his earpiece, Wolfe could hear Rowley's response. He moved to the front of the group and led them around the next bend and into a small clearing. Rowley and Rio stood to one side, to allow him to pass. He scanned the area. Two bodies, or what was left of them. One, male, propped up against a tree, had been secured and used as target practice and the other, a woman posed to gain a shock reaction, was brutally disfigured. Camping gear and pots and pans lay scattered on the ground, but all personal effects appeared to be missing. Set in the middle of the clearing, a fire circle of stones had been disturbed, ash spilled out onto the grass. He touched his earpiece. "Jenna, are you one hundred percent sure they have James Stone in custody?"

"Yeah." Jenna moved to the perimeter of the clearing and he caught her sharp intake of breath. "But this sure looks like his work. They'd contact me if he escaped, but I'll call county and make sure they have eyes on him." She walked away, pulling out her earpiece.

Wolfe turned to Kane. "Can you smell gas? This is another replica of one of Stone's crime scenes, but when he committed murder, he had an accomplice. This was a frenzied attack. He'd have been drenched in blood, and I didn't notice any blood spatter on the trail we came through and I was looking." He turned to Webber. "Document the scene as best you can from the perimeter but don't touch or walk in anything."

"Yes, sir." Webber took out a camera and began filming.

"I have my camera." Rio waved it at Wolfe. "I've taken a few preliminary shots, but I can cover the scene if you want? It might save time."

Wolfe nodded. "Knock yourself out." He turned to Kane. "I don't like this at all. It's as if a crime scene photograph was leaked. This entire scene is staged. I figure someone is playing games with us."

"Yeah, it's too close." Kane scrolled through the files on his phone. "Look at this—not exact but too close for a coincidence. The backpacks are missing, I'll bet the phones are as well."

There was so much blood someone must have left a trail, however minute, when they left. Wolfe scanned the area and could make out three trails leading from the clearing. He turned to Blackhawk. "Can you determine which way the killer left the scene?"

"I can try." Blackhawk shrugged and moved through the trees, disappearing into the shadows.

Wolfe took in the scene as a whole and set a probable timeline in his head. He'd use Kane's expertise in weapons trajectory to determine the height of the shooter. "Do you think there is more than one killer?" He pointed to the numerous angles the bolts made in the victims.

"Maybe, but this all looks up close and personal to me." Kane shrugged. "Is it possible to narrow down the time of death?" His gaze hadn't stopped searching the trees. "We've charged Adams with the murder of Payton Harris. There's a window of opportunity where he could have killed these people and then gotten himself into work on the day we interviewed him."

Wolfe shrugged. "I always use every resource possible to get the exact TOD, but there are many things against us here. We don't have a witness, so we have to rely on science. The best I can do is an approximate TOD."

"Approximate will be fine." Kane turned as Jenna moved into the clearing.

"Stone is still locked up." Jenna walked to Wolfe's side. "I asked the warden to send a guard to make sure. He didn't have to; he has him on CCTV. At this moment in time, would you believe Stone is in the prison library? He likes to read."

"The model prisoner, huh?" Kane shook his head. "We need to look into his time in jail more closely because something isn't right."

"Yeah." Jenna stood hands on hips. "I have the same feeling."

As soon as Webber and Rio had finished documenting the scene, Wolfe turned to Jenna. "You know the drill. We'll process the scene together. Mark any body parts, footprints, and blood spatter you find. I'll do a preliminary examination of the victims. I want to take their core body temperature ASAP, then we'll pack them up and get them to the lab."

"Okay." Jenna beckoned Rio and Rowley. "Do a grid search of the area, these people must have had backpacks or personal items. Hunt around until you find them." She turned to Wolfe. "I want to be with you when you examine the bodies."

"Yeah, so do I." Kane looked at Wolfe. "Do you mind?"

"Nope." Wolfe picked up his bag and stepped with care toward the body of the male and crouched beside him. "He's still in rigor and from the extent, I'd estimate death occurred longer than twelve hours ago, less than twenty-four." He lifted the man's shirt and used a probe directly into the liver. "The body temperature will tell me more. It's important I take the temperature first. The body cools to the surrounding temperature between twelve and twenty hours. I'll need to consider the overnight conditions and I'll be able to give you an answer when I get back to the lab. We have formulas to determine a more accurate TOD than the estimate I could make now." He looked at Kane. "We'll need to pry him from the tree to transport him, but if you could do a crossbow bolt trajectory analysis on him, I'll go and take the body temperature of his companion."

"Sure." Kane dropped his backpack to the ground and bent to retrieve his equipment.

Noticing Jenna staring at the congealed puddles of blood and body parts surrounding the woman, Wolfe moved closer. "It seems this killer had some insight to Stone's torturing techniques." He indicated to the blood. "The amount of blood tells us that her killer kept her alive until she bled to death."

"Yeah." Jenna looked at the woman's face. "That has to be Patti Howard. I recognize her from her driver's license. Her face is untouched, so we do have an anomaly. Stone chose every victim. To him they were me. He hated me and took it out on innocent women, but this isn't revenge or a crime of passion. This man enjoyed his work."

CHAPTER THIRTY-THREE

Overcoming the fight or flight response when confronted with a brutal murder scene was something Jenna had fought to control. Now, after so many brutal killings, she would have thought her mind would have gotten used to seeing carnage, but no. Right now she wanted to hightail it back to the Beast and hide under Duke's blanket. She turned to look at the dog, sitting patiently at the edge of the crime scene, his head on his paws and his eyes following Kane's every move. Her attention went to her deputies. Rowley and Rio were walking shoulder to shoulder back and forth across the clearing, collecting anything of interest and placing markers. Blackhawk arrived carrying the backpacks and she went to him. "Did you document where these were found?"

"Yeah, I'll forward the images to you and Wolfe." He handed her the backpacks. "This man knows the forest and moves like a spirit, he left only a whisper of a touch as he passed. There was no blood trail leading from the scene, and the killer left through the trees, dropping the backpacks before taking an obscure path from the crime scene. I've recorded and marked the path he took but it melts into the forest." He glanced at the blood-soaked ground and back at her. "He killed and then took the time to clean up." He pointed to a disturbed patch of grass. "He stood here, removed his clothes, and washed. The ground is still damp." He turned slowly and stared into the forest. "He'd have planned this well and stowed his change of clothes close by. The ground where I found the backpacks is disturbed. He dressed there, took his soiled clothes, and left."

Jenna nodded. "Thanks."

The IDs inside verified that the victims were indeed Emmett and Patti Howard out of Sleepy Creek. She waved to get Kane's attention. "The phones are missing but whoever did this didn't steal anything from them apart from their lives. What is the motive for killing them?"

"It looks like a thrill kill." Kane waved a hand toward the two victims. "Wolfe found a back injury, a stab wound. He disabled the man, just like Stone's MO. From the male victim's position, the killer likely made him watch while he tortured the female and then he used him for target practice. This time he left the bolts in situ and only used a crossbow." He gave Jenna a long look. "Stone used a rifle and crossbow. It's very close to Stone's murder spree, but there are differences. This is different from the Adams crime scene. What are the odds on two people deciding to murder a couple with a crossbow in the same week?"

"Astronomical." Jenna's attention slid to the staring eyes of the victims. "This has to be Adams, there's no other explanation."

"Aw, come on, Jenna." Kane's eyebrows rose. "In this county, trust me, anything is possible. We've had more than one killer in town before. How do we know there aren't two killers? It's possible. Anything is possible."

Unconvinced, Jenna shook her head. "This has Stone's MO all over it; he's getting his message out somehow. I'm calling Jo. I want her input on this killer. I'm finding it hard to believe this is the work of more than one man."

Jenna pulled out her phone and picked her way back to the trail and headed downwind. Glad of the respite the cool mountain air offered, she leaned against a tall pine nestled in a clump of snowberry bushes and made the call. She had to wait a few moments for Jo to pick up. "Hi, Jo, do you have time for a chat?"

"I sure do. It's been quiet here for days. Have you caught the person who invaded your home?"

"Yeah… well maybe." Jenna explained and gave details of both crime scenes. "So, we have three victims and one missing person."

"Do you mind if Carter listens in?"

Jenna could hear a chair scraping and Carter's voice in the background. "Sure. How are you, Ty?"

"Bored, so what's happening in Black Rock Falls?"

She brought him up to speed. "I'm on scene and the DA has charged a suspect. There are subtle differences to the James Stone murders. I figure someone leaked crime scene information and this is a copycat. If not, he's somehow communicating with an accomplice on the outside."

"From what you're telling me, we're dealing with an organized killer." Jo cleared her throat. *"Of course, I can't make a conclusion until I've analyzed the crime scenes for comparison. You say this scene is messy and the female is posed. This would indicate an organized killer. From the images I've seen of the Stone murders and the planning behind each kill, Stone was an organized killer as well."*

Intrigued, Jenna straightened and headed back to the crime scene. The suffocating smell of the bodies greeted her and seeped through the mentholated salve spread under her nose. "So what characteristics are we looking for in a man who kills this way?"

"Well, if we take Stone as an example, you can see if Adams fits the same profile." Jo sounded enthusiastic. *"Stone lived and worked in Black Rock Falls for a long time. He hunted and disposed of his victims within the local area. He used the caves as a special place to hide some of his victims and revisited the crime scenes and corpses."*

The file Jenna had on Adams filled her mind, and the profile fit. "Yeah, Adams is the same, but remember, Stone didn't act alone and at some point was receiving instructions on how to kill his victims."

"Which takes an organized, highly intelligent mind." Jo tapped away on her keyboard. *"I'm opening Stone's files now. Uh-huh, yes, very organized and yet his kills were spaced out a little more and he was triggered by a disagreement with you. The question is, Jenna: Is Stone capable of manipulating people to act for him? We have no proof that anyone has been communicating with him, but things happen in jail. Not every prison guard is honest. I figure we go and speak to him and see what pearls of wisdom he can offer us. Some psychopaths can't wait to tell their tales, especially if it's for research into the criminal mind. The entire beginnings of profiling came about because of the FBI's interviews with psychopaths."*

Jenna swallowed hard. Acid formed in her stomach at the thought of speaking to James Stone again. The confrontation on the mountain, the weeks and months afterward hoping Kane was alive, had been a nightmare. Could she face Stone again? "I'm not sure. Going in to see him might give the wrong impression."

"The wrong impression to Stone?" Jo chuckled. *"Seeing you will more than likely unlock his defenses, it's the last thing he'd expect. Facing a victim he failed to kill and one who put him behind bars might make him drop his guard."*

The confrontation with Stone played in her head like the rerun of a soap opera. She'd been outside the interview room watching when he'd blamed her for his killing spree. Her refusing to date him had triggered a psychotic episode resulting in people dying. Could she dare risk it? "What if seeing me unlocks the rage in him again? What if he decides to kill the inmates?"

"Unless Black Rock County jail decides to place him in the general population, I don't think so." Jo sucked in a breath. *"I could go with*

Carter and talk to him but I think the shock value of seeing you will loosen his tongue. It all depends on if you're able to cope with seeing him again, after what's happened."

Torn between her private hell and Jo's intentions, she needed to know more. "What do you expect to gain from seeing Stone? He's not going to tell you anything. He's smart and if he's playing a game with us, we're doing just what he wants."

"Exactly, but we'll be prepared, and he won't be." Jo sounded confident. *"I'll make arrangements to speak to him. I've interviewed some of the vilest human beings on the planet; he won't be able to manipulate me."*

Jenna turned and looked at the horror of the crime scene. "Maybe not you, because you haven't been threatened by him and you're not standing ankle deep in blood, like I am at the moment. I might let you down. He'll play to my weaknesses."

"Will he?" Jo sighed *"The last experience he had with you is you taking him down. You outwitted him and he knows it. You'll have the upper hand. Don't worry, we'll discuss everything beforehand and if it makes you more comfortable, we'll have Dave and Carter in the room with us."*

Jenna considered the options. "No, if we're doing this, I don't want him believing I need backup. He'll see you as a doctor and no threat. Having the guys in there with us will demonstrate my apprehension at seeing him again. I'd never give him the satisfaction."

"Then it's a go?"

Determined, Jenna straightened and lifted her chin. "Yeah, it's a go."

Keeping the conversation with Jo to herself, Jenna worked the scene with the team. She had to walk away numerous times to gather herself. She might have investigated more murders than most sheriffs, but she never at any time forgot the victims were people. Her imagination ran riot with the ordeal the victims had endured, and it tore at her heart. All she could think of when she looked at the perfect features of Patti Howard and the once handsome Emmett was that killing them had been such a waste. Two intelligent young people in the prime of their lives, struck down on the whim of a madman. She had to find out who was responsible. If not Adams, then she'd keep investigating until she found the killer.

The exhausting trek back up the mountain, loaded up with bodies and evidence, gave her time to think over her conversation with Jo. Her body ached as she climbed into the truck. As they drove down the mountain road, she turned to Kane. "As you know, I called Jo and she had a few ideas on the case."

"We already have someone in custody and I'm sure we can figure out this case on our own." Kane cut her a glance. "We managed to solve cases before they arrived on the scene."

"Yeah, but this one is different. I know we have Adams in custody but nothing will convince me that Stone isn't involved in some way. Not after seeing that crime scene." Jenna poured them coffee from the Thermos. "Jo wants to interview Stone and find out if he's involved. She has so many techniques she can use to pry information out of him and I need to find out if he knows anything about the attack on me."

"Do you honestly think he'd tell you if he did?" Kane snorted in obvious disgust. "The man is less than an animal. Depraved, brutal, and crazy doesn't come close. I can't believe you want to be in the same room as him, let alone speak to him."

"Well, I don't have to. We have one of the top behavioral analysts in the country at our disposal." Jenna recalled the long talks they'd had about the FBI behavioral analysts' convention, and why Kane had wanted to attend. "I remember you telling me how the FBI started analyzing psychopaths. How most of their information came from interviews? The agents learned a way to approach them to make them talk and get insights into their behavior." She yawned explosively. "Oh, sorry. Anyway, as we have copycat murders and an ongoing threat to me, interviewing Stone might give us the edge we need. Stone is so arrogant he might slip up and admit to influencing the killer. It's worth the chance. Don't you think Jo would be able to handle Stone?"

"I'm sure she has had experience with interviewing psychopaths worse than him." Kane turned onto Stanton Road and accelerated, making the forest flash by in a swirl of green. "Why would you give Stone the satisfaction of knowing you went to him for help? You know he believes you're in love with him and that you'll go back to him one day." A nerve ticked in his cheek. "You'd be playing into his fantasy."

The vivid memory of Stone shooting Kane and then gunning for her flashed across her mind. How could she ever forget? It had taken every ounce of willpower not to put a bullet into Stone's head. She'd known Kane would disapprove, and on the way back from the murder scene had thought long and hard about how to convince him. "I'm not planning on going in and straight-out asking him about this murder or my intruder." Jenna finished her coffee. "Jo will interview him on the pretense of writing a paper or whatever and ask him if he'd like to be involved in the research."

"He'll know from the newspapers about the first body in the forest." Kane slowed as they hit town. "By tomorrow, Rio would have the media release out. Stone will know the details."

"No, I've decided to restrict the media release to the search for June Harris." Jenna placed the empty cup in the console. "It will be generic and nothing will be mentioned about her husband or the other murders. Rio is an expert at saying nothing in media releases." She looked at him. "We can't stop Stone receiving newspapers; it would make him even more suspicious."

"An interview with Stone wouldn't be too easy to set up." Kane shrugged. "But Jo can cut through red tape. I hope you're not planning on going into an interview room with him alone, are you? You'll need Carter and me with you. Even in chains I don't trust Stone."

Jenna shook her head. "I don't either, but it will be just me and Jo. You'll be right outside watching through the two-way mirror." She shrugged. "Nothing can possibly happen, Dave. You and Carter and the guards will be a second away. We'll be safe."

"Jenna." Kane ran a hand down his face and sighed with a hint of desperation. "A man like Stone can kill in a second." He let out a long sigh that made Duke whine and looked at her. "There's no changing your mind about this, is there?"

Jenna turned in her seat and gave Kane a determined stare. "Absolutely not."

CHAPTER THIRTY-FOUR

It was like the lull before the storm. The only sound in Jenna's office came from Duke snoring in his basket under her desk. The media release had gone out, asking if anyone had seen either of the murder victims but not indicating that they'd been slaughtered in the forest. She had to admire the way Rio injected urgency into the notice by asking people to contact the sheriff's department without delay if they'd even seen a glimpse of the couple in town. The midday news bulletin had come and gone, and although the information would be repeated on the hour, she'd expected at least someone to have noticed them. She glanced up as a shadow fell over her doorway. "Do you have anything for me, Dave?"

"A timeline of the murder." Kane sat down in the chair before her desk and slid over his iPad. "Going on the way the camping gear was tossed around, I figure the couple had just entered the clearing when they were set upon." He leaned forward in the chair and scrolled through the images. "Emmett Howard was disabled first and dragged to where we found him. There is dirt on the back of the heels of his boots. Wolfe will confirm but from his initial findings, a puncture wound in the spine paralyzed him. There didn't appear to be any defensive wounds but we'll know more from the autopsy." He pointed to an image of the fire circle. "See here, there is a half-moon print of a small boot. It matches Patti Howard's hiking boots, which tells me the killer surprised her, she spun around and tripped over the fire circle. She didn't have time to react and was attacked. It looks like the killer carried her to the tree and secured her arms." He pulled his tablet back toward him and frowned. "In a few seconds, this person had overpowered both of them. They were at his mercy."

The sightless eyes of the victims filled Jenna's memory and she shuddered. "The gas was poured on both of them but the woman's clothes were still soaked. Is that possible? The rate of evaporation might give us a better idea of the time this happened."

"From what I could see, Emmett was doused in gas first. His clothes have the smell but appeared dry apart from the dew." A nerve in Kane's jaw ticked and his mouth flattened into a thin line. "Patti was soaked in blood. That alone might have some relation to the time the gas took to evaporate. There'd be many factors: the weather, temperature, and then there's the humidity… which, that close to the falls, is never less than ninety percent."

Jenna chewed on the end of a pen and thought for a beat. "I think she had tape residue on her face. The killer wanted her quiet, but why cover her husband in gas before her?"

"Maybe it was a threat." Kane shrugged. "He could've pulled out a Zippo and waved it around, threatening to light Emmett up if Patti didn't cooperate. Love is a powerful thing and she might have tried to protect him."

The phone on the desk buzzed and Jenna lifted the receiver. It was Maggie on the front counter. "Send him up." She disconnected and looked at Kane. "Someone met our couple in town." She heard footsteps on the stairs and pushed to her feet. "Mr. Long. Come in and take a seat. This is Deputy Kane."

"Ma'am." Long removed his cowboy hat and sat in the chair Kane had just vacated.

Jenna took out a notepad and took in the man. He was mid to late thirties, strong build, and had a pleasant face. "First up, can I have your details for the record?"

"Sure. Tyson Long, raised and now living out of Summit Heights." He glanced up at Kane as if assessing him.

Jenna cleared her throat to get his attention. "Okay, tell me how you came to meet Patti and Emmett Howard."

"I met them on Monday." Long's expression was earnest. "I was in the Wild Outdoors store and they spoke to me. They were arguing about satellite phones. Patti wanted to see the falls and Emmett wanted to have some time alone with his wife in the mountains." He opened his hands wide. "They just up and asked me if I could take them into the forest. They offered to pay me but I refused."

The story sounded too darn familiar, and the sudden feeling of being trapped in a recurring dream spilled over Jenna. It was too much of a coincidence not to be taken seriously. It was as if the man before her were Adams. She'd play along and see what else he knew. "So, I'm guessing you took them into the forest, left them all alone, and came back to town?"

"Yeah. Are you reading my mind, Sheriff?" Long met her gaze, steady and unwavering. "I didn't have much to do, so I agreed to take them up on Tuesday. We met at the Bear Peak parking lot at eleven-thirty and I took them down the mountain to a campsite I recalled. I left them there about an hour or so later and planned to go back up and bring them down this afternoon at four." He gave Jenna a sweet smile. "When I heard the news, I figured no one knows where they are and I'd come by and tell you."

Jenna exchanged a puzzled look with Kane and he returned it with the subtle lift of one eyebrow. She ground her teeth. It was as if he'd heard Adams' story and decided to repeat it. Some people would do anything for attention, but Long had put her on her guard. Could this man be Adams' accomplice, or was he here to throw reasonable doubt on Adams' arrest? "Did anyone see you with them in the store?"

"I'm not sure, the store is always busy—maybe." Long shrugged. "I guess the store has a CCTV camera. You could check the footage but I don't see the point." A flash of annoyance caught in his eyes for a split second. "Don't you believe me? I took them into the forest and showed them a secluded campsite."

"So, you'd be willing to take us to this campsite?" Kane pushed off the wall and dropped his combat expression on the man.

"Sure." Long leaned back in his chair and shrugged. "I've nothing better to do this afternoon."

Needing an excuse to speak to Kane alone, Jenna pulled her phone out of her pocket, looked at the blank screen and then at Mr. Long. "Can you give me a minute? Something's come up."

Not waiting for a reply, she stood and looked at Kane. "We need to talk."

"Sure." Kane opened the door and they walked into the hallway.

Jenna pulled him into the locker room. "What the hell is going on here? Is this guy playing us for fools? We have three homicides and one missing woman and they all just happened to meet strangers and ask them to take them into the forest? Am I missing something here or have people suddenly started to lose their minds? I mean, can people be gullible enough to go up to a stranger here in serial killer capital and *ask* them to lead them into danger, or what?" She paced the small area. "Once, I might believe, but twice?" Wanting to tear her hair out in frustration, she stared at him. "This guy gives me the creeps. He is so nice and yet I'm getting a really bad vibe off him."

"One thing for damn sure, this isn't a coincidence. I can't figure out his angle, but to be singing the same song as Adams makes me wonder if they've planned this little charade." Kane leaned against the wall. "This might be two different cases but having the exact same scenarios, same MO and both men admitting to everything apart from the actual killing is bizarre."

Jenna pushed two hands through her hair. "What if this is a ploy to get them both off a murder charge? Think about it, Dave. Long's testimony throws reasonable doubt on any case we might have against Adams, especially if Wolfe decides the TOD isn't in Adams' timeline. The second murder with the same MO, is reason enough for Adams to walk."

"The problem is without evidence both men could be telling the truth, and most people would ignore the subtle differences in the actual killings and believe the murderer is still in the forest, waiting for his next victims." Kane shrugged. "The autopsies will confirm, but from Wolfe's preliminary examination of the last victims, both MOs were slightly different. There is a possibility we're looking at two killers."

Incredulous, Jenna stared at him. "You think?"

"I'll go with the conspiracy theory but we'll need proof they're both involved." Kane rubbed the back of his neck. "You'll need to push Long a little harder and see if he cracks. Although I doubt it. Like Adams, he is so sure of himself he must have an ace up his sleeve or a get out of jail free card."

"It sure looks that way." Jenna pinched the bridge of her nose. "It's as if they know we haven't gotten a shred of evidence against them." She moved to the door. "I'll figure out a way to keep Long here to give us time to dig into his background. I'll call Kalo."

"Send Long to an interview room with Rowley to take his statement?" Kane followed her into the hallway.

"Yeah." Jenna nodded. "That will give us time to check out this guy." She pushed open the door to her office and smiled at Mr. Long. "Sorry about that—ah, where were we? Kane, do you have any questions?"

"Yeah." Kane narrowed his gaze. "Do you work here in town? Are you a shift worker?"

"Nope. I've been fixing up my ranch." Long rubbed his chin as if deciding to tell them and then sighed. "I've been away for a time. My pa passed and I inherited the ranch. I don't have any livestock so there's not too much to do, but I have plans to run some cattle. I'm waiting until spring to buy me some calves to raise."

Jenna frowned. "Why take the Howards to Bear Peak? It's not very romantic, with its history of murder." She pulled a face. "Darn right creepy if you ask me."

"What murders?" Long met her gaze with a wide-eyed, astonished expression. "I've been away for five years and I don't know about any murders."

"Really?" Kane pressed both palms on the desk and eyeballed him. "They made the news. Have you been off the grid? Living on the moon?"

"Yeah, something like that." Long shrugged. "That's beside the point. I came here to give you information on Patti and Emmett, not to be interrogated like a criminal. I want to leave now." He went to push to his feet but Kane laid a hand on his shoulder. Long laughed at him. "Are you trying to intimidate me, Deputy? I'm just trying to help the sheriff." He looked at Jenna. "Is he always so intense?" He turned back to Kane, obviously amused. "Chill out, man. The Howards will be right where I left them."

"We're asking questions is all." Kane's jaw tightened. "When people go missing in our town, we take it seriously. Right now, you're the last person to have seen them."

"That's not unusual, is it?" Long stifled a yawn. "I'm sure that happens all the time." He stared at Jenna as if challenging her. "You know they're in the forest, don't you? It's gotta be over a million square acres and only I know where I left them. Come with me and I'll be glad to show you."

And murder us as well? Keeping her expression neutral, Jenna stood. "Okay, we'll go with you to where you left them. I'm sure they're waiting there for you as planned."

She understood how many psychopaths enjoyed revisiting a crime scene and seeing the reactions to their work. Many would try to insert themselves into an investigation to relive the moment of their victim's death over and over each time the crime was discussed. Long fitted into this category and had fast gone from witness to possible suspect in a wink of an eye. The need to find out more about Long tugged at her, and she sat back down in her seat. "Do you like to hunt, Mr. Long?"

"Yeah." Long scratched his cheek. "It's all about the hunt for me. Stalking and then bringing down the kill."

Jenna leaned back in her chair. "What is your weapon of choice?" She asked the question but it was as if she already knew the answer.

"I like a crossbow." Long mimicked the motion of loading a bolt in a crossbow and aiming it directly at her. "Silent but deadly. They never see it coming. I can see the surprise in their eyes when I take them down." His gaze fixed on her unblinking.

She'd seen that stare before, many times. Many psychopaths she'd interviewed had the same cold, dead eyes. Empathy didn't exist in their world, for people or animals. Life meant nothing to them but a fast thrill as they extinguished it. Hairs raised on the back of her neck in a tingle of a warning. She nodded. "You hunt alone? How do you manage to field-dress your kills?"

"Same as everyone else, I guess." Long stared at the wall and his breathing increased as if he was reliving a memory. "It has a smell when you gut a kill." He looked directly at her. "The blood gets everywhere, even under your fingernails." He examined his hands and smiled at her. "It's almost as good as the hunt."

"I'm sure it is." Jenna looked at Kane. "Would you call Rowley for me, please?"

As Kane left the room, Jenna forced a smile. Something inside her had told her not to trust this man from the minute he'd walked into her office. His relaxed attitude was different from the behavior of the usual witnesses who came forward. Most displayed nervousness or even excitement, but this guy was so laid back and had kept up the act until Kane had leaned on him. It was as if he'd rehearsed his story and expected her to be gullible enough to believe him.

A few things had made her suspicious of Long. He claimed not to know about the Bear Peak murders, when stories about them had been on TV and in books. Some of the murders went back twenty years and it didn't ring true for a guy who'd been raised in Black Rock Falls not to know about them. Even if he'd been away for five years, surely his family would have mentioned the murders to him at one time. She moved files around on the desk and then looked at him. "Do you know Payton and June Harris?"

"I've heard of them." Long inclined his head. "The name has been on every news story. Is June Harris still missing?"

Jenna caught the flash in his eyes, the sudden change of expression. She couldn't describe it, but it made her skin crawl. She stiffened. "Yeah, she is." She couldn't look away. Had he noticed her change of attitude? "So, you must have been in town Thursday through Monday?"

"I was all over town." Long opened his hands. "I can't recall every second, but I went into the mountains and I was out by your ranch late last Sunday during that storm."

Jenna swallowed the bile creeping up her throat. "How do you know where I live?" She noticed the way he looked at her and how a smile played in the corner of his lips.

"I went by your neighbor. The snowplow guy." Long placed one booted foot on his opposite knee. "I heard tell he had a horse for sale. He mentioned you lived in the next ranch."

"I see." Jenna sipped from a cold cup of coffee and pushed it to one side. "Where were you Thursday night through to, say, Friday morning?"

"Thursday night, I went to Aunt Betty's for supper. It was late, I stayed for some time. I went home and was back there for breakfast." Long smiled. "I do recall seeing Tommy Jonas at the crossroads around eleven. I stopped and chatted to him about buying cattle but it was late and he had to get on home." He looked at her. "I can give you his number to call him if you like?"

Jenna nodded. "Yes, we'd like to check that out." She took down the details he'd found on his phone and then looked at him. "Where did you go after returning to town yesterday?"

"I hung around town." Long broke eye contact and stared into space as if thinking. "I decided to take a look at all the changes around these parts and drove around some. It was dark by the time I got home. I don't recall speaking to anyone in particular. The weather has been unpredictable. I didn't walk anywhere."

"Yes, the dry storm on Sunday night was unexpected." Jenna picked up her pens and dropped them back into the chipped mug on her desk. "Do you own a slicker?"

"What kind of question is that, Sheriff?" Long snorted. "Do you know anyone around these parts that doesn't have one to keep the rain off them? Or have I become a suspect in a crime? If I have then you need to tell me. I have a fine lawyer. Sam Cross is his name."

Same lawyer too, huh? Jenna looked away. "I was just making conversation." To avoid his eyes, she collected the files on her desk and pushed them into a drawer. She could play mind games too.

"Rowley won't be long. I'll get him to take your statement about the Howards and then we'll head up to the campsite."

As she stared at Long, the image of the man she'd seen in the alleyway slid into Jenna's mind. Long was the same height and build, he wore his black Stetson pulled low over his eyes, and Adams was in custody, so it couldn't have been him. Long also matched the man she'd seen at her ranch and he'd admitted to being close by on Sunday night. She couldn't allow Long to just walk out the door, not after listening to his story. He had too many strikes against him already. He was the last person to see Emmett and Patti Howard alive and he hunted with a crossbow. He couldn't account for his whereabouts between Thursday and Monday, when Payton Harris was murdered and her home was invaded. The implications had a red flag as big as Texas waving madly at her. What if they'd made a mistake and the circumstantial evidence on Adams was just that, and Long was the killer of Payton Harris and the Howards?

Relieved when Rowley arrived at her door with Kane close behind, she stood. "Take Mr. Long down to interview room one. Get him some refreshments and take his statement. It will be more comfortable for him to wait there while I make arrangements to go out."

"Okay." Rowley's dark eyebrows knitted into a frown. "Do you want me to wait with him?"

Jenna shook her head. "That won't be necessary." She waited for them to leave and called the number Long had provided. Tommy Jonas verified seeing Long on Thursday night around the time Payton Harris was murdered. Unconvinced, she called Bobby Kalo, the FBI super-hacker. "Hi, Bobby, it's Jenna. I need your help. I want everything you can find on Tyler Long out of Summit Heights, Black Rock Falls."

CHAPTER THIRTY-FIVE

Not comprehending what Bobby Kalo had said, Kane stared at Jenna's phone in disbelief. "He what? You have to be joking."

"How come we didn't hear about either of these cases?" Jenna drummed her fingers on the desk. "We're usually informed when anyone from our county is released from jail. Most have to report here as part of their probation. This can't have happened twice in—what? The last month?— and we're kept in the dark. You have to be mistaken."

"Nope, it's all here. Tyler Long had his conviction overturned, same as the last guy. He was doing ten years for murder in the second. He won an appeal and they set him free, no probation officer visits, nothing." Kalo tapped away on his keyboard. *"I've just sent you the details."*

Dumbfounded, Kane stood and went to pour fresh cups of coffee. It had been a long day and they needed to be sharp. "Did they have the same lawyers?"

"Yeah. They didn't have much choice. There are only a few attorneys conducting criminal law in your county, and they both selected the top guy, one Samuel J Cross. Do you know him?"

"Yeah, I'm afraid I do." Jenna sighed and rubbed her eyes. "He's good."

"Ah, is Dave with you? Jo wants to speak to both of you."

Kane handed Jenna a cup and sat at the desk opposite her. "Hi, Jo. If it's not urgent, do you mind if I bend your ear as we're discussing the current homicide cases? We've had a strange twist in the investigation."

"Bend away. My news can wait and Carter is here too."

Kane smiled at Jenna. "Great! This case has got us baffled." He brought them up to speed. "So, now we have this dilemma. What do we do with Long? From the evidence, he is just as guilty as Adams. It seems a stretch of the imagination to believe they're both not involved."

"I'd write up what you have and discuss it with the DA." Carter's voice came through the speaker. *"You have to inform him, as it reflects on the Adams case. With this much reasonable doubt both ways I can't see him proceeding unless you come up with solid evidence to prove either case. Right now, you have zip."*

Kane nodded and looked at Jenna and shrugged. "Jo, do you figure both these men are manipulating us by covering each other's asses to force reasonable doubt?"

"If you can prove they know each other, it's very possible. Are they showing any psychopathic or sociopathic tendencies?"

"Yeah, they both tick a lot of boxes, especially Long; he is classic." Kane leaned his elbows on the desk. "I could write a book about him. Adams is much the same. When we charged him, he was laid back and sure of himself. It's as if he knew Long would come forward with the same story."

"Is this the main reason you're suspicious of both of them? Did you ever consider the possibility one or both of them are telling the truth? People do help others, not everyone has murder on their minds." Jo sighed.

"Not at any time." Jenna's mouth turned down. "I've interviewed many serial killers and both these men slide right into the same category. Why Long just walked in to my office as if he wanted to be caught puzzles me."

"From what you've told me, it sounds like a collaboration or they're following instructions." Jo sounded animated. *"It would be an interesting case to pursue. Two men with almost identical stories and murders with the same MO is more than a coincidence. I know you've wondered if Stone was somehow involved in Payton Harris' murder. I can see why you'd consider this because as a one-time defense lawyer, Stone would be aware a good attorney would use the circumstantial evidence you have against both men to form a reasonable doubt in court. No one will be convinced two practically identical murders are a coincidence. Most people would believe both men are telling the truth and there's a lunatic running lose in the forest."* Jo cleared her throat. *"To be honest, if I was a juror in either case, given only circumstantial evidence and two possible suspects, I would be very reluctant to convict."*

Kane pushed a hand through his hair. "Yeah, we've come up with the same conclusion. We're between a rock and a hard place."

"You'll have to hope Wolfe finds something in the autopsy you can use." Carter paused a beat. *"You could hold Long until the autopsy results. Although unless you find something other than a hunch, Sam Cross is going to eat you alive."*

"Maybe." Kane sipped his coffee. "There has to be a connection between James Stone and these murders. What if they consider Stone a role model or cult figure and they're imitating him? The murders are staged like the actual crime scene images we took of Stone's victims, and as no one outside our team and now you guys have seen them, it's freaky. More so when two men just up and start talking like there's no tomorrow."

"This is the reason I wanted to speak to both of you." Jo sounded her usual calm self. *"I discussed this possibility with Jenna earlier. I feel the only way possible to discover a link between these homicides and James Stone is to go to the source. In my experience, serial killers like to relive*

their crimes, and he admitted to everything, didn't he, so he has nothing to hide. I figure by talking to him we might discover if he's found a way to kill through his followers."

"I agree. Have you been able to set it up?" Jenna straightened in her chair.

"Yeah, we have an interview with James Stone tomorrow at ten." Jo cleared her throat. *"He'll only speak to Jenna and me. He made it very clear he doesn't want Kane anywhere near him."*

Kane snorted. "Really?"

After receiving a gunshot wound to the head from Stone resulting in a near-fatal fall into a ravine, a busted knee, and memory loss, he'd wanted to confront the man who'd tried to kill him. In fact, something deep inside him had hoped Stone might attack him so he'd have the chance to even the score, but there was also something satisfying knowing the murdering SOB would be locked up for the rest of his life. He chuckled. "It amuses me to think that I intimidate him, but when you're interviewing him make sure you let him know I'm right outside."

"We'll be landing at your ranch around 0800 hours." Carter was all business. *"We'll have time for a chat before we head out to the county prison. They have a helipad, so we'll take the bird."*

Kane nodded. "Sure. I'll have a pot of coffee waiting."

"Thanks for your help, guys, we'll see you in the morning." Jenna disconnected.

Trying to keep all the information straight in his mind, Kane stretched. They had other commitments for the morning. "We'll miss one of the autopsies. Wolfe mentioned ten and two."

"I'll send Rio." Jenna leaned back in her chair. "Rowley can handle the office." She chewed on her bottom lip, staring into space. "Now we have to come up with a plan to keep Long here for a spell." She turned her attention back to him. "Write up what we have on Long and run it past the DA." She stood and pressed the button that made the whiteboard slide from its recess in the ceiling. "I'm going to enter all the information we have on the whiteboard. It will help us piece this together."

Kane stood. "Sure, I'm on it."

After getting the statement from Rowley, Kane picked up the phone and called the DA's office. Surprisingly, the secretary put him straight through. "Some information has come up you need to be aware of in the Adams case."

After going through the statement Long provided, Kane waited for the DA to process the information. "The sheriff would like to detain Long pending the autopsies. We've considered a collaboration between Adams and Long or maybe they're part of a cult imitating James Stone's murder spree. They both display psychopathic tendencies and we're wary about allowing Long back out on the streets."

"Stone will have him out in a second. Let him out before he figures out you suspect him." The DA swore under his breath. *"It also means the circumstantial evidence we have on Adams is shot to hell. I'll have to drop the charges until you have more evidence. If we take him to trial now and he walks on reasonable doubt, which he will once Long's statement is presented, we'll be faced with double jeopardy if you establish, he did indeed kill Payton Harris."*

Kane grimaced. It wasn't the news he wanted. "I'm sure Adams killed Harris and probably his wife too."

"Then bring me the evidence. Until then, I suggest you keep both men under surveillance. I'll speak to the judge and explain why we're dropping the charges. I'll see if he'll agrees to allow your department to track both men via vehicles or phones. As they're both ex-cons, we may be lucky. I'll let you know." He disconnected.

Shaking his head, Kane climbed the stairs up to Jenna's office. He stared at the notes on the whiteboard and then headed back down the steps and hustled to the interview room. He flashed his card and walked inside. Long had his chair tipped back against the wall, boots on the table, and cowboy hat pulled down over his eyes. He cleared his throat. "Good news, we don't have to trek up the mountain. The Howards have been found."

He waited for a reaction and when Long jerked up, spilling his hat to the floor, it was all Kane needed. The surprise on the man's face was evident.

"You sure it's them?" Long bent to retrieve his hat.

Kane rested one hip on the table and looked at him. "Yeah, they're on their way back as we speak. Thanks for coming in." He paused a beat. "Something I forgot to ask you: You did time in county jail, didn't you? What's the scuttlebutt on James Stone?"

"Men talk, you know." Long shrugged but his eyes shifted from side to side. "I seen him one time but he didn't look like a serial killer. No one hassles him, that's for sure. The guards treat him like royalty."

Kane narrowed his gaze. "Really? I'd have thought the opposite, as he was a defense attorney."

"Nah." Long gave him a slow smile. "I figure it's because he could kill them all and they know it."

CHAPTER THIRTY-SIX

Somber didn't adequately describe Jenna's mood; morose, depressed came close. After receiving the news from Wolfe that the ear found pinned to her porch was indeed from June Harris, she had to concede the chances of finding her alive were now remote. There had been no sign, not as much as a strand of hair from June Harris, to assist them since the few drops of blood Rio had discovered. Search and rescue, along with cadaver dogs and the usual volunteers, had combed the forest, including the riverbeds and lakes. With hunters, wardens, and hikers constantly roaming the forest, someone should have found her or smelled her remains, but the woodlands were vast and Jenna had no option but to bring in the search parties. The poor woman had more than likely been murdered along with her husband and her body hidden. There was little or no likelihood of finding her remains after all this time.

After Kane had spoken to the DA, the two suspects she'd considered for the current murders had walked free. The only good news was that the judge had granted them permission to track Adams and Long. She'd contacted Bobby Kalo and he'd promised to set up an alarm system to notify her if either of them left town. When he'd called Kane with the details, she'd been on a call listening to Sam Cross crow in her ear about Adams' release.

Jenna had never been a person to give up and believed the Wild Outdoors store and Aunt Betty's Café could be possible hunting grounds for couples the men planned to kill. On the way home she'd stopped by both stores and showed the photographs of Adams and Long and had asked to be notified if the men happened to drop by. Both the café and the hunting goods store had CCTV cameras, and the proprietors were more than happy to call her and keep any footage if the men visited. The latter had placated her some, but a murderer still walked the streets. Until she had a suspect in custody, nothing would remove the terrible feeling of responsibility cramping her gut. Every minute that passed, another couple could be butchered in her town.

Without any other possible suspects to investigate, Jenna sat on Kane's sofa and watched the news. The media release she'd worked on with Rio gave few details about the bodies they'd found in the forest and requested information about anyone in the area acting suspicious in the vicinity of Bear Peak at the times of the murders. She leaned into Kane and sighed. "I hope someone comes forward. I feel like I'm stuck in quicksand. I'm convinced we had our killers and now all we can do is wait until one of them tries to kill again and hope we get there in time."

"We'll get there." Kane pulled her under one arm. "You've trained a fast-response team. Everyone knows their jobs and we can rely on them one hundred percent. The suspects aren't going anywhere without us knowing."

"How so?"

"Kalo has many tricks up his sleeve, and face recognition software is one of them." Kane smiled. "He is utilizing the feed of every CCTV camera in town. Trust me, if those guys as much as jaywalk, we'll know about it and in real time." He gave her a squeeze. "You and Jo will be able to make Stone give up information. If those two men are involved, he'll be crowing about it. For him it will be a triumph. He won't be able to help himself. Knowing someone is killing for him will make him careless."

Jenna sighed. "Oh, I hope so. The idea of facing him again makes my skin crawl, but it's necessary, and I don't like being beaten by a killer or killers." She turned to look at him. "No, dammit, I refuse to be. Those guys are heading back to jail. We'll find the evidence and June Harris. I'm never giving up."

"That's my girl." Kane grinned.

CHAPTER THIRTY-SEVEN

Opting to wear civvies rather than stir up hatred at the prison, Jenna stood on the stoop of Kane's cottage and glanced at the men crawling over her ranch house like ants. She hoped they'd be through soon, although the awful feeling of not being safe in her own home hadn't gone away. A cold wind with the bite of frost blew from the mountains, and she wrapped her coat around her and turned to watch Carter go through his preflight check. It never ceased to amaze her how he turned from a laid-back, easy-going guy to a professional in the blink of an eye. He had his FBI hat on this morning and had been very vocal over coffee about visiting James Stone.

After inhaling the clean pine air, Jenna turned as Jo moved beside her. "Ty seems different this morning. Is he always like that?"

"Not usually, no." Jo pushed her hair inside her hood and shivered. "He's read everything there is about Stone and doesn't believe we should be interviewing him. He watched the interview you taped after his arrest and has the court transcripts. Ty has it in his head Stone can manipulate people to his will, and maybe he can, but he won't be able to manipulate me, that's for sure."

"Who is trying to manipulate you?" Kane walked out behind them and pulled the door closed.

"Ty thinks that Stone will walk all over us." Jo snorted. "As if."

"Really?" Kane smoothed his hair and pushed on his black Stetson. "What do you think?"

"Ha." Jo grinned at him. "You are too nice, Dave. That's a classic reply from someone who hates to be involved in disagreements."

"You don't know me at all, Jo." Kane chuckled. "All this geniality is a front. I'm hiding a dark and dangerous past." He winked at Jenna.

"Sure, you are." Jo tucked her bag under one arm and pulled on gloves. "Ah, it looks like Carter is ready to leave." She headed for the chopper.

Jenna stared at him. "You're pushing your luck. One of these days she'll see right through you."

"Carter has hinted at knowing my past." Kane shrugged nonchalantly and buttoned his overcoat. "He doesn't have details, but he's not stupid. He recognizes a brother in arms, just like I picked you as an agent the moment we met. He just knows not to discuss it. To be honest, if Carter did discover our past lives, I don't think it would go any further. He's solid and I trust him. Wolfe believes he is a loose cannon, but I've never seen that side of him."

Jenna headed for the chopper. "Me neither; now he has his filter back in place, I find him professional and an asset. I like his dog too."

"It's just as well Zorro gets on so well with Duke; they'll keep each other company while we're away." Kane strolled beside her. "Although, I figure Ty wanted to take his dog into the prison with him. He sure loves that dog."

The flight to county would be swift, and Jenna took the time to take in the scenery and absorb the peace the Big Sky Country gave her. Flying over Stanton Forest and the mountains gave her a special sense of wonder. The mountain had been there since the beginning of time and held the secrets of the ages. The peaks stood like sentries protecting Black Rock Falls with an impenetrable boundary, strong and resilient, like the people who lived in its shadows. She sighed as she searched the forest looking for the herds of elk and deer. It was as if she could reach out and touch the snowcapped granite and brush her fingers through the tips of the pines. She loved watching the eagles soar and, being so high, she had their perspective on life. High above the earth, the beauty of her county... *her* county, *her* people, *her* responsibility, thundered home. The townsfolk expected her to keep them safe. She had to solve the crime for them and bring the person or persons responsible for the murders to justice.

How different the scenery became as they approached the county jail. Set in the lowlands, surrounded by nothing but wilderness, the massive red brick building did justice to the word *depressing*. High walls, triple lines of fencing, and razor wire was the theme. No greenery, no gardens. Guard towers overlooked the building and armed men looked out as they flew over. Jenna peered into the exercise yards. Separated into sections, they were little more than pens with reinforced wire fences surrounding a dusty dirt rectangle. The chopper dropped, and through her headphones she could hear Carter advising of their arrival.

Guards and a man in civilian clothing waited near the helipad on top of the county jail, all keeping close to the wall as they landed. The wind buffeted the chopper and it swayed back and forth unnervingly before Carter finally set it down. As the engine whined to a halt, Jenna removed her headset and turned to Kane. "You haven't offered me any advice about talking to Stone. Do you have any pearls of wisdom for me before I go and speak to him?"

"Nah, you'll do just fine, but if I was in with Jo, I'd allow her to take the lead. I've seen her work and she's very good. She has a way of manipulating psychopaths without them knowing, and that in itself is a gift." Kane smiled at her. "She was amazing at the conference; her insights have really helped me up my game."

Jenna laughed. "You sound starstruck. It's just Jo, our friend, or is there something you're not telling me?"

"I've always been a great admirer of her work, but I've yet to be starstruck by anyone. I do have respect for people's talent, but to me everyone is equal no matter their rank or position in life. I've never been intimidated or in awe of anyone, not even POTUS—he's just a man." Kane shrugged. "I figure we're lucky to be able to call Jo our friend."

Jenna nodded. "Absolutely." She gathered her things and followed Kane out of the chopper.

The warden greeted them and they went through the usual procedure of removing their weapons before being allowed inside the prison. Inside, the mood was gloomy and the place had the smell of unwashed men and boiled cabbage. Jenna followed the warden through many electronic doors and along walkways that took them through areas filled with inmates. The men glared at them and some whistled, sniffed, or made kissing noises. A knot of uncertainty crawled into her belly. It was like walking into hell. She recalled movies about people trying to escape a never-ending passageway with locked doors on each side, and this place was the same. It was a nightmare. No windows and a lingering presence of despair. The urge to turn around and run back outside was overwhelming; each step into the continuous gray interior suffocated her.

Fluorescent strip lights flickered, threatening to plunge them into darkness. Ahead, an inmate cleaned what looked like blood from the floor with a smelly mop and licked his lips as she walked past. She could feel Kane beside her and valued his solid presence. Behind her, Jo walked with Carter, but as they passed more inmates, they had to dodge spittle even with the guards issuing warnings to stay back as they passed through different areas. She wanted to speak to Kane but kept her thoughts to herself and her eyes on the men's backs before her. She sighed with relief as they entered a small room with a window on one side. From here she could see into an interview room. It was bare apart from a table with two chairs on either side. All the furniture had been secured to the floor and the table had a loop for securing the prisoner. The room was brightly lit and two cameras sat high on the wall.

"We'll have the cameras switched off. This is a confidential session." Jo turned to the warden. We'll make our own recording. I find the subjects are more cooperative if they know they're not being watched by anyone." She nodded to Carter, who waved a camera at him.

"Your safety is our priority, Ms. Wells." The warden looked taken aback. "This man is a mass murderer and psychopathic killer. You can't possibly want to be alone with him."

"But we do." Jo smiled at him. "Agent Carter and Deputy Kane are highly skilled. They are the only protection we require. Thank you, Warden. We'll give you a call when we're ready to leave."

"I'll be posting guards outside the room." The warden rubbed his chin, obviously concerned. "I'm afraid that is a condition of allowing you to interview Stone."

"Very well." Jo pulled open the door to the interview room and waved Jenna forward. "Bring in the prisoner."

CHAPTER THIRTY-EIGHT

Heart thundering in her chest and with a sick feeling in her stomach, Jenna stood at the table staring at the door as it opened slowly. It had been some time since she'd laid eyes on James Stone. The couple of dates they'd been on had been a disaster. As an attractive man and a wealthy lawyer, he'd been quite a catch, but the connection hadn't been there. He hadn't been good company. In fact, he'd become a problem, almost stalking her and not taking her refusal for more dates as final. It had taken Kane's man-to-man chat with him to make him back off. From all accounts her refusal to see him again triggered a killing spree. Well organized, Stone ran a service through the dark web for hunting humans. Jenna hadn't discovered who was behind the murders until she'd come close to being his next victim, but she'd brought him to justice with the help of her team. The last time they'd met, Stone's hatred for her had been palpable and he'd threatened to get even. The man entering the room had committed unspeakable crimes and he was dangerous with a capital *D*.

Sucking in one last deep breath to calm her nerves, she lifted her chin and met Stone's cold gaze as he shuffled into the room, his feet shackled, hands cuffed and secured by chains to his waist. He hadn't changed much, and the prison T-shirt showed off well-developed muscles. Startled out of her fear paralysis by the sound of Jo's voice beside her, Jenna gripped the back of the chair.

"Remove the shackles." Jo placed her books on the table beside a voice recorder.

"Ma'am?" The guard couldn't hide his shocked expression. "That's not what we do here."

"Well, you do now." Jo smiled at him. "Mr. Stone is allowed to use the library unshackled and I'm told he is a model prisoner. Why would he want to have his privileges revoked? Do as I say." She looked at Stone. "You understand the terms of my visit, Mr. Stone? There will be a reward for your cooperation."

"Yeah, I understand." Stone smirked at the guard. "See, Harry? I told you sooner or later Jenna would come by and see me." He turned his attention on her. "I knew you couldn't keep away for long."

Fighting the need to escape the room and run as fast as her feet would carry her back to the chopper, Jenna stood rigid as the chains were removed. She could see a flash of amusement in Stone's eyes, the twitch of his mouth in the corner. She'd seen the same when he tried to kill her; his overconfidence astounded her. Gathering her senses, she nodded to Jo in a silent communication to inform her she wanted to continue, although her gut instinct was telling her the opposite.

"You can wait outside." Jo waved the guard away. "We can handle it from here." She sat down, pressed the button on the recorder, and a red light flashed.

"It's your funeral." The guard flashed his card to exit the room but through the glass panel she could see him take up a position outside.

Although the room was comfortably cool, sweat trickled down Jenna's back. Squashing the rising panic that seeing Stone had incited, she turned her attention to him. His pleasant expression hid the crazed mass murderer within. "Hello, James."

"How did you get mixed up with her?" Stone indicated to Jo with a jut of his chin.

Pressing a smile on her lips, Jenna stood her ground and kept her tone conversational, as Jo had advised. She didn't intend to antagonize him or cower. Yeah, he frightened her, but he'd never know it. "This is Special Agent Jo Wells. As you're probably aware by now, she is researching criminal minds for the FBI. She asked me about some of my more notorious cases and I thought of you." She waved to the chair. "Why don't you sit down."

"Why don't I just reach across the table and strangle her so we can be alone? We have unfinished business." Stone dragged his thumb across his throat and grinned.

Refusing to be intimidated by him, Jenna met his amused gaze with an eyeroll. The idea of being nice and acting like his friend to get information had left on the last train. *Damn you to hell.* "You just can't get over being beaten by a woman, can you?" She waved a hand to encompass the room. "You're never to be released, James. Locked up in here real tight, all on your lonesome. All you have are empty threats."

"I'm not restrained, Jenna, and you don't have a weapon. I could kill you in a second and you know it, but I'm more interested in Jo here." Stone's lips curled into a smile. "Maybe I'll break her neck just to prove I can? What do you say, Jenna? You choose. Won't that be fun?"

"That's not your usual MO. Sit down, or we're leaving along with the benefits we offered for the interview." Jo remained relaxed, just leaning back, crossing her legs, and looking at him as he slumped into a chair. "I'm sure you wouldn't get much of a buzz from just strangling me. I've read your files. The only reason I'm offering you another chance to cooperate is because you interest me."

"Do I now, Agent Wells?" Stone polished his fingernails on his orange coveralls. "How so?"

"You're IQ is bordering on genius and yet you turned to crime." Jo raised one eyebrow. "I'm interested to know why."

"What? You don't want to know how I felt when I watched the life slipping from my victims' eyes?" He barked a laugh. "'Victims' is a very strange word to use for the people involved in my business, Agent Wells. Competitors, or perhaps contestants, really describe them better."

"An interesting analogy." Jo opened her notebook and lifted a pen. "You can call me Jo."

"Are you married, Jo?" Stone glanced at her fingers. "I don't see a ring."

"No, I'm not married, but I didn't come here to talk about me." Jo leaned forward a little. "You fascinate me. I want to know everything about you. You'll be immortalized in my book."

"That's nice." He turned to Jenna, moving his gaze all over her. "You still haven't found anyone yet, have you, Jenna?"

The question made Jenna's skin crawl but the few tips on the FBI interviewing technique that she had gotten along the way fell into place. She'd already broken the first rule and antagonized the subject. She had to pull back and go along with his delusions to loosen his tongue. She shook her head. "I haven't found anyone like you, James."

"Ha." Stone slapped the table, sending shards of panic up Jenna's spine. "I knew it." He turned to Jo. "You're way too pretty to be single." He sighed. "Okay, one question: Is this a one-off deal or are you planning on visiting me regular?"

"That depends on your cooperation." Jo smiled at him.

The way he changed from serial killer back to the man she'd dated astounded Jenna. He'd relaxed and had taken on a friendly attitude. She gave Jo a meaningful stare. She'd remain quiet and allow Jo to work her magic.

"I want to know everything, James." Jo leaned forward with her hands clasped on the table. "Start at the beginning."

"That would take years." Stone yawned. "Give me specifics."

"Sure." Jo made a note in her book and smiled at him. "You mentioned the breakup with Jenna triggered a killing spree, so although you've told psychiatrists you had no empathy toward the people you murdered, this would indicate you're not a person lacking of feelings, or are you?"

"Jenna would have slid into my life perfectly and she'd have been the wife of a wealthy lawyer." He slid his gaze over Jenna and snorted. "She was an ornament is all." He turned his gaze slowly back to Jo. "I have empathy, so I can't be classed as a psychopath—is that right? Don't answer, because I know about the Hare Psychopathy Checklist. Trust me, most of the high-profile people in this country wouldn't pass that test." He chuckled.

"Do you want the truth or are we playing games?" Jo shrugged. "You know as well as I do psychopathy isn't an exact science. Many I've interviewed can turn empathy on and off like a tap. Tell me, did you have empathy for the people you killed at Bear Peak?"

"See, you're looking at what I did all wrong, Jo." He let out a long sigh. "It's simple to understand. If I went out hunting to put meat on my table, do you think when I sink the bolt into an elk or whatever, I care about its feelings or if its friends will miss it?" He wiped his mouth with the back of his hand. "When you eat your burger or cut into a prime ribeye, do you feel sorry for the steer who gave its life so you could eat? Do you worry over how it felt being shuffled onto the killing floor and getting a bolt in the brain?"

"No, that never enters my mind." Jo didn't show any emotion. "I'm not a vegan. I don't have a problem with eating meat."

"And what do you think about the people who slaughter animals for food, Jo?" Stone leaned forward, watching Jo's reaction closely.

"It's business." Jo made a few notes. She appeared relaxed and in control.

"Exactly." Stone gave Jenna a triumphant smile. "Business. What I did was business. I ran a hunting business to make money. Once the transaction was completed, I walked away and didn't have a reason to think about the contestants in the game."

"What about the ones you left in the cave and visited?" Jo looked up, an interested expression on her face as if she were hanging on his every word.

"Have you seen elk heads hanging on walls, Jo?" Stone opened his hands wide. "I'm no different to anyone else who likes to keep trophies of his kills. Tell me, are all the folks with taxidermy in their homes psychopaths?"

"No, I guess not." Jo wet her lips.

"What else do you want to know?" Stone smiled at Jenna. "I like her, she understands me."

"The method of keeping your targets alive while increasing their pain levels was ingenious. How did you learn how to do that?" Jo stared at Stone.

A shiver of disgust slid down Jenna's spine and she moved her eyes to the mirror. Knowing Kane and Carter were just outside helped some. She found herself leaning forward a little, waiting for his reply to Jo's question.

"Practice." Stone leaned back in his chair, relaxed, and then moved forward and leaned on the table. "I didn't start in Black Rock Falls. I was in foster care and there was a lot of kids coming and going. Some would tell me about how they'd been treated and so we got together and killed their foster parents." He laughed. "They never expect it. They think they can do whatever they please and many do, but you should have seen their faces when four or five kids arrived with knives. I showed them what to do, most times."

"How wonderfully interesting." Jo smiled at him. "How old were you when this happened?"

"Eight, maybe ten." Stone shrugged. "Many more followed, and then I received a scholarship to attend law school. I like to study and the urge for blood died down some. I was quiet for a couple of years and then a bunch of girls started to mess with my head. One girl, I kept alive for five days before I pushed her into a wood chipper."

"You did that alone?" Jo took notes.

"Yeah, that one I did, but her friends knew she'd dropped by the ranch where I was living and I had to get my buddies to deal with them. We enjoyed the hunt so much, and everyone wanted more, so I devised the plan to use the dark web. There are so many likeminded people out there. People who want to hunt down and kill humans, so I decided to make it into a business."

"Do you often encourage people to kill for you?" Jo looked up from her notes.

"Ah, if I say yes this could be construed as entrapment. I'm in jail for murder. I know this, but the lawyer side of me is very astute." Stone's eyes changed from soft to hard in a flash. "Trying something like that would be a very stupid move."

"I'm only here to listen to your story and if I'd wanted to use anything you say, I'd have read you your rights." Jo shrugged. "I have no reason to lie to you. You must have heard about the FBI's behavioral analysis program? We want to learn from you is all. There is no ulterior motive." She smiled. "You must have quite a few admirers in here and outside. Do you communicate with them?"

"Outside the prison?" Stone shook his head. "I have no way to communicate with anyone on the outside. I don't mix with other inmates. I'm not allowed visitors. You see, I'm considered too dangerous and I spend most of my time in my cell. My only respite is the library."

Jenna stared at him. It couldn't be true, he had to be lying. Stone must have a partner in crime they didn't know about. "If you didn't communicate with anyone on the outside, how come we have a killer using the same methods you used out of Bear Peak? Unless you're the copycat?"

"They were all mine. I don't need to copy anyone else." Stone's eyes flashed with anger. "No one before or after me has ever devised such a plan. Before me, no one knew how to disable a person and keep them alive. Paralyzing a man is incredible fun. I can tie a torniquet around any part of his limbs and remove them while he watches. There's no pain and they take forever to die, but the look on their faces makes up for it. They fight for life, but not the women. Those usually beg me to finish them."

Jenna laughed. "That's not true, James, and you know it." She slid a photograph out of Jo's folder and pushed it across the table to him. "Look at this: he has the same MO as you, right down to the severed spinal cord."

"This isn't my work, but close." He sniffed the image and ran a fingertip lovingly over it. "They say imitation is the sincerest form of flattery. Can I keep it?"

"I don't think that's a good idea." Jo lowered her voice. "What if I told you this happened just the other day. How do you feel about someone imitating you?"

"I love it… mmm, I can smell her: perfume and the metallic scent of blood. Nothing like it." Stone looked at Jo and a slow rumble of laughter spilled from his lips. "Can you hear her screams? How many got to look at her before Wolfe took her away? Has he cut her up yet? Can I see the autopsy photographs?"

"I can't answer that, sorry." Jo closed her notebook. "I think that's enough for today. Thank you for the chat. I'd love to talk with you another time."

"Next time, come alone. I like the way you smell. Chanel Number Five, I believe." Stone turned his gaze slowly toward Jenna. "Am I making you jealous, Jenna?"

Jenna ignored him.

"I'll see what I can do." Jo pressed a buzzer on the table and stood.

The guard came in and shackled Stone, and Jo headed for the door. Jenna wanted to leave, but her legs had turned to Jell-O. When Stone shuffled closer and bent over the table not a foot away from her, his expression had changed and the psychopath had risen to the surface. The guard was just watching with an amused look on his face and hadn't attempted to stop him. A wave of dread hit Jenna full force and, vulnerable, trapped between chair and table, she leaned back, getting her feet under her, and stared into Stone's dead eyes. She could smell him; rancid sweat and his onion breath washed over her.

"I'd have killed you slowly, and made you suffer." He ran his tongue slowly over his bottom lip. "It's not over, Jenna. You'll never be safe from me. You should have put a bullet in me on the mountain."

Jenna snorted. "Trust me, I wanted to, but seeing you locked up in here like a rabid dog is much better."

"Next time we meet, I'll win and you'll be dead. I don't lose twice." He chuckled deep in his chest. "Mmm, I can almost taste your blood on my hands. I'm coming for you, Jenna. Don't close your eyes, because when you do, I'll be right behind you."

CHAPTER THIRTY-NINE

Rigid, Jenna stared at the retreating back of James Stone. His words seemed to echo in her mind on a loop of insanity. She sucked in a deep breath, tasting the smell of him on her tongue, and moved away from the chair. The blinking light on the recorder caught her eye, and she pressed the button to turn it off and then just stood there staring at it. Seeing him again and hearing his threats had shaken her to the bone.

The door behind her opened and Kane's voice seemed loud in the small room.

"Jenna. Are you okay?" He touched her arm. "What did he say to you?"

Jenna picked up the recorder and handed it to him. "I'm fine. I was expecting him to threaten me. It's on here." She ignored the rising panic and forced herself to act nonchalantly. She had no need to be afraid of Stone. He had no way to escape and hurt her. It was all smoke and shadows, nothing more. "He's crazy is all." She led the way outside and looked at Jo. "I think we should speak to the warden. I'd like to see for myself how they contain Stone. He needs to be informed we have a copycat killer and we suspect Stone is somehow involved."

"Sure, but I played to his ego. Most psychopaths can't resist boasting they have the power over people to make them kill for them." Jo shrugged. "I'll go over the tape and listen again to his replies, but he gave me no indication of being involved. He'd like to be, but he's not."

"Sorry, but I disagree." Kane pulled an earpiece from the voice recorder and placed the device on the desk. "Listen to this."

Jenna stared at the wall as Stone's last words to her filled the room. She swallowed hard. "Open threats, nothing more. The ravings of a lunatic."

"Maybe not." Jo frowned and looked at Kane. "You may have something there."

"It sure as hell sounds like he's planning something, to me." Carter rested one hip on the corner of the desk. "But how? Without contact with the outside world, it would be impossible."

"Did you see the way the guard smiled when he went close to Jenna?" Kane straightened. "He did nothing. Guards can be bought—hell, many people have their price. Stone has millions, cash no one but he knows about is hidden in bank accounts worldwide. He'd still have people in his employ just waiting for the chance to break him out of jail."

Jenna nodded. "Yeah, what Wolfe found on the dark web would indicate he had a network of people moving money for him."

"How come you didn't call in the FBI to track it down?" Carter looked amused. "Wolfe is a medical examiner. You needed someone like Bobby Kalo."

Annoyed, Jenna turned to him. "Wolfe is an IT specialist as well, but by the time we uncovered what Stone was doing, a fail-safe was used to eradicate everything on the dark web. Trust me, Wolfe did everything to uncover details but he only found fragments. Stone used the best in the business to build his page and to hide his money." She sighed. "We're getting way off track here. We have murders to solve and June Harris is still missing. Right now, all I want to do is make sure they have Stone under surveillance day and night." She looked at Kane. "Let's go. The guard outside the door will take us to see the warden. Let's hope we're not paraded in front of the inmates again."

"Don't listen to them." Jo moved to her side. "Here." She pulled sets of earplugs from her pocket in neat plastic bags. "Shove these in your ears and hum. It blocks out the obscenities and they don't get the reaction they're expecting."

"I don't need them." Kane grinned at Carter. "Do you?"

"Hell no." Carter laughed. "I don't think the kissy sounds were aimed at me."

Jenna pushed the plugs in her ears. "Okay, stop messing around. I want to get out of this hellhole as soon as possible and take a shower. I figure we'll carry this stink on us for weeks." She pulled open the door and beckoned the guard. "We'd like to see the warden before we leave. Can you take us to him, please?"

"This way." The guard walked beside her. "You might have to wait for a time. He don't stay in his office all day."

"Just let him know we want to speak to him." Kane moved behind Jenna. "We won't hold him up for long."

The guard took them through an outside area and they moved through more exercise yards, but the abuse had become background noise behind the humming. As they moved into a different, more modern area the layout of the prison changed as they climbed a staircase to another floor. The same concrete and tiles, but offices replaced the interview rooms and the noise of the inmates came from below them. Luckily, the warden was in his office and waved them all inside. After removing the earplugs, Jenna explained her concerns and the warden dismissed them with a wave of his hand.

"Come with me." The warden led them down the hallway and into a control room lined with screens showing CCTV footage of vast areas of the prison. "See here." He pointed to an array. "This is maximum security. The guards here watch the inmates twenty-four/ seven. The cell doors are controlled from a central area. Two or more guards are in control of the opening and closing of doors and gates at each checkpoint."

"What about when Stone goes to the library?" Carter stared at the screens. "Who does he meet and why is he really there?"

"The library is a privilege he earned by being a model prisoner." The warden gave them an impatient shrug. "They have to have an incentive to behave. He put in a request to have his lawbooks added to the library, he also offered his services to any prisoner who believed they'd been railroaded by the system."

Jenna gaped at him. "So, he does have contact with other prisoners. You said he wasn't in contact with anyone."

"That's right. He's not, apart from the guards, the medical staff, and one prisoner, who is a trustee. He collects orders for books, delivers them, and returns them to the library. Trust me, Stone is under guard the entire time and there are no conversations allowed between the trustee and Stone." He gave Jenna a long look. "He doesn't speak to the prisoners who seek his help. He's given their case files and makes suggestions is all. The files don't get to him via the inmates. They come from the previous counsel on the case. All his notes are read before they're handed to the inmates via a guard."

Unsettled, Jenna met the warden's gaze. "Can you assure me that there is absolutely no way Stone is communicating with the outside world?"

"Yes." The warden nodded emphatically. "We have many maximum-security prisoners here. Some are so high profile they're kept in solitary confinement for their own safety. They all would find some reason to kill each other, and the slightest thing can trigger them. Most are cunning and very smart. It wouldn't take long for them to devise a plan of escape. This is why they're not permitted to speak to others of like mind in the max wing."

Unconvinced because her gut was insisting something wasn't right, Jenna reluctantly nodded and turned to Kane. "I've seen enough." She looked at Jo and Carter. "Are you ready to leave?"

"Yeah." Jo smiled at the warden. "Thank you for your coopera-tion. The visit with Stone was very illuminating. I hope I'll be able to speak to some of your other prisoners in the future?"

"Only too happy to assist, you Agent Wells." The warden beamed at her. "The guard will take you back to the helipad." He waved them into the hallway. "Good day to you."

Not making eye contact with anyone, Jenna moved swiftly through the jail, earplugs firmly in place and humming like a deranged lunatic. When she finally climbed into the chopper she slumped back in her seat, totally drained, and looked at Kane. "I'm sure glad that's over."

"You can say that again."

CHAPTER FORTY

Back at the ranch, Jenna stared at the recording device playing back on the kitchen table in Kane's cottage. The sound of Stone's confident voice sent chills through her. The constriction in her throat was like a cord tightening, and she touched her neck just to be sure there wasn't really one there. As the last few threatening words echoed in her ears like a death knell, she closed her hands around her coffee cup just to feel the comforting heat, and found the cup empty. Trying to keep her voice steady although her mind was racing one hundred miles an hour in panic mode, she lifted her gaze to Jo. "What is he planning?"

"More like, what *has* he planned." Carter moved a toothpick across his lips and raised both eyebrows at her. "He sounds way too overconfident to be making those threats without having some type of plan to back them up. He must be communicating with other prisoners and not those in maximum security—I doubt he could trust them, as most of them have their own form of psychopathy. He'd more likely chose those inmates who have regular visitors or are allowed to correspond with the outside. Remember, this guy is loaded, he could be bribing anyone inside the jail. You never caught his accomplices on the outside or those who control his fortune. I believe he still has contact with a few very well paid and dedicated followers."

"His affairs were put in the hands of a lawyer he trusts. I doubt he is corruptible." Jenna rubbed her temples. "You heard it straight from the warden's mouth. It's impossible unless he has every guard on his payroll."

"Then we ask for the CCTV surveillance from the prison and spend the time to go through it for ourselves." Kane refilled the coffee cups from a fresh pot and slid a plate of sandwiches he'd just made onto the table. "Stone is a smart man. He'd have found a way, somehow. Maybe it's something to do with the cases he's supposedly helping with." He looked at Jenna. "How vigilant are the guards? I heard a ringtone during our visit to the warden's office. How many guards are playing with their phones in the control room?"

Jenna nodded. "True, but will the warden release the tapes?"

"I could ask to use them as a follow-up to my behavioral studies." Jo placed a sandwich on her plate and examined the contents. "It would be a normal thing to do, as in observing a person in their day-to-day activities. I'll call as soon as I've eaten this delicious sandwich Kane has made." She smiled at him. "A man of many talents, I see."

"Food is a passion, so I learned to cook good food, real fast." Kane grinned back. "I was making my own meals as a boy."

Trying to keep Kane away from his favorite subject, Jenna tapped on the table. "Moving right along." She turned her attention to Jo and Carter. "I guess you don't have plans to hang around?"

"Not today, no." Carter removed his toothpick, flicked it into the trash, and selected a sandwich. "We'll head home but we'll be right back if you need us." He shrugged. "Right now, without any leads on any possible suspects or the missing woman, there's not much we can do to help." He motioned with his sandwich to the open front door. "How come you have guys in military fatigues working on your house, Jenna?" He flicked his gaze to Kane. "There's an entire camp out there. What gives?"

Jenna searched her mind for a plausible excuse. "After my house was trashed, I had the damage repaired, but the mayor wanted my security upgraded. This"—she waved her hand absently toward the door—"is part of a military training program. Apparently to see how fast they can secure the perimeter of a sensitive area." She shrugged. "It works for me, but I'll be glad when they're through checking us back and forth through my own gate. It's a pain and I'm sure Dave is sick of me living here by now."

"Right." Carter gave Kane a wink. "I'll go do a preflight check and then we'll be on our way." He snapped his fingers and Zorro jumped to attention. "Wheels up in five." He strolled out the door.

"I'll make that call." Jo pulled out her phone and called the warden.

After some delay and back and forth, she disconnected and smiled at Jenna. "He uploads everything into the Cloud, he's texting me a link so we can access the files direct." Her phone chimed a message. "That was fast. I'll forward it to you."

"Got it." Kane looked at his phone. "We'll get Rowley and Rio onto it this afternoon."

"Mind if I take the tape we recorded today? I'll send you a copy." Jo finished her coffee and stood. "I'd like to study it some more."

Jenna pushed to her feet. "Sure. Thanks for coming. That was an experience I won't forget in a hurry. I'd like to do it again but with psychopaths who don't want to kill me next time."

"They are interesting to study as long as you know how to play to their ego." Jo collected her things. "Or get down to their level. Being their best friend usually works well, but never fall into a misguided state of false security. They're killers, without feeling, and most would kill you without a second thought."

Jenna frowned. The list of killers from her town had never left her mind; she recalled them and their victims vividly. "Yes, I know how dangerous they are, Jo. Learning how to deal with them is my goal. If I can think like them, I'll be able to catch them easier."

"Well." Jo smiled. "We all live in hope of that. See you soon." She hurried out the door and looked over one shoulder. "Don't come out, the rotor blades will kick up a pile of dust. I'll call you soon."

Jenna followed her outside, gave them a wave, and closed the door against the rush of wind. She took her coat from the peg and tossed Kane's to him. "We'll drop by the office on the way to the autopsy and get the guys onto the footage now. I'll be interested to find out if there's been any calls on the hotline from the media release. I also want to know what our two suspects have been doing."

"Sure." Kane bent and rubbed Duke's ears. "You stay here, Duke." He went to the dog's feeder and topped it up. "There you go, plenty of food to keep you going."

Duke licked Kane's hand and went to his basket, turned around three times, and lay down with a sigh. Jenna smiled at him and chuckled. "He'll be asleep before we leave."

"Yeah." Kane pushed on his black Stetson. "It must have been a hard morning for him entertaining Zorro."

CHAPTER FORTY-ONE

He strolled through town, unable to keep the smile from his face. Everything had worked out as planned. He'd gotten to enjoy himself and hunted down a couple of tourists. Soon he'd be famous. The body he'd stashed in a cave was the talk of the town. He'd walked past the Black Rock Falls newspaper office and read the headlines about the missing woman. They'd searched for a week now, but he'd hidden her in a secluded place he'd found as a boy, far from any regular trails. The urge to hunt again had become a nagging ache but he'd wait until the time was right. Being smart and taking his time to plan each exquisite move had worked so far. Confidence filled him with power. He would control destinies and no one would be able to touch him as long as he remained patient. He'd seen the sheriff's team, like a pack of wolves hunting him down, but they'd never find him. They'd run in endless circles. He could be nowhere and everywhere at the same time, and, like a Halloween illusion, he'd vanish into the mist.

He slowed to examine the Halloween displays. Man, they got bloodier every year. As a kid, wearing a sheet over his head with holes in it and screaming "Woo woo" had been his Halloween highlight, but the excitement of scaring people didn't last long. He'd return home expecting the beating his father would give him for cutting holes in his ma's linen. He'd learned long ago that crying didn't satisfy his pa's brutality, it made it worse, so he'd never made a sound. He understood the feeling just fine—the rage when women screamed or pleaded with him made him want to shut out the noise. This Halloween would be different and nothing would come close to the feel of warm blood on his hands. The smell from his last kill still lingered in his nose, like a beautiful memory to savor, and he found himself moving close to the macabre displays and inhaling just in case.

He strolled on, enjoying the fresh air mingled with the fascinating aromas drifting from Aunt Betty's Café. During his time away, he'd had dreams about the diner. The quality of the food never changed, although Susie Hartwig had replaced the old lady he'd remembered as the manager. The menu had grown from a small greasy sheet to a foldable plastic-covered list of delights, and he planned to spend every day eating there to make up for lost time. He had money to burn. In fact, he doubted he could ever spend all the cash hidden in his home.

Fall leaves spun in wind funnels across the sidewalk and the sky darkened as clouds passed the sun. The dry storms still threatened, and he noticed quite a few folks glancing skyward nervously. He chuckled. Nothing frightened him, not even the threat of death. He'd just make the best of the time he had left, one day or fifty years made no difference. He didn't care.

The sound of a powerful motor moving down Main drew his attention and he stared after the vehicle driving Sheriff Alton to the sheriff's department. He'd been watching them for over a month now, and he could just about set his watch to her arrival each morning. Yet here it was way past noon and she'd only just arrived. He shook his head. Trust the woman to be tardy when he had plans. He removed his hat and scratched his head. Maybe she'd be on time tomorrow.

CHAPTER FORTY-TWO

The sky darkened as Kane followed Jenna inside the morgue and his mind went straight to Duke alone at home. His dog had been through a traumatic event with Jenna during a storm and he wondered if he would cope alone if another storm hit. "There's a storm coming. I hope Duke will be okay."

"He'll hide under your bed." Jenna led the way to an alcove outside an examination room with a red light glowing, indicating an autopsy was in progress.

Taking in Jenna's pale, drawn complexion, Kane touched her arm. "That was pretty bad meeting Stone again, huh? I wanted to charge in the moment he moved close to you but figured it would only make things worse."

"I'm glad you didn't." Jenna shrugged out of her jacket. "What could he do to me? He had both hands chained to his waist and his legs shackled. Trust me, I was getting ready to punch him in the nose if he made a move to hurt me." She handed him a set of scrubs. "He likes to control and intimidate. I didn't want him to know he'd scared the life out of me. That's why I stood my ground." She looked at him. "It beats me why I immediately tied my intruder to Stone. I mean, Stone never wore a slicker. Well, not when I confronted him in the forest. He wore camouflage gear as far as I know. It was just the way he stood, holding the crossbow." She shrugged. "Then the other day in the alleyway, the menace that flowed from that guy, it was just the same hate I felt from Stone in the interview room."

Kane touched her cheek. Her flesh was cold under his fingers and matched the frigid air in the morgue. "You know it wasn't him. That doesn't make this killer any less dangerous. This guy may be a copycat, but most times they're more vicious than the real thing. They like to prove they're worthy of the notoriety. You're right to be worried. It's a perfectly normal response."

The door whooshed open and Wolfe stood at the entrance. Kane nodded to him. "Are we late?"

"Nope, right on time." He waved them inside. "Em is at school so I only have Webber, and another pair of hands would make life easier."

As he followed Wolfe into the examination room, the smell of decay and gasoline crept through his mask like evil twins of murder. Kane pulled on his gloves. "Sure, who do we have first?"

"Emmett Howard out of Sleepy Creek." Wolfe indicated toward the X-rays on the screen. "As you can see, a crossbow bolt penetrated the frontal lobe, causing a significant skull fracture. Even without removing the cranium, the lack of hematoma from the injury is indicative that this is the cause of death. I'd say it was instantaneous. The penetration through the skull and the depth the bolt dug into the tree would indicate the shot was taken within six feet."

Kane moved closer. "I can still smell gas. Can you tell if it was poured over him before he was shot?"

"Yeah." Wolfe lifted the eyelids. "As you can see, the damage to the eyes is significant. The redness and swelling wouldn't have occurred post mortem as in Patti Howard. When we get to her, it's obvious the gas was used post mortem."

"Stone only ever used gas on the male victims." Kane lifted his gaze from the blank, staring eyes of Emmett Howard. "I figure he wanted the women he murdered eaten by wildlife as a final desecration."

"Yeah, I have to agree." Wolfe stared at him over his facemask. "This killer wanted everyone to see what he'd done to these people.

He's proud of his work and wants to display it. Stone was more interested in murdering his clients and keeping them in his private viewing gallery. The couples on the trail were just short-lived entertainment, they meant nothing to him once they'd died."

"What about the spine?" Jenna moved closer, adjusting her facemask. "Is it severed like Stone's victims'?"

"Again, from the X-ray and initial examination of the body at the scene, I'd say affirmative, but of course the findings today will prove or disprove that theory." Wolfe used a remote to bring up the images of the spine. "See here." He pointed to the screen. "The notches in the bone? This is what I'd normally find in this type of deliberate injury. The knife must be moved through the bone to the spinal cord. It takes skill and practice."

Kane glanced at the blue skinned man on the gurney and shook his head. The mental torture he must have suffered watching his wife being mutilated and unable to help her must have been horrendous. His gaze never wavered as Wolfe proceeded to examine the body. The weighing of the organs, checking the stomach contents and the spinal column, and finally removing part of the cranium to examine the damage from the crossbow bolt. Each action was recorded, and finally Wolfe handed the closing to his assistant, Colt Webber.

Kane gave himself a mental shake. The entire process had been hypnotizing, or he'd placed himself into a sniper state without realizing it. He glanced at Jenna, who had said nothing during the examination, and she gave him a nod indicating she was okay. He moved his attention back to Wolfe. "Did you find anything significant?"

"Yeah." Wolfe removed his gloves with a snap and replaced them with a fresh pair. "Whoever inflicted the injury to the spine was right-handed." Wolfe gave him a thoughtful look over his mask. "I'd assumed the injury was an attack from behind, but from the angle of the wound it was a frontal attack. I don't think Howard saw it coming. There are no other signs on him to indicate a struggle."

"So, he knew his attacker?" Jenna folded her arms across her chest and leaned her back against the counter. "Like his guide, for instance?" She raised both eyebrows. "It has to be Adams or Lane, doesn't it?"

Kane nodded. "They seem to be the most likely candidates, but without new evidence the DA won't prosecute them. Because the murders are alike and you can't prove either man committed both murders, you have too much reasonable doubt to convict either of them."

"Have you found anything to link these men?" Wolfe looked at Jenna. "Have you gone right back? For instance, were they at school together?"

"Nope. Apart from murder scenes, we've come up empty." Jenna cleared her throat. "They both did time in the county jail but deny knowing each other. They were in different areas of the prison and I can't prove they met. They both belong to the firing range, but so does just about everyone in town." She looked at him. "How close have you gotten to the TOD?"

"My findings haven't changed. Emmett Howard died from a projectile to the head. His time of death is between the last time he was seen alive, which, according to Tyson Long's statement, was at eleven-thirty on Tuesday, and when his body was discovered at nine on Wednesday morning."

"Which, if we can believe Long, puts Adams in the clear. He was at work at eleven on Tuesday and in custody at the TOD." Jenna glanced at Kane. "And Long has an alibi for Payton Harris' TOD. Which makes it impossible for one of them to have committed both crimes. Although, they could be collaborating and timing their crimes to give the other an alibi?"

Kane shook his head. "We've found no evidence to suggest they know each other. It won't play for a conviction unless we can link them."

"Okay, let's push on with Patti Howard." Wolfe pushed a gurney under the light and pulled back a sheet."

Although Kane had already seen the brutality one person had inflicted on this poor woman, the sight of her laid out was no less of a shock. He straightened and stood feet apart and shoulders back and forced his mind to be objective. Murder was never pretty, and although he'd served in a warzone and as a government assassin taking out targets to protect his country, nothing in his experience prepared him for this level of carnage. He noticed Jenna shiver and wanted to reach out and hold her hand but when her chin rose and she stepped closer, a sense of calm descended on him. Jenna had that effect on him. Seeing her upset concerned him deeply, and it would seem the opposite soothed his nerves.

"From the lacerations, the killer used a hunting knife." Wolfe examined, measured, and documented each deep incision on the body. "As we observed at the crime scene, Patti Howard was secured, her arms extended with tape and then at one point pinned to trees with crossbow bolts. I'd say he did this not for any other reason than to prevent her from fighting back. There are no defensive wounds on the arms, but the lacerations to the legs show she fought long and hard before he subdued her long enough to restrain her."

Kane ran his gaze over the woman's body. The injuries appeared methodical, not what he recognized as a frenzied attack. He turned to Jenna. "This looks calculated to me. Look at the cuts to her torso: they are evenly spaced."

"None of them look deep enough to have killed her." Jenna scanned the body. "He wanted to torture her, make her suffer, just like Stone's victims." She glanced up at Wolfe. "What killed her? I can't see any signs of strangulation, or anything else fatal."

"I'll examine her heart for any signs of a coronary, but heart failure from blood loss due to sharp force trauma is the most likely cause of death. After examining the lacerations, although some are gaping, the one here, on her thigh, killed her." Wolfe pointed to the narrow incision. "If you look at the crime scene image, blood has pooled all around her, but in this area it was most concentrated, which made me examine this wound closely. This was a fatal wound. It sliced through the femoral artery and death would have occurred in five minutes or less."

The autopsy continued and Kane watched as Wolfe examined Patti Howard's organs, but his findings didn't change. It was getting late by the time he climbed behind the wheel of his truck and headed back to the office. He turned to Jenna. "These murders have me baffled. Everything points to Adams and Long."

"Whichever one it is, he'll make a mistake or he already has." Jenna chewed on her bottom lip. "Or one of the witnesses backing up their alibis is lying. For instance, we only have the word of the receptionist at the nursing home to confirm Adams arrived there at the time she said he did. My gut tells me he's involved."

Kane nodded. "We just have to prove it." He pulled into his parking space outside the sheriff's department.

"Well, we've found needles in haystacks before." Jenna gathered her things. "I'm not waving a white flag just yet."

CHAPTER FORTY-THREE

Exhausted emotionally and physically, Jenna dragged her legs up the steps to the sheriff's department and headed toward the front counter. She noticed two teenagers sitting on the row of seats beside the main entrance and went to them. "Are you waiting for me?"

"Yeah." The boy stood and gave her an angelic smile. "I'm Cade Rio and this is my sister, Piper. Zac wants to know if we can hang around here until he finishes work? We don't mind helping out. Answering phones, sweeping up, or whatever."

Jenna looked from one to the other. She could see the resemblance the twins had to their brother. "Yes, of course. Is there a problem at home?"

"No." Cade shook his head. "Our housekeeper is polishing the floors and she doesn't want us walking all over them until they're finished." He chuckled. "She likes things nice."

Trying not to laugh, Jenna waved them toward the receptionist. "Maggie will find you something to do, won't you, Maggie?"

"I sure can." Maggie gave them a beaming smile, her brown eyes twinkling.

The silence in the office surprised her, and Jenna flicked a glance around the room and found it empty. Leaning on the counter, she looked at Maggie. "Where are my deputies?"

"They had a few calls on the hotline and went to check them out." Maggie lowered her voice. "Someone else was seen with the Howards. Wendy at Aunt Betty's Café called and they headed down there."

Jenna nodded. "Okay. I'll be in my office with Kane. Send them up when they get back."

Hopeful of a lead, Jenna climbed the stairs to her office and inhaled the smell of brewing coffee. She could always trust Kane to go ahead and fill the coffee machine. Inside, she dropped wearily into her chair and stared at him across the desk. "Please tell me that's good news."

"Maybe." Kane handed her the scribbled note in Rowley's handwriting. "It says after the Howards left the Outdoors Store, one of the CCTV cameras in town picked up them speaking to someone outside Aunt Betty's Café. They're hunting down the person right now."

Jenna stood and took out cups and the fixings and then stared at the dripping liquid filling the jug. "So, no mention of the Stone surveillance tapes, and what about our suspects? Have they left town?"

"Nope, both have moved around town but not at the same time or places." Kane scrolled through the files Rowley had uploaded. "They've both been working all day. The entries in the file track Adams' and Long's movements. They have watched a small portion of the footage from the prison but that's going to take forever. It's a long, tedious job, we all need to take turns or something will be missed." He held up a finger before she could reply. "Nothing on June Harris either."

After pouring the coffee and adding the fixings, Jenna slid a cup across the table to Kane and then noticed the yellow slip of paper under the old chipped mug on her desk that housed her pens. It was a note from Atohi Blackhawk. She glanced at it and lifted her head. "Ah, here's a note from Atohi. He's been searching the area around the Payton Harris murder scene again in the hope of finding which way June Harris went. He is concerned her trail wasn't picked up by him earlier and is convinced she must be close by. He'll be searching again tomorrow. He doesn't give up easily."

"There wouldn't be much left of her now if she died in the forest." Kane sipped his coffee and sighed. "Payton Harris' murder, with his wife going missing and all, convinces me this is a copycat of Stone's murders. I figure Payton Harris' killer stashed June's body in a cave up there somewhere."

Jenna pushed a hand through her hair. "'Somewhere' is the operative word. There are thousands of caves up there. Many have entrances that are so overgrown no one would ever find them. So yeah, that's a distinct possibility."

Footsteps on the stairs interrupted their conversation. Jenna stared at the door. It was Rio.

"We've brought in a person of interest for the murders." Rio was trying hard to control a smug smile. "I think you should come down and speak to him."

Taking in his excited demeanor, Jenna held up one hand. "Slow it down, Zac. Give me the details, so I know what to ask this guy."

"First up, we received a call on the hotline this morning from Morgan White out of Maple Way. He and his girlfriend, Fern, were out hiking in the forest on Monday and noticed a man following them. The guy kept off the trail but he was carrying a crossbow and wore a slicker and a cowboy hat. As luck would have it, they met up with a forest warden on horseback patrol and he escorted them back to their vehicle." Rio frowned. "The man had vanished into the shadows and with the mist rising from the river, the warden didn't want to risk hunting him down without backup. White gave me the warden's name and I called him; he didn't see anyone or any tracks but he made note of it in his report. He figured the couple were spooked because of the murders and the fact people act a little crazy around Halloween."

"It gets better." Rowley walked in the door. "We get back here and there's a message from Wendy at Aunt Betty's. Her curiosity got the better of her and she checked out the CCTV footage of the day Long said he met the Howards. She recalled they dropped by to pick up some supplies for the hike and wanted to see if they met anyone in the diner. When they left, she saw them speaking to another man, and Wendy knew him. She identified him as John Foster, he lives out on Pine, two doors down from Wendy. We dropped by and he was at home and only too happy to come down and answer some questions."

Jenna exchanged a look with Kane and he raised one eyebrow. She looked up at her deputies. "Good work. Write it up and we'll go and speak with Mr. Foster. Have you read him his rights?"

"Nope." Rio shrugged. "We asked him if he'd mind coming in to talk to the sheriff and he agreed."

"What is it with these suspects coming in willingly and talking?" Kane scratched his head. "Have I walked into another dimension, or is this one giant conspiracy? Nothing is making sense anymore." He turned his attention to Rio. "Tell me you did this by the book. You did show White a six-pack?"

"Yeah, don't worry, I made sure we had a photo lineup. I pulled Foster's driver's license and showed the image, along with five others selected at random, to White and his girlfriend and they made a positive ID on Foster." Rio looked at Jenna. "Think about it. If Adams and Long were telling the truth about the couples they took into the forest, this guy might have been waiting somewhere along the trail for them. He could be our killer."

Unconvinced, Jenna narrowed her gaze at him. "So, you figure Foster just hangs around the trails up at Bear Peak, the most isolated of areas, on the off-chance a couple might wander by so he can kill them?"

"He just happened to be hanging around the same places at the same time as both the couples who met with Adams and Long." Rio shrugged. "We have him on CCTV footage and he was close by in both instances. It's not unreasonable to assume he overheard the

plans the victims made with Adams and Long and followed them…
or headed out there before they arrived. He would have had time."

"So, we brought him in for questioning." Rowley straightened.
"He's in interview room one."

Jenna waited for them to leave and blew out a long breath. "I'm
with you on this one. Have we stumbled down a rabbit hole or
something? Foster throws doubt on both our possible suspects. With
the three of them admitting to being involved at least before the fact,
we'll never get a case to stick against any of them." She glanced out
the window at the gathering darkness and swirls of mist. It was as if
the chill was creeping toward the windows with its long, fingerlike
tendrils reaching out to her, and she hurriedly looked away. "This
is the weirdest Halloween week ever. It's like we're living the same
day over and over again. If this guy gives us the same story as the
other two, pinch me good and hard, because as sure as hell I must
be dreaming."

CHAPTER FORTY-FOUR

In the interview room, Foster appeared to be relaxed. He sat turning his to-go cup of coffee in his fingers, patiently waiting as if he had nothing else to do with his time. Jenna looked him over: he'd be in his mid-forties, rugged, with corded muscles in his forearms. The calluses on his hands and a weathered complexion would indicate he spent a lot of his time outside and likely did manual labor. There was an odor of freshly sawn wood around him, and she noticed a peppering of sawdust on the front of his T-shirt. He actually smiled as Jenna walked in and dropped a statement book beside her iPad on the table. She didn't return the smile, turned on the recorder, and gave the date, time, and who was present. This interview would be by the book. "Mr. Foster, we'll be interviewing you in relation to an investigation into the deaths of Payton Harris and Emmett and Patti Howard." She read him his rights. "I believe when you spoke to my deputies, Zac Rio and Jake Rowley, you mentioned speaking to the Howards outside Aunt Betty's Café on Tuesday morning. Is that correct?"

"Yeah, that's right." Foster clasped his hands on the table. "Nice couple."

Jenna opened the statement pad and then raised her gaze back to him. "Tell me in your own words how this came about."

"I was heading into Aunt Betty's for a bite to eat and Patti bumped right into me." Foster eyed her with an amused expression. "Feisty woman that one, she told me to mind where I was going. I apologized, and Emmett said there was no harm done and Patti had walked into me. So, we got talking about the weather and hunting and such. They mentioned their plans to head up to Bear Peak. I told them straight it's not safe up there and they told me they were going with some guy who was heading that way."

"How did you know their names?" Kane looked dubious. "I'm sure most folks don't offer their details to people they bump into on the sidewalk."

"Oh, yeah." Foster's eyes danced with amusement. "I offered to buy them a cup of coffee so we could talk some more about the trails, but they had to get along."

Jenna made unnecessary notes to appear uninterested and casual. Everything she needed would be in a transcript of the tapes. "What took you to Stanton Forest today?"

"I was collecting firewood." Foster raised his eyebrows. "No law against that, now is there? Clearing the forest floor of dead wood is a good thing. You never know when a dry storm will trigger a wildfire."

"Do you usually take a crossbow with you when you're collecting firewood?" Kane leaned forward in his chair.

"I sure do." Foster rubbed his chin. "You're not from hereabouts, are you, Deputy? No man in his right mind would go into the forest without some type of protection. A crossbow is my weapon of choice."

Wanting to push Foster a little harder to see how he'd react, Jenna eyeballed him. "So why stalk the couple in the forest? You must have known that after the recent murders they'd be suspicious of strangers?"

"Is that what they said?" Foster bellowed a laugh. "That I stalked them? I tried to get close enough to warn them to get the hell out of Dodge, that Bear Peak wasn't a safe place to be right now, but they hightailed it like scared rabbits."

Jenna shook her head. "So, if it was too dangerous for hikers what made you believe you were safe? A killer running in the forest would be just as dangerous for you."

"Me?" Foster shook his head. "They wouldn't see me unless I wanted them to, Sheriff. In the forest I'm a ghost."

Recalling the man in the alleyway, Jenna pushed down an involuntary shiver and scrolled through her iPad. "Where were you last Thursday night through Friday morning, Sunday night and last Tuesday between ten and four?"

"I can't remember." Foster scratched his head. "Around. I had a few things to do on Friday but I work at the produce store most days. Loading and unloading trucks. The other times, I went many places: stores, Aunt Betty's, the new outdoors store to purchase bolts for my crossbow. I got gas at George's Garage."

"Okay." Jenna stood. "I've written down what you told me about meeting the Howards and seeing the couple on the trail at Bear Peak. Read it through and if it's correct, sign it. I'll be outside."

She scanned her card and left with Kane close behind her. She leaned against the wall in the hallway. "What do you think?"

"To me he is no more than a witness. Yeah, we could make a case using circumstantial evidence, but with Adams and Long in the mix, it will never fly." Kane shrugged and joined her, pressing his back to the wall. "We'll get Rowley to check out his story, but I think we have zip against him."

Jenna huffed out a sigh. "There's my gut feeling again. I figure they're all involved and somehow, by magic, telepathy, or whatever means he used, that James Stone is controlling them."

"You should trust your gut." Kane smiled. "Give his photograph to Bobby Kalo to add to the face recognition program he's currently running to keep tabs on Adams and Long. If he acts suspiciously or any of them meet up, we'll haul them back in."

Tired from a long day, Jenna pulled open the door to the interview room. She collected the statement. "Thank you for your cooperation, Mr. Foster." She waved him out the door.

As they followed him, she turned to Kane. "I could really go for a steak at Antlers tonight." She glanced at her watch. "If we eat now, it won't be too late to tend the horses when we get home."

"They only need to be led from the corral into the barn." Kane followed her up the stairs to her office. "I fixed up their feed and water before I left this morning."

Jenna dropped the statement on her desk, collected her coat and weapon before locking her office door and heading downstairs. Rio and his siblings were behind the front counter and Rowley was at his desk. The office was deserted and a heavy mist pressed against the glass front doors. Maggie had finished for the day. Jenna turned to Rowley. "Are you done?"

"Yeah." Rowley closed his laptop and slid it under one arm. "The files are all up to date."

Jenna smiled. "I have a statement from Mr. Foster but I'll file that in the morning and some follow-up work for you. Head off home now. Sandy will be worried about you."

"I called her earlier, she's fine." Rowley laughed. "I won't be able to get my arms around her soon. The twins are growing really fast."

"That's good to know." She walked to the front counter. The usually disorganized area looked spick and span. "Wow! I'll have to get you guys to drop by more often. Thank you."

"Time to go." Zac waved the twins toward the door and looked at Jenna. "One thing I don't have to worry about is cooking meals. My housekeeper is a dream come true."

"Except when she's polishing floors." Cade pulled a face. "Then she's like she's possessed by a demon."

Jenna laughed and followed everyone outside. They all moved away, heading for their respective vehicles. She locked up and mist rose up around her, the dampness touching her cheeks in a cold caress. As the trucks pulled away, darkness surrounded her. She hastened her step to Kane's truck. Main seemed to be deserted apart from the ghoulish Halloween displays. The glow from the street lights poured over the pure white cloud of mist, turning it opaque, and in the distance the only lights spilling onto the sidewalk came from Aunt Betty's Café. Movement and a churning of mist caught her attention. At the entrance to the alleyway opposite, she made out a figure of a man. Her heart skipped a beat as the cowboy hat and slicker loomed out of the shadows. She pulled her weapon and edged closer to Kane's truck, not taking her eyes off the man. When Kane buzzed down his window, she spoke to him through her teeth. "The man with the crossbow I saw in the alleyway. He's right over there."

"Stay here and use the Beast for cover." Kane climbed out and peered into the darkness. "Where is he?"

Jenna stared into the shadows. "Right there." She indicated with her Glock.

Beside her Kane scanned the area, moving his head from right to left. "I don't see anyone."

Heart pounding, Jenna stared into the shadows. "He was in the mouth of the alleyway. Where could he go? It's a dead end down there."

"Did you see a crossbow? Or any weapon?" Kane's stare remained fixed on the alleyway.

Jenna wound back the fleeting image in her mind: the swirling slicker, the cowboy hat, and his stance, with his feet apart. His hands were down by his sides, maybe in his pockets. She shook her head. "I don't think so, but I'm not sure with the mist and all."

"I'll go take a look." Kane grabbed a Kevlar vest from the back seat and pulled it over his head. "Stay here. I'm not his target." He stepped out from cover and strode across Main, almost vanishing in the rising clouds of water vapor.

Fighting back the need to follow, Jenna rested her forearms on the hood of the Beast, tightened her hands around the handle of her weapon, and aimed. An arc of light filled the alleyway as Kane entered and moments later it was extinguished. Panic grabbed her by the throat. It was so quiet she could hear a pulse beating in her ears. "Dave, where are you?"

"I'm right here." Kane emerged from the darkness and walked a few yards in both directions before crossing Main and returning to her side. "There's no one there."

Incredulous, Jenna stared at him but holstered her weapon. "I saw him. It was the same man who wrecked my house and the same person I saw in the alleyway the other night."

"It must have been a trick of the light." Kane put his arm around her and squeezed. "I've checked it out, and there's no one in the alleyway, all the doors are locked up tight, no footprints, zip. It was your imagination playing tricks on you is all. These things happen when we've been traumatized, it's a normal reaction to be overcautious." He waved a hand at the headless ghoul riding a full-sized horse and brandishing a sword outside the liquor store. "Halloween does spike the imagination. That figure looks as if could come alive and ride down Main." He chuckled and slid behind the wheel.

Unconvinced, Jenna peered over one shoulder at the dark alleyway before climbing into the passenger seat. The space where the man had stood was empty, but she hadn't imagined seeing the man. Someone was out there watching her, and she darn well knew it.

CHAPTER FORTY-FIVE

Friday, Week Two

Dark clouds hung over the ranch like a warning to stay home as Jenna stepped out of the barn. She turned to Kane. "Yeah, looking at that sky, we're in for a storm sometime today. It's best we leave the horses in the barn."

"Heads up." Kane motioned to a man wearing fatigues with a captain's insignia heading in their direction. "I hope they've finished at last."

Jenna looked at him and turned her mouth down. "Can't you wait to see the back of me?"

"Nah." Kane gave her a hug. "I just like it better without a yard filled with soldiers. The smell reminded me of my last tour of duty."

Jenna chuckled. "Well, if it ever decides to rain, it will freshen things up a bit." She headed to meet the man.

"We're all done here, ma'am." The captain motioned toward the house. "I'll walk you through the changes and then we're bugging out."

"Sure." Jenna followed him to the house and up the steps to the porch.

The freshly painted front door had changed considerably. Gone were the glass panels on either side, and the front windows had security mesh installed. She walked inside. The smell of paint lingered, but the house looked much the same as before the intruder had trashed it, apart from a black circular leather sofa that curled around the rug in front of the fireplace and was large enough to sit eight. Two matching overstuffed chairs sat on either side.

"Do you like it?" Kane walked up behind her. "Surprise."

She turned and looked at him. "You bought that for me?"

"Yeah." He grinned.

"Okay, ma'am." The captain cleared his throat. "As per my instructions, entry to the house is by fingerprint. You can scan one to four fingerprints into the system. It's run on an independent power supply and backed up with batteries. You'll get a notification on your phone if the batteries are running low. You also have a backup generator in the house now—it's in the cellar beside the gym. As requested, there is an escape hatch inside the office, situated under the desk. It is one-way. It can't be opened from the outside. The front gate is the same, and the perimeter boundary has been extended to twelve feet high. It has been calibrated so you won't be troubled by birds, horses, wildlife, or your dog setting off the alarm." He sighed. "If everything is to your satisfaction, we'll be on our way."

"I'll take a look at the generator." Kane headed off in the direction of the cellar.

After moving around the house and setting up the entry alarm, Jenna thanked the captain and his regiment for their assistance. She stood at the door with Kane and watched the trucks disappear down her driveway in a cloud of dust. "I'm glad we started early this morning." They headed back to the cottage. "We'll just have time to eat before we head out to the office."

The sky rumbled and a few flashes of lightning zigzagged the sky over the horizon as they headed for town. The whine from Duke made Jenna turn up the tunes on the radio. "It's okay, Duke. I brought cookies and you'll be safe in the office today."

"He doesn't sound too convinced." Kane slowed the truck as they joined a stream of traffic into Main. "What's going on here?"

Jenna peered ahead. "The road must be blocked, there's no oncoming traffic. An accident maybe?" She buzzed down her window and beckoned to a man walking on the sidewalk. "What's happened?"

"Car wreck." The man pushed his hands into his pockets. "Three vehicles blocking the road."

"Thanks." Jenna turned to Kane. "Can you get closer?"

"Sure." He hit the lights and sirens and headed up the wrong side of Main.

Ahead, Jenna made out smoke and pulled out the fire extinguisher from under her seat. "Pull into the alleyway beside the soup kitchen."

They jumped out and ran along the sidewalk, pushing through a group of onlookers. A trio of vehicles greeted them. One was pouring steam into the air from a busted radiator, and the others all had damage. She tossed the fire extinguisher to Kane and went to the huddle of people exchanging details. "What happened here? Is anyone hurt?"

"No ma'am, and we have tow trucks coming from George's Garage. Deputy Rowley is on his way." A man in his sixties with silver hair and wearing a thick brown coat and gloves looked at her. "Some idiot came flying out of the alleyway. I swerved to miss him and hit the Toyota, the GMC ran into the back of him."

"Did you get a plate number of the truck?" Kane raised an eyebrow. "The make, model?"

"No, we were just saying that it came out so fast and took off at high speed." The man frowned. "It was a white pickup, Ford maybe. I was kind of busy trying to save myself at that point." He looked at the crowd. "Anyone see anything? Any camera footage?"

Not one person put up their hand. Jenna looked at the three car owners. "I'll take some photographs and file a report for your insurance companies. We'll need to clear the road as soon as possible." She sighed with relief as Rowley jogged into view.

"Rio is at the other end of Main diverting traffic. We have a clear path for the tow trucks." Rowley looked behind her at the vehicles at a standstill. "Do you want me to walk down and detour the traffic via Maple?"

Jenna nodded. "Yeah, thanks." She took the fire extinguisher from Kane. "Can you drop this into the Beast on your way past? We'll capture the scene for the insurance and get everyone's details."

"Sure." Rowley took it from her and headed through the crowd.

It took forever to get the wrecks onto the tow trucks and clear up the mess. She'd collected everyone's details, had no witnesses that had actually seen anything but the aftermath, but it didn't bother her too much. The CCTV cameras along Main would have picked up the truck and she'd be able to hunt it down easily enough. When Kane came back with a sour expression, she went to his side. "What's up?"

"I pulled up the CCTV camera footage on my phone and we have nothing from six this morning. I'm not sure, but it looks like they used a laser pointer to disable it. There's a flash and the camera goes offline." The nerve in Kane's jaw twitched. "I hope it's not kids planning something spooky and illegal for Halloween."

Jenna sighed. "So, our chances of catching the guy in the white truck are zero?" She looked up at him. "All these so-called coincidences are starting to freak me out. Things happen, but this is darn right weird. If you find the door back to our dimension, pull me through with you. I'm so over this week."

"I'll keep a lookout." Kane chuckled. "I have to admit this has been the weirdest week I've ever worked, and we've experienced every ride at the fairground." He looked up as another flash of lightning lit up the sky and thunder rolled. "No rain again. These dry storms are darn right dangerous when the ground is so dry."

They arrived at the Beast and Jenna slipped into the passenger seat. She heard Kane mutter under his breath and then a whistle that almost burst her eardrums. She leaned across the seat to look out the open window at him. When he repeated the whistle and walked back and forth staring in all directions, concerned, she climbed out of the truck and went to his side. "Who are you whistling?"

"Duke." Kane's expression was distraught. "He's gone."

CHAPTER FORTY-SIX

Jenna pulled open the back door and stared at the blanket Duke was snuggled in when they'd left him. She spun around to Kane. "You did secure him with his harness, didn't you?"

"Of course I did." Kane paced up and down, rubbing the back of his neck. "He can't unclip himself. His leash is missing as well."

Jenna stood beside him and touched his arm. "Are you sure he couldn't have unclipped his harness? I've seen him biting at the clasp—he knows what it is and how it works. He's very smart."

"Then we'll take a closer look." Kane turned back to the Beast and leaned inside. "There are toothmarks on the seatbelt clasp. They could've been there from before. He can't get out of his harness, but if he managed to unclip the seatbelt, he could slip right out of the truck. His leash was attached, he'd be trailing it behind him." He removed his Stetson and ran a hand through his hair in an agitated manner. "Why would he leave the safety of the truck? He's never jumped out the window before."

Jenna pointed skyward. "The storm could have frightened him, and he was alone. You know he likes to hide and he needs someone to comfort him. If he jumped out in fear and couldn't find us in the crowd, he'd look for the safest hideout. We'll have to figure out where he'd go. He knows his way around town." She looked at him. "Who does he trust?"

"Me, you, Atohi, Maggie." Kane rubbed his chin, thinking. "He likes Carter and I guess Susie Hartwig, because she always feeds him something special." He shrugged. "Or he's hightailed it to the office to hide under Maggie's desk. I'd say Aunt Betty's would be the closest place, and it has food." He buzzed up the window and locked the Beast. "We'll walk and ask people as we go." He shook his head. "If he was close by, he'd come back. Duke always comes when I whistle. I've got a real bad feeling about this."

"I'll call Rowley and then Maggie in case they've seen him. You keep whistling." Stomach cramping, Jenna pulled out her phone. "Hey, did you see Duke in Kane's truck when you returned the fire extinguisher?"

"Nope. I figured you'd left him home today." Rowley sounded concerned. *"Is he missing?"*

Jenna gripped the phone. "Yeah. He was wearing a harness and secured as usual. We don't know how he got out, but the window was left open for him. Are you back at the office?"

"Yeah. I'll see if he's here." After a minute or so, Rowley cleared his throat. *"He's not here. What do you want me to do? I can't put out a BOLO on a dog."*

"No. We'll hunt him down. He can't have gotten far." Jenna chewed on her bottom lip. "While we're gone, check Foster's alibis at the times of the murders. Call Bobby Kalo, and get Foster's image to him. I'd like eyes on the movements of all our suspects." Jenna thought for a beat. "And ask Rio to put out a media release asking for anyone who witnessed the car wreck on Main to come forward."

"Yes, ma'am, and I'll call you if Duke shows up here." Rowley disconnected.

Kane was on his phone as she walked to his side. "Duke wouldn't go willingly with anyone he doesn't know, not after that asshole tried to starve him to death. Yeah, I agree, he might well be heading to the res. He feels safe there." Kane listened for a time. "Okay, yeah, I'll do that, thanks, Atohi." He disconnected and turned to Jenna.

"Atohi said due to the dry storms coming through this week, the fire department has wildfire watchers back in the towers. He knows most of them and will call them to watch out for Duke just in case he's heading for the res, same with the forest wardens." He shrugged. "I know it sounds farfetched for Duke to head into the forest, but he's a dog—who knows what goes on inside his head?"

Jenna continued to scan the sidewalk. "What did Atohi suggest?"

"Duke likes familiar places but, in a storm, could hide anywhere." Kane shrugged. "I figure, first up we should talk to people in the immediate area. The car wreck had people's interest but they might have seen Duke, especially as he was dragging his leash."

They walked to Aunt Betty's, stopping familiar faces and asking if they'd seen Duke. The bloodhound was so well known around town that the locals' concern was evident. Jenna pushed open the door to Aunt Betty's Café and went to the counter. Susie Hartwig came right over. "Hi, Susie. Has Duke wandered by this morning? We can't find him."

"Duke?" Susie's forehead creased into a frown. "No. When did he go missing?"

"Not long ago, maybe in the last hour." Kane had removed his Stetson and was curling up the rim. "He hates storms, we thought he might have come by as he likes you."

"Aww, poor Duke." Susie shook her head. "I'll make sure to keep him here if he shows and I'll call you." She thought for a beat. "Does he know his way home? He might be heading there where he knows it's safe."

Jenna nodded. "Maybe. We'll keep searching around town. Thanks."

They walked up and down Main for over an hour, checking all the stores and the park, with Kane whistling intermittently. As they returned to the truck, she turned to Kane. "I think we should head home. Duke has been your close companion for years now. I figure if he couldn't find you, he'd head home. It's been a couple of hours, we should check—it's the most logical place."

"Okay. It's worth a try." Kane scanned Main one more time and got reluctantly into the truck. "Like you said, Duke has been with me for some time now. I know all his little idiosyncrasies, but not since the day I rescued him has he left my side. You said how he pined for me when I was in Walter Reed. This doesn't make any sense. He wouldn't just run away, storm or no storm. He'd be more likely to bury himself under his blanket and wait for us to come back."

They drove slowly back to Jenna's ranch, both searching all around, but found no sign of Duke. As they entered the gate, Jenna waved Kane passed her ranch house. "He might be in the cottage."

"I don't figure he could have gotten this far in two or so hours." Kane pulled up outside and headed for his front door. "Did you leave your doggie door open?"

Jenna shook her head. "No, it was locked when we checked out the house this morning."

She followed him inside and they looked under beds and in Duke's usual hiding places. The house was empty. As they headed for the front door, Kane's phone chimed.

"Unknown number." Kane accepted the call and put his phone on speaker. "Dave Kane."

"Hi there, this is Jo Prichard. I'm one of the forest wardens out at the station just down from Bear Peak. I had a call from a hunter, he said he could hear a dog howling out near the ravine. Atohi called earlier, and said you were looking for your hound? Maybe it's him. I'd go and take a look but I'm alone here all day."

"Yeah, I've lost my dog, a bloodhound by the name of Duke." Kane looked at Jenna and raised an eyebrow. "I'll head up that way now. Thanks." He turned to Jenna. "I'll get my horse and drop you back at the office. You have a case to solve. I must go see if it's him. Maybe he got his leash caught up and can't move."

Jenna frowned. "The ravine? How did he get that far?"

"It's been over three hours now, Jenna." Kane grabbed a backpack and stuffed it full of supplies. "I'll take a med kit in case he's been injured."

Jenna frowned. "Then take one of the trail bikes from the office. It will get you there faster."

"No, Duke would run from the noise." Kane frowned. "He'll be terrified and won't recognize me, especially if he's hurt."

Gut cramping from the implications, Jenna went into the bedroom she'd been using and took out her backpack from the closet. She went back into the kitchen and filled it with supplies. "I'm coming too. There's a serial killer hanging around Bear Peak and although the ravine is west of there, it's safer if we both go. None of the victims wore Kevlar vests or sheriff's department jackets and that alone may put off a killer. We'll take our rifles and plenty of ammo just in case. I'll call Rowley on the way and give him the heads-up."

"Sure, grab the horses and I'll hitch up the trailer." Kane hurried out the door.

In no time they were heading for the forest. Thunder rolled across the heavens as Kane pulled up at the end of a fire road and jumped out. Jenna collected their gear, they mounted, and headed in the direction of the ravine. The wind had picked up and the lightning cracked all around them as they moved along the trail. Jenna's white mare, Seagull, danced sideways; her ears flattened against her head. She didn't like storms either, and shied away from the moving branches swirling in the gusts of wind. As they reached the fork in the trail leading around the ravine before joining up again a mile or so ahead, Kane gave an ear-piercing whistle. They stopped and listened. A howl unmistakably from Duke echoed through the forest and continued for some moments.

"That's him. I'd know that sound anywhere." Kane blew out a breath. "We've found him. He must be close by."

"But where?" Jenna searched the dense trees. "I hope he's not fallen into the ravine. Did you pick up a direction?"

"I'm not sure." Kane whistled again and a long howl carried on the wind. "Dammit, the echo from the mountain distorts the direction of the sound." He scanned the area and frowned. "We'll need to check both trails. If you recall, the trail on the right crumbles into the ravine in places. Your mare isn't sure-footed enough to risk taking her there."

The sky had darkened in the last few minutes, a storm imminent. Jenna shrugged. "Then we split up and meet up at the end." She leaned toward him and squeezed his hand. "Don't look so worried. I doubt a killer will be out in this weather. I haven't seen a hiker or anyone else since we entered the forest."

"Are you sure, Jenna? If the storm gets any worse our earpieces won't work. If you run into trouble, you'll have to use the satellite phone and hope the storm doesn't interfere with the signal." Kane turned his head as another long howl came from the forest. "We can do both trails together. It will be safer."

Jenna patted her Glock. "Duke could be dying for all we know. It's less than a mile, five or six minutes on horseback. I'll be fine. Just to be sure, I'll check in with Rowley and Rio and give them our position. They'll use trail bikes to get here if needs be."

A crack of lightning lit up the sky, the replying thunder a second behind it. A gust of wind blew up pine needles in a dust cloud and a panicked howl came from the forest. Jenna waved Kane away. "Go, that's the obvious trail to the res and he more than likely went that way. I'll ride fast along this track and meet you at the cut-through."

"Stay safe, Jenna." Kane pulled his horse around and took off in a cloud of dust.

As the storm raged around her and lightning zigzagged across the darkening sky, Jenna pulled out her satellite phone and called Rowley to give her position, but the reception was breaking up. She could only grasp the odd word from Rowley's urgent reply. "I can't understand you. You're breaking up." She texted him a message with her coordinates and tried again. "Rowley are you there?"

"We've been trying to reach you… Agent Wells called…. Hospital… might be…" The line went dead.

CHAPTER FORTY-SEVEN

The wind buffeted Kane as it whistled through the trees and lifted his massive black gelding's long mane like a woman's hair in a shampoo commercial. The trail was easy going at first, but subsidence caused by the last melt had left it narrow in parts. Wide gashes had gnawed at the edges. Soil and rock had crumbled away and spilled into the ravine. Pine trees tilted over the chasm at unnatural angles, their roots exposed, and some had fallen far below, their once green needles now brown and crumbling. The sight saddened him. It reminded him of the way some people ripped young pines from the ground and left them to die, as a Christmas tree, to be put out with the trash. He snorted. To him killing a tree didn't seem right when he was celebrating a birth. Oh, he loved the tradition of decorating a tree for the holidays, but the plastic one he dusted off and decorated each year looked just fine in his cottage.

He whistled again and heard the response, but again the direction was distorted by the echo. He cupped his hands around his mouth. "I'm coming, Duke."

Lightning cracked around them and thunder roared loud enough to rally the Vikings in Valhalla, but his horse didn't so much as flinch. He urged Warrior forward; the sure-footed gelding reminded him of a horse trained for a knight in days gone by. He'd read about the ways the warrior horses were trained to move from side to side to enable a knight to keep his seat as he swung a heavy sword, and during battle they'd rear and use their flying hooves to take out a foot soldier. Fearless and brave, they rarely allowed anyone but their owners to ride them and would return to a fallen knight rather than run away. His horse, Warrior, was fearless, and he could trust him to pick his way without guidance through just about any terrain. He'd taken to Kane at once and they'd bonded.

As they moved up the trail, Warrior stopped and snickered in a greeting. Kane scanned the trees and the path ahead. A fallen pine blocked the way, but it was narrow enough for the horse to step over. Perhaps Jenna had already made it to the cut-through. But no white horse or anything else came down the path. Thunder rolled and a whine came on a gust of wind. "Duke? Where are you, boy?"

The next second, Duke's head appeared from behind the fallen log, but instead of his usual happy dance, his mouth pulled back, exposing his teeth, and he barked in a savage warning, his head turned toward the forest. Warrior shivered and stepped sideways. Kane pulled out his rifle and scoped the shadows. Something was there, and Duke considered it a threat. Sniffing the air for the scent of a bear, Kane dismounted and, holding his rifle shoulder high, moved along the tree line, using each pine to cover his back. He caught sight of a shadow, man or bear it was hard to tell with the trees in constant motion. Behind him Warrior had remained where he'd left him, head held high and ears pricked. A twig cracked behind him and the next instant a crossbow bolt slammed into the tree two inches from his nose. He dived to the cover of the trees and belly-crawled to one end of the log. Crossbow bolts hit the log with sickening thumps. *So, not a bear, then? Who are you? Adams or Long?*

The idea that someone had used his love of his dog to lure him to his death annoyed him. He reached for his combat mode and everything slowed—it was as if the distance between one second and the next had grown a thousand times longer. His mind went to Jenna and he tapped his com. "Jenna. Jenna, do you copy?"

Nothing.

"Jenna, do you copy?

The storm raging above him was interfering with the signal. Keeping his head down, he moved closer to Duke. "Good boy." He reached out to rub his ears and Duke tried desperately to crawl closer. "Stay. I'll get you untied. Lie down." He pushed on Duke's back.

Someone had secured Duke to the fallen tree using his leash. Kane edged closer and had him untied in seconds. He needed to get to the cover of the trees and, with one hand on Duke, urged him forward. The dog moved on his belly just as he'd taught him, and they edged their way back to safety.

Before Kane could get to his feet, two bolts came at him from different directions. They were close. Too damn close. "Sheriff's Department. If you take another shot at me. I'm going to take you down. I don't give second chances."

Zing. Thwack. Another bolt just missed him and hit the trunk behind him. As he rolled behind a snowberry bush, he caught a glimpse of something shiny in the shadows. He lifted his rifle and took the shot. Lightning flashed and in that millisecond of light, he saw a man in a cowboy hat and slicker tumble into the ravine, his hat falling from his head as he fell, arms wide. Kane scanned the forest. With another unknown intent on killing him close by, he needed to move right now. Making sure Duke was well hidden under the bush and supplied with water, he cupped the dog's face and looked him in the eyes. "I know you're scared but you must stay. Understand? Stay."

Moving swiftly, Kane used the dense forest as cover and headed back down the trail. The shooter was to his left, and he needed to come around behind him. The wind howled and the lightning intensified, but Kane used it to his advantage. When the lightning lit up the sky, he waited for the roll of thunder and then ran through the dry bushes, using the noise to cover his movements. This was what he'd been trained for and it was as natural as breathing. With his back and front protected by tall, fragrant pines, he waited for the man to make his next move. The one thing being a sniper had taught him was patience. He could stay frozen in time for hours if necessary. It didn't take long at all before the shape of another man dressed the same, in cowboy hat and slicker, with a rifle over one shoulder and carrying a crossbow, appeared in the distance heading to the fork in the trail and in Jenna's direction. He shook his head in disbelief. Jenna had insisted someone was stalking her and now he'd seen two men on the trail and both had shot at him. She'd been in danger, and it hadn't been her imagination after all.

His stomach tightened. With the coms down he'd try the satellite phone to call Jenna to warn her. The call didn't connect, the screen displaying a NO SERVICE message, and he swallowed hard. If the men had been stalking Jenna, why did they try and take him down unless they wanted to pin his head to a tree with a crossbow bolt? Had they captured her and wanted him to watch their macabre show? He stared toward the retreating man. *Good luck with that— your buddy can't help you now.*

If the men had captured or hurt Jenna, it was his fault. He should've known they'd use his Achilles heel to get him into the forest and no doubt had dragged Duke from his truck. The plan had been ingenious. They'd have known he'd drop everything to find his dog, and any local would know that during the search he'd send Jenna along the safest trail. He'd been so concerned about Duke he'd let his guard down and allowed Jenna to fall into their trap, but he'd turned the tables. One was dead. His shot had been dead center with zero chance of survival. Rage could easily take control, and he couldn't allow his feelings for Jenna to influence his emotions. He breathed in and out, pushed everything out of his mind, and dropped into his combat zone. Cold determination to take down this man enveloped him. Through the scope on his rifle, he could see the man clearly as he moved along the trail across the ravine, heading in Jenna's direction. This animal who killed without mercy had just met a superior predator. In the forest he moved like a ghost. He dropped back into the deep shadows and trained his rifle on the man. He slowed his heartbeat and aimed. The shooter had just become a target. *And I never miss.*

CHAPTER FORTY-EIGHT

"Rowley?" Jenna stared at the phone in disbelief. She pressed her com. "Kane, can you hear me?"

Nothing.

Against her legs, Seagull's skin rippled in fright and she flung her head high, her nostrils flaring. Jenna reined her in, turning her in small circles. "It's okay. It's just a dry storm, we'll be fine." She leaned down and stroked the mare's neck, keeping her voice calm. "As soon as we find Duke we'll go home. We just have to keep moving down the trail."

As she lifted her head, a blinding flash of lightning revealed a glimpse of a man watching her from the shadows. Dressed in a cowboy hat and slicker with a black balaclava covering his face and carrying a crossbow, he was too familiar. Blinking away the red spots in her eyes, Jenna shook her head, not believing what she was seeing. She reached for her weapon and searched the forest, but by the next flash the man had vanished. Had she imagined him? She'd seen the man who'd invaded her home three times in succession now, and each time had found no one there. Could she be suffering from PTSD? The possibility was staring her in the face, and the last thing she needed slap-bang in the middle of a murder investigation was flashbacks. She'd be no good to anyone if she couldn't function properly. "Am I losing my mind?"

Frantically looking around one more time as the lightning flashed, illuminating the forest, and finding nothing but trees groaning in the wind, she holstered her weapon. Her horse danced around, the rolls of thunder and flashes of lightning like gunshots cracked around her terrifying the mare. Heart thundering in her chest, Jenna urged the terrified horse onward, soon reaching the exact place where Stone, some years previously, had shot Kane in the head and she'd been unable to prevent his fall into the ravine. The wind howled around her, plastering her exposed flesh with dust and pine needles. She bent low, keeping her attention on the narrow trail ahead. Not much farther and she would be at the cut-through, but the going was slow with a reluctant mare.

A sound like a man laughing sent shivers down her spine. Her pulse quickened and she turned in the saddle and scanned the trees behind her. Terror slammed into her as her worst nightmare stepped from the forest. James Stone stood grinning at her not twenty yards away. How could he have escaped prison? It was impossible. Blinking through the mist, she gaped at the sight of him, not believing her eyes. It was as if fate had re-created a terrible loop and flung her back in time.

"Hello, Jenna." Stone's voice carried toward her over the noise of the storm like a hideous memory as he removed the balaclava and dropped it to the ground. He carried a rifle but wasn't pointing it at her. "Haven't you dreamed about rewinding our time here together? I sure have." He took a few steps toward her. "This time without the cavalry, like it was supposed to have been." He leaned his rifle against the tree, peeled off the slicker, and tossed the hat to reveal army camouflage. "Just you, me, and maybe my hunting knife." His laughter was muffled by the wind. He opened his hands wide. "One on one. A fair fight." He shook his head. "No? Your choice." He reached for his rifle.

Survival instinct had Jenna's hand going for her Glock but with lightning flashing all around her, a gale force wind, and a terrified horse moving below her, the chances of even winging Stone would be remote—and he had a rifle. She had one option: run. She spun her horse around and, keeping low, she bolted down the trail. As they turned a bend not twenty yards away from the fork on the main trail and safety, Jenna's hair rose all around her face and a prickling sensation crawled over her head. The next instant, in a flash of brilliant white light, a tall pine exploded and fell in a wall of fire across the trail. Flames danced across the ground, hungry yellow and red tongues licking the dry forest floor, climbing trunks, and leaping from branch to branch in milliseconds. In a mighty roar the forest ignited into a wild, uncontrollable beast. Seagull reared, screaming in terror, and twisted, launching Jenna into the air. The ground came up fast and she landed flat on her back, gasping for air. Flying hooves barely missed her face as Seagull stamped and reared inches from her. Jenna's fingers had instinctively tightened around the reins.

The air filled with smoke as flames claimed the dry pines in a *whoosh* of crackling and sparks showered down, igniting everything they touched. In seconds Jenna's way back to Kane and safety was blocked by a wall of fire and thick clouds of smoke. Dragged by her horse, Jenna finally staggered to her feet, but there was no calming the mare. Seagull's eyes rolled in terror and she reared, flailing her front legs. Fighting to get her horse under control, Jenna remounted, but the jittery mare wanted to bolt. Thickening smoke filled her lungs and, coughing, Jenna pulled a facemask from her pocket and with some difficulty pressed it over her nose. The fire was like a roaring freight train as the flames reached the top of the pines. A whining noise surrounded her as if the forest was screaming. She searched for a way through the dense undergrowth, but the ravine blocked the way on one side, the fire on the other. She turned Seagull around. Behind her the flames would kill them in seconds, and ahead was a serial killer. It was catch-22, and her chances of survival had just dropped to zero.

CHAPTER FORTY-NINE

A crack of lightning like a cannon exploding hit a tall pine and split it in half. As it tumbled to the dry forest floor, the uppermost branches ignited in a *whoosh* of flames, so intense they heated Kane's exposed flesh. The cowboy had been close to the strike and Kane doubted he'd survived. Fingers of flames danced across the ground to the surrounding pines and ran up their trunks like liquid fire. Branches hissed and crackled as trees exploded into fireballs. All around him, pine needles fell like burning matchsticks, igniting everything they touched.

Kane ran to Warrior and grabbed his reins. After pushing his rifle into the scabbard attached to his saddle, he dashed to where he'd hidden Duke and hauled the dog onto the horse. He mounted and rode away from the fire and headed to the fork in the trail. If Jenna was in trouble, he had to get to her before the fire reached her. A wide river ran from the mountain not far from the trail and heading there would be the best option. They could travel on horseback up the river and reach the firebreak, the Beast, and a way out of the inferno. He urged Warrior up the track as smoke filled the air, making it hard to breathe. The raging dry storm overhead had darkened the sky, and through the smoke the sun had turned into a dark-orange moon.

It seemed to take forever to reach the fork, and once there Kane turned Warrior around the corner and headed downhill. The smoke was thick, and glowing sparks spiraled down, setting small fires where they landed. He pushed Warrior on and the horse responded without hesitation. He called out for Jenna, but his voice was drowned by the roar of the fire as it gorged itself on the dry forest. She should have turned back and been on her way by now. Coughing, and eyes streaming, Kane pulled on a facemask. In front of him Duke whined and he dismounted and lifted him down. "Stay. I'll come back for you."

He looked at Duke's trusting face and climbed back into the saddle. His dog wasn't stupid. If the fire came closer, he'd head for the res, but with the wind heading away from him, unless it changed, he'd be safe enough. Sweat trickled down Kane's back as he pushed on. In front of him, an orange wall of flames reached for the heavens and spread out as every gust of wind sprinkled the dry forest with sparks. Cold wind seeped through his clothes from the ice-capped mountain peaks behind him, offering a respite from the heat, but as the storm intensified the howling wind pushed the fire down the mountain toward Black Rock Falls. The wind came in huge gusts over the mountain peaks and whistled down the hillside. The lightning flashed and a crack like a shotgun exploded a tree farther down the mountain. He rounded a corner. Ahead spot fires had taken hold in the ravine, and wildlife dashed across the trail looking for a way out of the heat. Thick gray smoke blocked his way and he couldn't see more than a few yards ahead of him. The next second a blood-curdling scream came from down the trail. Male or female, he had no idea. The leaping flames roared like a jet engine as trees exploded into fireballs. Heart racing, he dismounted and knotted his reins. Warrior would wait for him or run to safety. He had to find Jenna and couldn't risk taking him any closer to the fire. He settled his backpack on his shoulders and, taking his rifle, ran headlong into the choking smoke.

CHAPTER FIFTY

Screams pierced through the howl of the fire and fear bunched Jenna's stomach as her mind went to Kane. She tried again and again to reach him on the com, without success. Lungs bursting, she scanned the forest. The screams sounded human, and fear created images in the swirling blaze. She stared at the uncontrollable, greedy band of red and orange flames. The smell of burning hair singed her nostrils as a man, his clothes on fire, staggered from the forest, waving a knife. She gaped in horror as flames engulfed him, but he kept on coming, his blackened mouth stretched in a hideous grin and brown eyes staring out of a ruined face. He took a few steps and then fell face down in a smoking, charred heap. Before Jenna could process the sight before her, the man stirred, rising up on his elbows to drag himself toward her, knife still clutched in his fire-ravaged hand. The remnants of a cowboy hat fell to ashes as the man sank to the ground and remained still as flames lapped around him.

Bile rushed into Jenna's mouth as she stared at the man. "Oh, my God!"

The man wasn't Kane or James Stone. Stone had been wearing army fatigues, which meant he was still out there waiting for her. Fast running out of options, Jenna scanned the trail for a way out of danger. At her back the fiendish, hungry blaze consumed the forest in deadly delight. Trees exploded, shooting fireworks high into the air as boiling sap ran down the trunks like molten lava, and ahead, if she rode back up the trail, she'd face James Stone, a brutal serial killer intent on dismembering her. He'd already fired a warning shot. She'd heard it above the murderous screeches of the blaze but she'd ridden hard and used the smoke to shield her. Without doubt, the rifle shot would bring Kane. Thinking it was a call for help, he'd walk straight into James Stone. The storm raged above her, lightning flashed, and the mountain shuddered as thunder pealed out like a stampede of elephants. She had to warn him. She pressed her com again—if one or two words got through it would be enough. "Kane, Stone on trail. Do you copy? James Stone is here."

A crackle came in her ear but not a sound from Kane. She repeated the message three times. Had she gotten through to him? Swallowing the fear threatening to strangle her, she examined the line of fire. The black edge and smoldering stumps had grown wider in the past few minutes. The wind was at her back and pushed the fire down the mountain. She'd move deep into the forest, using the trees and dense smoke to conceal her, in an attempt to go around Stone, and hopefully meet Kane where they'd parted. She urged Seagull from the trail and through the trees. The terrified mare bucked and snorted and Jenna's soothing words were lost in the deafening noise. Seagull dug in and refused to move. Jenna dismounted and tied the mare's reins around a tree. She shrugged out of her backpack, vest, and jacket and then removed her T-shirt. After dressing quickly, she pulled her T-shirt over the mare's head to cover her eyes. When Seagull settled, Jenna untied her and led her through the forest, following animal tracks and keeping as far away from the main trail as possible. Behind her the forest moaned in agony and above her the storm raged, lighting up the fast-moving dark clouds.

"Jenna."

The voice carried on the wind like a whisper in her ear. Who was calling her? Kane or Stone, she couldn't tell. Jenna stopped to listen and the call came again. She turned to look behind her, but only an orange glow greeted her, shrouded by thick smoke. She stroked Seagull's neck and carefully removed the shirt from her head and stuffed it into the saddlebags. The mare had calmed some and snickered, rubbing her nose against Jenna's pocket, searching for sugar or the apples she carried as treats. "Okay. We have to find Dave."

Mounting the mare, she urged her in the direction of the voice. If it was Stone, she'd take him down and end this nightmare once and for all. Her mind was set. There'd be no second chances for him this time. The moment he aimed his rifle at her, he was a dead man.

CHAPTER FIFTY-ONE

Kane stopped walking and listened intently to his com. The broken transmission from Jenna had mentioned one name: Stone. That was all he needed, and he melted into the trees alongside the ravine. If somehow James Stone had escaped from jail and engineered this entire fiasco by stealing his dog and calling the forest warden to lure them here, he'd been smarter than he'd given him credit for. The jigsaw fell into place. Adams and Long had been the decoys. Both had likely committed murder and by coming forward had thrown enough doubt to avoid conviction. He shook his head and moved through the trees, sporadically calling Jenna on his com. He'd seen her after interviewing Stone, her back rigid as she attempted to shake off the terrifying memories provoked by meeting him again.

A blast of cold air shifted the smoke into curling waves and the forest moved. He raised his hunting rifle to peer through the scope and scanned the trees. Walking through the forest as large as life was James Stone. He strode confidently, keeping between the safety of the trees. Stone obviously believed his henchmen had taken him out and Jenna was alone. Kane scoped the forest up and down the trail and spotted Jenna's white mare moving between the trees. He swallowed hard. She was riding straight toward Stone. He picked up his pace, leaping over fallen trees. The injury he'd suffered a month previously hampered his movements. Two stab wounds to the chest had come close to killing him, and breathing in the thick smoke didn't help. The storm had moved on, now only a rumble in the distance, but the wildfire still roared and crackled toward town, devouring everything in its path. He heard Stone calling Jenna's name and pressed his com again. "Jenna, do you copy? I'm on my way. Stone is calling you, not me. Take cover."

To his relief, the com crackled in his ear. Jenna had heard him.

"Copy. I know he's there, but I don't have eyes on him yet. He's carrying a rifle but he doesn't plan on killing me outright and I doubt he knows I'm wearing liquid Kevlar. He wants to have some fun first, so won't risk a headshot. I'll have the advantage and he's out of second chances. The moment he draws down on me, I'm taking him out."

Kane swore under his breath and pressed his com. "Stone is ten yards ahead on your left. I'm one hundred yards from you. Wait for me to get to your position. We'll be able to flank him."

"I need to face him alone, Dave. It's the only option. I want this nightmare to be over. Jenna out."

Her voice rang with a finality that alarmed him and he broke cover and ran down the trail. Over the roar of the fire, he could just make out sirens—the fire spotters had activated the plan that brought volunteer firefighters from Black Rock Falls and every surrounding county to fight the blaze. Everyone had been on standby, waiting for the inevitable, and would be out in force to protect the town. Moving his attention along the tree line, Kane searched for Stone. His camouflage gear was doing a fine job of concealing him, and Kane could be running into his firing line. He zigzagged along the tree line, the smoke offering him a modicum of cover, and then slowed as he approached a bend in the trail. He'd be close to Stone's position and in Jenna's line of fire if she planned to confront him. Slipping into the cover of the trees, he edged his way through the forest. He made out Seagull, her back legs dancing impatiently, head jerking at the reins Jenna had attached to a sapling. A conversation carried to him. Stone had raised his voice to be heard above the roar of the fire. He sounded excited but in complete control. Kane's stomach cramped into knots as Jenna stepped out of cover. She had her rifle tucked into her shoulder and a determined look on her face.

Kane crept through the trees and took up a position ten yards away. He lifted his rifle and took aim. Jenna wanted to deal with Stone and bury the ghosts that haunted her. Killing him the first time they'd met would have saved three, maybe four, people's lives, and he understood how, as sheriff, she'd feel responsible. He listened. The voices were clearer now. He placed his eye on the scope and aimed for Stone's head. Jenna would be taking the collar, but he'd cover her back. He pressed his com. "I'm ten yards ahead on your left. I have eyes on Stone."

Kane heard a tap, her signal she'd understood his message. He controlled his breathing and slowed his heart rate. Whatever happened next, he'd be ready.

CHAPTER FIFTY-TWO

Disgust flowed over Jenna in an overwhelming hatred for James Stone. She'd heard Kane's message in her earpiece, and having him close by offered her some modicum of comfort, but it didn't diminish the fact that the man taunting her was a manipulative psychopath intent on killing her. She'd seen his mutilated victims, all the same type as her, killed to appease something in his twisted mind because he'd been unable to control her. She would be his ultimate goal, his grand finale, until someone else bruised his incredible ego. It made her sick to her stomach knowing she'd been the trigger that led to him committing such atrocities, the true facts so vile they were never released in open court. She'd spared his life that day on the mountain and, somehow, he'd manipulated his followers to kill in his stead, and now he'd found a way to escape a maximum-security wing to wreak havoc again in Black Rock Falls. Killing didn't come easy to her. She'd believed that given a chance everyone could change—until she'd met James Stone. He was the psychopath's psychopath, the one they all admired, and seemingly unstoppable. She took in his smug, self-satisfied expression and her stomach roiled.

Jenna pulled out her phone, turned on the video recorder, and slipped it into her top pocket. It might not record everything but would get the audio. For her own peace of mind, she'd play it by the book, but she kept her rifle aimed at his head. *No more deaths on my watch. You're out of chances.*

"Come out, come out, wherever you are." Stone stepped out onto the path, his rifle aiming in all directions. "You came to see me and I know you've never stopped thinking about me—have you, Jenna?" He chuckled. "Have you been chasing your tail trying to find someone to convict for the recent murders? I'll tell you everything you want to know."

Knees trembling, Jenna sucked in a breath of smoke-tainted air and gathered her cloak of professionalism around her. Stone played on weaknesses, trying to make himself appear superior. She understood so much more about psychopathic behavior since working alongside Kane and Jo. Confident she could handle him and get the answers she needed, she gathered her courage around her and, using a thick tree for cover, raised her voice. "Are you so frightened of me you need to keep a rifle aimed at my head to talk to me? Your reputation will be torn to shreds when the inmates at the jail discover you acted like a coward with a woman who took you down and had you jailed for ten life sentences."

"Really? I don't think so. They respect me but they spat on you, didn't they, Jenna?" Stone's cruel mouth turned up in a wry smile. "I *chose* not to kill you. I could have picked you off at any time, but a quick death wasn't what I wanted. Dying fast was too good for you. I wanted to make you suffer." He chuckled. "I still do. So as sure as hell, I'm not planning on shooting you in the head. A knee, maybe, so you can't run away."

Jenna aimed her rifle at his head. "I'm not alone, but you're smart enough to figure that out by yourself, I'm sure."

"I'm not alone either." His grin widened. "That shot you heard was one of my disciples taking out Dave Kane. You're alone, Jenna. No one is going to save you. Not this time." He lowered his rifle a little. "If you want to play fair, we'll talk."

A shiver of apprehension slid down Jenna's back. If she hadn't known better, his smooth talking would have convinced her he was really a nice guy. She could play his game and stood her ground, never taking her eyes off him for a second. "Okay, start talking. My patience is wearing thin. What do you need to get off your chest, James? Spit it out—this conversation is getting boring."

"Don't you want to know how I escaped?" He laughed. "I'm a genius. It was so easy."

In Jenna's ear, Kane's voice whispered. *"Ask him about his disciples. How he recruited them. If there's more out there we need to know."*

Jenna tapped her com. "I don't care about the jailbreak, James. I want to know how many men you've invited to the party."

"Three fascinating sexual deviates." A wide grin spread across Stone's face. "I think sadomasochists would come close to a description, they enjoy torturing and raping their women before they kill them. I thought they would be a perfect match for you and you know how I love to watch—well, for a time, anyway."

Three? Three other men in the forest. One had died in the fire, so two more were close by. She could be surrounded. An uncontrollable tremble went through her and she clenched her teeth. Stone would never see her fear of him. She pressed her com and dropped her voice to just above a whisper. "Three others, one dead in fire."

"Two dead. I shot one." Kane cleared his throat. *"Keep him occupied. I'll scope the forest."*

The skin on Jenna's arms pebbled, the uncanny feeling that someone was right behind her was making her skin crawl. She tried to keep her voice calm. "I don't believe you. I know you had no contact with anyone in the prison. No one from outside or inside could get near you. All this is a figment of your imagination, James, just like our relationship. It never happened."

"I'm going to cut you so bad no one will recognize you as human." Stone lifted the rifle. "I'm not lying, Jenna. It was easy for someone with my intelligence to influence people of like mind. I selected cases of men I knew would be capable of working with me. I gave them freedom as an incentive. I have money and enough power to change magistrates' minds, if I presented a sound case and backed it up with a hotshot lawyer."

Jenna forced a laugh. "Rave on, that's the story in your head. I know you couldn't communicate with anyone. You didn't have a chance to enlist anyone as a disciple, as you call them, or do anything. It's all in your mind, James. You're sick."

"Really? I used the custodian in the library. I placed a note in a book and he took it to one of my selections. I was allowed visits from my lawyer. Private visits, Jenna." Stone chuckled. "He hired a specific lawyer for my chosen ones and it was he, a dedicated disciple of my work, who explained the situation to them. It was all planned before I was convicted. I knew they'd try and cut me off from the world, so I made a contingency plan. You see, I have many people in my employ, Jenna. People who don't exist in your reality but thrive in the world of the dark web. People who look after my finances, my businesses, my escape from jail." He stared at her. "Does that sound like a sickness or genius? Now come out. I'm tired of waiting—or do I have to get someone to coax you out of your hiding place?"

Jenna swallowed hard. She couldn't believe what he was saying. "I find it hard to believe you have Sam Cross in your employ." She stared at him. "He's Adams' and Long's lawyer. He might be a pain in the ass, but he's not corrupt. He plays it straight down the line and to the letter of the law." She snorted. "More lies, James. You're losing your edge."

"That's why I chose him." Stone glared at her. "Incorruptible Sam Cross. He's the best, isn't he? A lawyer who is wasting his life in Black Rock Falls but perfect for my needs. He was handed a file, Jenna, from another out-of-state lawyer. He knew the deal that I'd worked on the case and out of his civic duty he took the offered fee to represent Adams and Long. No money came from me, Jenna. I'm not that stupid. Adams and Long have more than enough in their bank accounts to pay for him and then some."

Jenna took aim but moved slightly out of cover. "Put down your weapon. I have you surrounded. Do it nice and slow and we'll take you back to your nice cozy jail cell."

"I hear the hesitation in your voice and I know you're not a very good shot." Stone raised his rifle. "I remember our first date. You said after becoming sheriff you'd have to get down to the practice range more often. I offered to take you because I'm really good. I'll take you down before you pull the trigger and then I'll show you a real good time."

Heart pounding so loud she could hear it in her ears, Jenna gritted her teeth. "Put down the weapon. If your finger moves to the trigger I will fire."

"No, you won't. You're weak without backup but now it's just you and me. I always win, Jenna. I'm so going to enjoy hearing you beg me for mercy… but I'm not a forgiving guy. I'll make you scream until you die in agony." He laughed in an excited giggle. "I knew it would end like this." His finger went to the trigger.

CHAPTER FIFTY-THREE

The bang deafened Jenna and when Stone fell back in a red mist, to sprawl on the trail, she wanted to spew. She dropped her rifle down to her side and flopped against the tree. Hand trembling, she pressed her com. "Stone is down."

The duty of care instilled in her bellowed in her mind. She should go and check Stone's vital signs, but her legs refused to move. His legs twitched, and the idea he might be alive terrified her. What would she do if he'd survived? She took out her phone with trembling hands and stopped it recording. Moments later, Kane's voice came in her ear.

"That was a righteous kill. You okay?"

Jenna couldn't drag her eyes away from the body. "Not really. Is he dead?"

"Very. Great shooting."

Jenna sighed with relief, but it wasn't over yet. "There's another bogey in the forest and we need to get out of here. If the wind changes, we won't be able to outrun the fire. What's your position?"

"I'm across from you, alongside the ravine. I can't see anyone. Maybe he's hightailed it out of the forest but I'll cover you just in case. Go and get Seagull. Warrior is waiting on the trail."

Heaving a sigh of relief, Jenna straightened. Hearing Kane's voice had calmed her nerves, but she'd killed a man and that would stay with her forever. "Copy. Did you find Duke?"

"Yeah, he's fine. SOB had tied him to a log."

Jenna sighed with relief. "Soon as I grab Seagull, I'll call it in. The phones should work now the storm has passed." She hurried to her mare and slid her rifle back in the scabbard attached to her saddle.

The wind was blowing the smoke down the mountain, fanning the roaring wildfire closer to town. Fear clenched her belly. So many people lived off the grid in Stanton Forest. Hundreds of houses lined Stanton Road, and schools and the hospital would be in danger if the fire wasn't contained. Trembling from shock and looking all around, she called Rowley and tried to keep the hysterics from her voice but, in truth, her flight response was in overdrive. Right now, she wanted to be anywhere but here and not ten yards from James Stone's dead body. "I'm on the ravine trail near Bear Peak. James Stone was in the forest along with three of his disciples. I took him down and Kane took out the second, the other one burned up in the wildfire. We have three bodies and one man still at large. What's the situation with the fire?"

"We heard shots, and knew something was going down. We've been trying to contact you since you left town. We know about Stone's escape. I'm with Rio on the opposite side of the river from you at Bear Peak, not far from the firebreak. You won't believe who I have in custody—John Foster and he hasn't stopped talking. Stone recruited him to kill you and Dave, which makes the other two dead guys Adams and Long. They were all involved just as you figured… including Stone. He sure didn't fool you, though, did he?" Rowley cleared his throat. *"Latest news is that the fire is being contained, there are crews from all over surrounding it now. It hasn't crossed the firebreak below your position, and the fire chief is convinced it won't get past the falls. Crews are on their way to your position now in case the wind changes."*

Jenna turned to look at the massive orange glow in the sky and shook her head. "It sure doesn't look contained. We'll need to retrieve the bodies, but it's too high risk at the moment. Call Wolfe and let him know the situation and we'll do the retrieval once we get the all-clear from the fire department. Stay where you are. We'll come to you."

"Yes, ma'am." Rowley disconnected.

Jenna pressed her com. "Rowley has John Forest in custody on the other side of the river. He's admitted to being involved and is singing like a canary. We're good to go."

"Copy."

Footsteps pounded on the trail and she swung around, reaching for her weapon. She dropped her hand at the sight of Kane bending over Stone, checking his vital signs. When he straightened and turned toward her, she waved. Once Kane had wrapped crime scene tape around the trees surrounding Stone's body, she led the reluctant Seagull onto the trail. The mare bucked and danced sideways, snorting. The fire and smoke had terrified her. Jenna heaved a sigh of relief as Kane hurried toward her. She stared at him, so glad to have him in her life. He'd taught her so much, protected her with his life, and all the while living with a secret misery. How he'd remained steadfastly by her side when she'd given him such a hard time she'd never understand, but that was the essence of Dave Kane. She fell against him when he walked to her side. "I can't believe they were all involved." She held up her hand and closed her index finger an inch away from her thumb. "They came this close to killing us, Dave." She shivered. "I've never been so scared in my life."

"It didn't show." Kane hugged her. "The way you handled Stone was by the book, Jenna. He'll never hurt anyone again."

Jenna tapped her phone. "I recorded everything. I'm sure the FBI will want to know what went down here, but right now we need to get more distance between us and the fire. We can't do anything about the bodies. Shane will want to see them in situ, and right now we need to concentrate on getting out of the forest."

"I'm sure Duke is getting anxious too." Kane picked up the mare's reins and took Jenna's hand. "I'll lead Seagull as she's in such a foul mood."

They ran up the trail and Jenna kept her eyes straight ahead as they passed the body of Stone. Kane had kept the mare on the outside and shielded her from the gruesome sight. By the time they'd rounded the corner and Warrior came into view, shock hit Jenna in a tidal wave of tremors. "Wait up." Her voice was shaky to her ears.

"Just a bit further and then we can ride the rest of the way." Kane pushed on. "Seagull will settle down once she's with Warrior."

Breathless, she pulled on Kane's hand. "Slow down, I need a drink of water. The wind is blowing the fire down the mountain. We should reach the river by horseback in no time."

"Okay." Kane stopped and pulled a bottle of water from her backpack and handed it to her. His concerned expression moved over her face. "Take a minute and catch your breath. You're sheet white."

The horror of the last hour slammed into Jenna. Tears welled in her eyes and she brushed them away, angry at herself for being so girly. She'd looked away, but eagle-eyed Kane had noticed.

"It's over." Kane pulled her into his arms and stroked her hair. "If you hadn't taken the shot, I would the moment his finger went to the trigger." He held her away and looked into her eyes. "The world is a better place without him."

Jenna burrowed into his chest and held on tight. "Today I watched a man burn to death and shot another. The forest is on fire. Everything is going to hell. So many killers come to Black Rock Falls, all out to prove they can take us down. Are we doing the right thing staying here? How many more people are going to die, Dave?"

"Don't you believe we've been sent here for a reason?" Kane rested his chin on the top of her head. "Not by POTUS, I mean by fate or whoever pulls the strings. We both know that murders were committed way before we arrived here and those killers escaped justice. The bones found in the forest would be the tip of the iceberg. The killers don't come here to challenge us, Jenna, they come here because our county is vast with millions of places to hide, commit murder, and dispose of bodies." He sighed. "Over six hundred thousand people go missing in the United States every year, and there are currently way over two hundred thousand unsolved murders, so how many were the victims of serial killers? It may seem like we have way over our quota of cases in Black Rock Falls, but in truth, we don't touch the surface—and so far, we've caught every darn one of them. I'd say we're doing a fine job."

Still shaken, Jenna leaned back to look up at him. "I'm not sure what I'd do without you, Dave. You always say just the right thing to make me feel better." She held her breath as Kane hugged her, rubbing her back. When he released her, she stared into his eyes. "You make me feel safe."

"I like that." Kane tucked a strand of hair behind her ear.

Reluctantly, Jenna stepped away and looked behind him at the flames waving high above the distant pines. "Come on, we need to keep moving away from the fire."

"Sure." Kane pulled down his facemask and whistled for Duke. "Even Duke knows to be careful when shots have been fired." He waved a hand toward his dog as he made his way through the trees, keeping low. "See? Duke is careful."

Jenna didn't have time to reply. Duke launched himself at them, backside wiggling and making snuffling sounds. Laughing, she rubbed his ears. "It's good to see you too. Maybe Dave will teach you how to bite the next person who tries to steal you."

"Somehow, I think he's learned that all by himself." Kane rubbed Duke from head to tail. "Haven't you, boy?" He straightened and looked at Jenna. "He warned me someone was close by. He went ballistic." He offered Jenna his linked hands to hoist her into the saddle. "I'll tell you all about it when we get home."

EPILOGUE

Sunday, Week Two

Halloween

The first rain had arrived to help extinguish the wildfire before Jenna and her team had left the mountain on Friday. It lashed the forest right through Saturday, sending torrents of ash-filled rivulets of water down the mountain to muddy the pristine rivers, but the discoloration wouldn't last for long. Black Rock Falls would replenish the lakes and rivers with clean water in no time. The fire had left a blackened scar, but after winter the forest would renew and it would become a distant memory. Although the horror of Friday would stay with Jenna for a long time.

After the bodies had been retrieved—the man shot by Kane identified as Long, and the burned corpse as Adams—Jenna had spent the rest of Friday interviewing the suspect Rowley and Rio had apprehended in the forest. John Foster, dressed in cowboy hat and slicker, the uniform, it seemed, for James Stone's disciples, had told an interesting story.

The scheme for Stone's escape had been set into action following his arrest. His contact with the outside world hadn't been restricted until after his conviction. As a lawyer himself, he'd known he'd be sent to jail for life and set a plan for escape in motion. It had taken time to organize. He'd selected suitable likeminded candidates for his disciples, working on a sure-fire defense to have them released from jail and by having guards ready to look the other way for the right price. Late Thursday night, Stone had complained of severe stomach cramps and convinced the medic at the prison that he was suffering an acute appendicitis. An ambulance had been called and the guards paid off to not resist the ambush by his disciples on the highway.

Foster insisted he hadn't killed anyone but laid the blame for June and Payton Harris' murders on Adams. He'd taken Jenna and the team to the cave where Adams had displayed June Harris. The poor woman had been retrieved and her body would be laid to rest beside her husband. It had also been Adams who'd broken into Jenna's ranch by stealing the gate fob from Wolfe's van. It had taken only a short time observing her ranch to discover who carried the controls to the gate. He'd tried to break into the Beast, but the bulletproof glass had proved too great a problem. Adams used a wireless blocker to disable Jenna's phone and, after switching off the generator, had cut the power to the house.

Continuing to deny any involvement, Foster gave a detailed account of the brutal murders of Emmett and Patti Howard, saying he'd been in the forest as a lookout when Tyson Long arrived with the couple. Late at night, he'd distracted Emmett by crashing through the trees and grunting like a bear. Long had instructed Emmett to sit behind the tree and then used his crossbow to kill him. Patti's murder had been brutal, and the gruesome details were verified by Wolfe's autopsy findings.

Foster explained how, unrestricted in the jail, the disciples had been able to pass messages and plan where to meet in Black Rock Falls. On their release from jail, they'd placed a message in the personal column that read: *I am a disciple.* At the following meetings, held in the cave out of Stanton Forest, they'd planned every move and kept Stone in the loop by posting cryptic messages in the newspaper.

To cause chaos, Stone had chosen Adams and Long to commit copycat killings and made sure the men had alibis for each other's crimes in order to shed reasonable doubt on any convictions. Knowing Sam Cross would see an injustice if one of them was arrested, he used the man's integrity for his own twisted needs. He wanted Jenna to be confused and chasing her tail. When Stone's plans fell into place, the disciples organized his escape, and as Stone's only concession in jail and link to the outside world was a local newspaper, they posted a message in the Thursday edition of the *Black Rock Falls News*: *Meeting of the disciples, 1:00 am Friday, Stanton Road.*

With his disciples ready, Stone had only to follow the plan. Getting Jenna and Kane to the mountain had been easy. Kane's love for his dog was well known, and causing an accident in the middle of town to coincide with the time they went to work enabled Adams to steal Duke. Later, Stone made an anonymous call to the forest warden, and all he had to do was wait in the forest for them to arrive. He had his men in position and only had to ambush her and Kane as they searched for Duke. The wildfire had been an unexpected bonus, driving Jenna into Stone's clutches.

Foster had been stationed on the bank of the river just in case Jenna slipped through Stone's net, and had been waiting for Stone to return when questioned by Rowley.

Jenna had interviewed Foster in the presence of Sam Cross, whose outrage at being a pawn in a deadly conspiracy was palpable. It was obvious that Cross was as honest as the day was long, but when he excused himself and refused to represent Foster, it was the first time Jenna had seen him vulnerable. After waiting for another lawyer to arrive, Jenna, with the DA present, had charged Foster with felony murder and a list of other charges. There was no deal offered, as he was a repeat offender. It would be very unlikely he'd ever walk free again.

Exhausted but with a huge weight lifted from her shoulders, Jenna had returned to Kane's cottage and showered, scrubbing the stink of fire and death from her body before sleeping like the dead right through until lunchtime Saturday morning. She'd spent the rest of the day in the office with her team, tying up loose ends. Sunday would be a day to kick back and relax at home with Kane.

It was late when she woke on Sunday morning, but for once she didn't care. She staggered out of bed, still drowsy, and headed toward the smell of coffee. She loved living with Dave, and having him close by was like living a dream. The thought of going back to her ranch house left a pit of loneliness in her stomach. She went into the kitchen, poured a cup of coffee, added the fixings, and took the cup to the window to stare at her beautiful home. Would she be happy there after what had happened? Would she ever feel safe again?

When Kane's arms came around her, she leaned back into his embrace. "If I told you how much I love being here with you and I'm worried about moving back into my house, would you think I'm stupid?"

"No. I'd probably figure it was your roundabout way of asking me to move in with you." Kane's voice had gained a very bad Transylvanian accent. "Of course I will, my dear. I'll move my coffin into your cellar as soon as the sun goes down. Ha, ha, ha."

"Your what?" Jenna, turned to look at him and burst out laughing at his plastic fangs and long, red-lined black cape. "Oh, I'd forgotten today is Halloween."

"You did?" Kane grinned, showing his fangs. "I'm going as Dracula... ha, ha, ha."

A LETTER FROM D.K. HOOD

Dear Readers,

Thanks so much for choosing my novel and coming with me on another thrilling adventure with Kane and Alton in *Cross My Heart*.

If you loved this book and would like to stay up to date with all of my new releases, sign up here for my mailing list. You can unsubscribe at any time and your details will never be shared.

www.bookouture.com/dk-hood

It is wonderful continuing the stories of Jenna Alton and Dave Kane and having you along. I really appreciate all the wonderful comments and messages you have all sent me during this series.

If you enjoyed my story, I would be very grateful if you could leave a review and recommend my book to your friends and family. I really enjoy hearing from readers, so feel free to ask me questions at any time. You can get in touch on my Facebook page or Twitter or through my blog.

Thank you so much for your support.
D.K. Hood

       @DKHood_Author

       dkhoodauthor

       www.dkhood.com

       dkhood-author.blogspot.com.au

ACKNOWLEDGMENTS

Many thanks to all the wonderful readers who took the time to post great reviews of my books and to those amazing people who hosted me on their blogs.

I must give a shout-out to Gary for being an incredible sounding board for my story ideas and to the fantastic #Team Bookouture who have supported me every step of the way.

1-24
c mw

CPSIA information can be obtained
at www.ICGtesting.com
Printed in the USA
BVHW031738290621
610742BV00003B/39